Marie could feel the sheriff watching her

When she was far enough away from the barn and well out of his view, she circled back through the woods and found a place where she could spy on him.

After a few minutes, he left the barn and walked to the trailer. Finally he came out and began walking straight in Marie's direction, moving fast, whistling loudly.

Marie looked around for a better hiding place. The whistling was getting louder. In desperation, she climbed a gnarly old live oak.

To her horror, Whittington came to a stop under the very tree where she hung precariously. He leaned against the trunk and fished a cigar out of his jean jacket. He seemed very relaxed, and continued to smoke for what seemed an eternity. Marie struggled to control her breathing in soundless little puffs.

Finally he coughed a short bark, and Marie almost slipped off her limb.

"Mrs. Manning," he said quietly from under his hat, "I think you can help me. Want to come down?"

Dear Reader,

There are places on this earth, fortunately, that never seem to change. I set this book in the fictitious town of Deep Springs in the Texas Hill Country because that area—so wild, open and beautiful—has always had a magical appeal for me. The rolling hills and winding rivers seem to go on forever, remaining basically untamed, even as we enter the twenty-first century.

Marie Manning, Jim Whittington and the other characters in Deep Springs are similar to real Texas farmers and ranchers I have known all my life. I love these people because they exude a hearty, no-nonsense approach to life and are as softhearted as they are tough.

This is my first novel. The characters and story come straight from my heart. I hope they go straight to yours and give you hours of pleasure.

So join me now on a journey to the heart of the enchanting Hill Country…and to the hearts of Jim Whittington and Marie Manning.

Darlene Graham

IT HAPPENED IN TEXAS
Darlene Graham

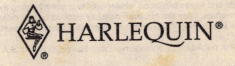

HARLEQUIN®

TORONTO • NEW YORK • LONDON
AMSTERDAM • PARIS • SYDNEY • HAMBURG
STOCKHOLM • ATHENS • TOKYO • MILAN • MADRID
PRAGUE • WARSAW • BUDAPEST • AUCKLAND

ISBN 0-373-70812-2

IT HAPPENED IN TEXAS

Copyright © 1998 by Darlene Gardenhire.

This edition published by arrangement with Harlequin Books S.A.

® and TM are trademarks of the publisher. Trademarks indicated with ® are registered in the United States Patent and Trademark Office, the Canadian Trade Marks Office and in other countries.

Printed in U.S.A.

To my husband, Gary, and to my children,
Damon, Devyn, Kathleen and Jennifer.
They laughed at my jokes, pitched in with the housework,
wrote me poems and always, always believed I would be a
novelist someday.

CHAPTER ONE

HER PANTIES WERE pure silk, her sheets Egyptian cotton. She bought hand-painted china from the Czech Republic and Thoroughbred horses from Joe Kirk Fulton's. Her kids were brilliant, her pets precious, her friends plentiful.

She lived in a charming seventy-year-old house outside Deep Springs, Texas, atop a knoll surrounded by one thousand acres of the most scenic ranch land in the beautiful Texas Hill Country.

And this morning, like every morning, Marie Manning woke up and reassured herself that everything, *everything,* was fine. *Just fine.*

But everything was not just fine.

Not *this* morning. This morning there was a dead body.

And halfway to that dead body—as Marie plowed through the clumps of sage and scrub—it occurred to her that what she was doing was truly dumb. Besides the fact that her ankle throbbed with pain and her heart pounded with fear and her mind reeled with panic, she was inappropriately dressed and her hair was a mess.

But she ignored the pain and the fear and the panic—and even the stupid pink leotard and the wild hair—and scrambled down the steep slope toward the body. She had to see for herself that he was dead.

She grabbed at sapling limbs, slipped and slid on the muddy bank and muttered castigations to herself. *Brilliant, Marie! Rushing out of the house like that, charging across that bar ditch, twisting your ankle.* She wondered what exactly she hoped to accomplish down in the draw. Heroic CPR?

Behind her, Alice Croft, twenty years Marie's senior and fifteen pounds heavier, stopped at the edge of the bank, breathing hard. "Marie, honey…slow down!" she called down the slope. "I told you…there's nothing we can…do for him now."

Marie slowed down. Years of infallible emergency-room assessments undoubtedly qualified Alice to pronounce any body "dead." And Marie had seen her share of fatalities in the E.R., too. Surely this was no different.

But she stopped short and clamped a hand over her mouth when she saw the body.

Oh boy.

This was way different. A dead body neatly laid out in a clinical setting and a dead body twisted in the mist and mud at the bottom of a ravine on your very own ranch were about as different as a baptism and a drowning.

He looked exactly as Alice had breathlessly described him: facedown, overalls, boots…and…dried blood everywhere.

Marie moved a step closer, got a sharp report of pain from her ankle, but stubbornness and her nurse's instincts won out. She gathered her unruly hair over one shoulder and folded her tall frame to feel for a carotid pulse, then reconsidered. He'd been dead for hours, maybe days. She stood and tried to blot the most obvious—and most nauseating—indicator from her mind. She knew her olfactories would give up in a minute and, mercifully, she would smell nothing.

The puncture wounds and blood made it all too obvious what had killed him. Something sharp, or rather, somebody wielding something sharp.

With eyes fixed on the body, she slowly backed up. "Nothing to do now but wait for the sheriff," she said.

Alice finally maneuvered herself down the bank, came up beside Marie and covered her nose and mouth. For a moment, the two women merely stared in horrified silence at the wretched old man.

When Alice caught her breath, she said, "Told you," beneath her palm. "Mercy. I can't think of a soul who'd want to kill poor old Cudd McCombs."

Marie gaped at Alice in disbelief. *Poor old Cudd McCombs?* Amazing how death sanitized the memory of the deceased. "Offhand," Marie said, "I can think of half a dozen."

Alice's eyes looked genuinely shocked. "Mercy, Marie! What a thing to say!"

"Oh, come on, Alice. This is *Cudd McCombs.*" Hearing her own cold tone, Marie wondered, not for the first time, if her heart hadn't hardened a little since her husband, Carl, had died.

"You never particularly cared for him," Alice mumbled through her fingers. That's an understatement, Marie thought. It would be more accurate to say that she could barely stomach the sight of Cudd alive, much less dead, much less in *rigor mortis.*

It wasn't that Cudd was evil. He was just thoroughly disgusting. A dirty old prevaricator who divided his time between making up lies, manufacturing moonshine and tinkering on the carcasses of the worthless vehicles that littered his weedy yard. Marie turned away and craned her neck to see up over the side of the ravine.

"Where in blazes *is* that sheriff?" Alice said. "You don't suppose he's taking his time because I told the dispatcher that Cudd was already dead?"

Marie gave Alice a little frown. "Good Lord, I hope not! Even with some of the doubts Carl had about the Law here in Carville County, Whittington's got to be more professional than that. Besides, since they closed off that old road across the Bishop ranch, we're almost seventeen miles from town." She resumed her watch over the rise.

"Have you ever met him?" Alice asked.

"No, but there's no time like the present." Marie nodded toward the road where a black Ford Bronco threw an arch of mud and gravel as it sped toward the ravine.

JIM WHITTINGTON gripped the wheel and downshifted, then brought the Bronco to an abrupt halt at the edge of the ravine. He was always keyed up when called to the scene of a major crime; he thrived on the challenge. But this morning something more was churning around in his gut. He hated to admit it, but he knew exactly what was bothering him: one of the ladies down in that draw was none other than Mrs. Marie Manning. Owner of the enormous Manning Ranch.

Marie Manning. Texas Highway Commissioner Carl Manning's widow. Four kids. A leader in all the usual society stuff. Picture in the paper all the time. A prissy, proper community watchdog.

Funny that he'd been back in Deep Springs for almost three years and they'd never met. But then, they didn't exactly move in the same social circles. She'd be a real pain in the butt, sticking her nose out here at 7:30 a.m., asking a lot of pointed questions.

Well, he'd have a few pointed questions of his own and then maybe she'd go away. He wanted her and that other woman out of his hair as quickly as possible so he could get this mess cleared up. Nothing like an unsolved murder to raise his stock among the venerable voters of Carville County three weeks out from the election. Beautiful. Just beautiful.

He spotted the two women standing below. Why didn't they come up into the sun instead of staying down there in that damp ravine? The younger one—Mrs. Manning, no doubt—wasn't even wearing a jacket. She had on one of those gaudy skintight exercise things. He took a closer look. Maybe this job *did* have some compensations.

They were hovering near the corpse. People act so damn dumb at the scene of an unattended death. Focusing on the body as if they could do something for the poor devil.

He put his camera over one shoulder, jerked the parking brake on and left the engine running. Then he stomped down the incline.

ALICE STEPPED UP behind Marie.

"What d'you suppose he's doing?" she whispered.

Marie gave no response—she was watching Whittington.

He'd squatted beside the body, his broad shoulders straining against his jean jacket, then pulled a pair of latex gloves from his pocket and tugged them on. After feeling for a pulse, and then peripherals, he stayed down, resting an arm across one long muscled thigh as he examined the blood-caked body.

"It's just plain awful," Alice mumbled to Marie's back. "I know you and Cudd had your differences, but he and I got along pretty decent when Thelma was alive. She used to drag him to church pretty regular."

Marie sighed. She loved Alice Croft with all her heart. The woman was the salt of the earth. But "the salt" tended to prattle on, and standing here in a leotard covered with mud, with a smarting ankle and the sheriff within earshot, Marie was in no mood for a gabfest.

Alice made a tsking sound, indicating she had more to say.

"Why, I remember one time," she continued. "Thelma came by to see me in the middle of the day, in the middle of the week. Just dropped by. And do you know what she said to me? She said, 'Alice, if anything ever happens to me, I want you to marry my Cudd and take care of him.' Can you imagine that? Marry old Cudd? Why, I nearly retched every time he came near me, he stunk so bad—"

Marie gave Alice the eye for mentioning stench.

"Sorry. But honestly, you never smelled such a powerful case of B.O. It'd just ruin your lunch. Shoot. *Me* marry Cudd? Isn't it amazing how once you're a widow, people assume you'd put up with any old fart just to be married again?''

Marie was silent, hoping Alice would get it. She didn't want to discuss being a widow, not with Jim Whittington crouching less than twenty feet away.

"Has that happened to you, honey?" Alice persisted. "Since you've been a widow, I mean? People trying to shove every available man at you?"

Available men? What in blazes was Alice thinking? Maybe discovering Cudd's body had rattled her marbles a little. Of all times to bring up available men. And *what* available men? With the exception of the one whose backside Marie was now studying, the "available" men in all of Carville County could be squeezed into Alice's root cellar.

Besides, Alice knew better, knew that Marie's days had been nothing but work and worry since Carl's death. Work and worry. Raising four kids alone, running a huge ranch, straightening out their tangled finances. When would Marie have time to think about available men? This whole train of thought intensified her irritation.

She could feel Alice eyeing her, waiting for a reaction.

"Alice," she snapped, "let's don't talk unkindly about Cudd while he's lying here like this. It isn't right."

"Talk unkindly? A minute ago *you* were getting ready to tick off the names of people who'd like to kill him."

"Shh," Marie hissed. *That'd* be a fine thing for the sheriff to hear: that Marie had a handy list of suspects. The sheriff slowly stood, planted his hands on his hips and looked down. Then he started taking pictures. This apparently distracted Alice enough to shut her up.

When he finished with the pictures, he started walking toward the women, then froze, bent and nudged a tiny object free of the mud. He wrapped it in the glove he had peeled off, and stuffed the wad into a plastic bag he withdrew from his breast pocket. Finally, he came forward and gave the women his attention.

"Mrs. Manning," he said as he turned to Marie and tipped his Stetson. "I'm Sheriff Whittington. I was acquainted with your husband."

When Marie looked up from the body, Whittington was startled by the vivid green of her eyes. You couldn't see *that* in the newspaper. Nor had the society photos captured that hair. The morning sun reflected off masses of wavy dark copper, flowing down over her shoulder like a sheet of wrinkled silk.

As if reading his thoughts, Marie self-consciously gathered her hair in her hands, twisting it into a tight knot. She looked away from him, back at the body.

"Yes, Sheriff. Carl mentioned you a time or two. Thank you so much for coming," she said, as if welcoming him to some kind of church meeting.

"My pleasure, ma'am," he said. But she didn't seem to catch the sarcasm. And she didn't offer her hand.

She kept a tight grip on that hair and glanced nervously at the older lady. "This is my neighbor, Alice Croft. She is the one who actually discovered the body."

"I was out for my morning walk." The Croft

woman extended her hand and kept talking as he shook it. "And I was coming up over that far ridge there—that's Marie's property—and I saw something bright blue through the brush down here." She pointed to the body. "It was Cudd's shirt, of course—what's left of it. First I tried to see if there was anything I could do—I'm a registered nurse—but, as you can see... Then I ran to Marie's to call the Law and then she came running back here with me." She finally stopped for breath, sighed and shook her head.

During Alice's story, Whittington had sneaked a few glances at Marie. She sure looked tense and self-conscious standing there in that—what would you call that thing? A ballet costume? And she sure was a beauty.

"Did either of you ladies touch anything, move anything?" he said.

"Certainly not," Marie answered, green eyes snapping up to meet his.

Could be this is particularly upsetting for her, he thought, *considering her husband's death a little over a year ago.* Carl Manning had fallen asleep at the wheel and driven his car into the river. Jim decided to question the older woman first.

"You live around here, Mrs. Croft?"

"Right down the road. Been Marie's neighbor for sixteen years, ever since she married Carl."

"And that makes you Mr. McCombs's neighbor as well?"

"Oh yes, although I haven't seen much of Cudd these last couple of years. Cudd got more and more peculiar after Thelma passed on." Alice shook her head.

"Does anyone else live out here besides you, Mr. McCombs and the Mannings?"

"No. The old Bishop ranch is abandoned, of course. But Toots Daniels lives up the road. I bet you know of Toots, Sheriff. Carl Manning's uncle. Married Carl's mother's sister, the nice one—not Bernice—"

Whittington squeezed one eye shut, trying to follow as Alice jabbered on.

"Everybody in Deep Springs knows Toots. Toots and Cudd go…uh…went way back. In the war together and all. That Toots is the soul of loyalty. Even when nobody else could stand Cudd, Toots'd never forsake him. You might visit with him about Cudd's recent doings."

"Yes, I'll be sure and *visit with* Mr. Daniels. You said you were out for your walk. Did you notice anything else unusual, unusual noises or anything?"

"No."

Marie lifted her gaze from the body and gave Alice a baffled look. Whittington wondered about that. Maybe she'd never heard the old girl give a one-word answer before.

He proceeded.

"Would anybody else out here have seen or heard something?" He turned to Marie now. "Don't you employ ranch hands?"

Marie felt her cheeks grow warm. She was used to being in the public eye because of her late husband's politics, but she always found it mortifying to have strangers know about her private life especially now that her financial situation was so uncertain. "I only keep one now. Henry Honicker."

Jim frowned. "Okay. Where is Mr. Honicker?"

"Back at the main house. I left him in charge of the children while I came out here."

He looked surprised. "Why didn't you send your hired man out here?"

How dare he stand there and question my judgment, Marie thought, and felt her color rise higher. "Sheriff, Henry's a simpleminded man, not exactly the kind of cool head that's needed in a crisis."

"Yes." He drew the word out while his eyes surveyed her burning cheeks, the tight rope of hair she still clutched, the mud-smeared hot-pink leotard. "A cool head is always appreciated in a crisis."

Marie released her hair. Was he implying that she was some nervous, nosy woman, running down here out of morbid curiosity, like a pesky onlooker at a highway accident?

Her face must have communicated her ire, because he cleared his throat and said, "Why don't you ladies go up to my truck and warm up. I'll finish here and take your statements in full in a moment."

Marie turned on her heel, intending to stomp up the incline in indignation. Instead, with her first step, she let out a yelp and pitched sideways into Alice.

"Marie, honey!" Alice cried, trying to break Marie's fall, which was like a fat hen trying to stop a tumbling colt.

Whittington lunged forward and said, "Whoa there," as if she *were* a colt and caught her from behind. He steadied her against him and gently assisted as she lowered herself to the ground. "Mrs. Manning," he said, "are you hurt?"

Marie put her forehead on her knee, clutching her

ankle and gritting her teeth because it hurt. Her hair was all over the place, blocking her face, and a vain little thought permeated her pain. Why hadn't she braided this mop before she started her workout this morning?

Her eyes were clamped shut, but she knew that he was right there beside her, down on one knee, she could feel him. She let out a moan, partly out of pain, but mostly from acute embarrassment.

"Mrs. Manning?" he repeated.

"I'm okay," Marie said, but the strain in her voice contradicted her.

"Marie, what's wrong?" Alice asked.

"My ankle." Marie winced. "I must have sprained it when I tripped in the ditch by the road."

"Let me look at it," Whittington said, and without waiting for her consent, he lifted her foot and delicately peeled away Marie's mud-caked tennis shoe and sock.

She peeked at him as he did this. *My God,* she thought. *He really is as handsome as they all say.* Square jaw, thick clean eyebrows, the densest, blackest eyelashes she'd ever seen. This close, she could even see a few faded boyhood freckles on her prominent nose.

"It's swelling badly," he said. "Let's get you up to my truck. I've got a chemical cold compress in the first-aid kit. Can you stand up if we help you?"

"Yes, I believe so." Marie threw her hair back and pushed the ground with her palms.

But it was no good. As soon as she moved the affected limb, pain shot through her ankle and lower leg. Serious pain.

"I'll have to carry you up," Whittington said matter-of-factly.

Marie's eyes widened. Carry her? "I can make it on my own," she said. She held her jaw firm, but her face felt as hot as a bowl of four-alarm chili. Damn those cheeks. She could never conceal her emotions with those cheeks always broadcasting in neon red.

He eyed the steep side of the ravine, then gave her a look that said, *"Nonsense,"* but aloud he said, "All right. If you insist."

She fought the pain and managed to stand with his help. He and Alice steadied her from either side, but no sooner had they started up when Alice slipped to her knees on the mud.

"*Okay,* here we go," he said. He scooped Marie up in his arms as easily as if she were a rag doll.

"Sheriff—"

"Now," he said, and shifted her weight in his arms, "put your arms around my neck and press in tight against me or we'll never make it up the side of this ravine."

Marie did as he asked. How could she argue? He was being so solicitous, and the look on his face was grave and businesslike. Yet here they were, all but fused together by the sheer force of gravity.

Suddenly, Marie wished she were wearing *anything* but these few ounces of pink spandex. Jeans, a rain slicker. A nun's habit.

She avoided looking at his profile, as if he might feel her eyes on him. But she couldn't avoid his scent. It poured up with his body heat out of the open collar of his cowboy shirt and from his thick, dark hair. She almost forgot the pain in her ankle as she breathed it in: piñon pine, cigar smoke, leather, strong soap and starch all mixed together.

He tightened his embrace as he struggled up the side of the ravine, and the warm pressure of his hands, arms and chest actually made Marie feel weak.

Alice was struggling along behind them, out of breath, but still clucking on about what a terrible morning it had been and now this and what next.

When they got to the Bronco, Whittington interrupted her. "Mrs. Croft, open the door, please."

She did and he gently lowered Marie onto the back seat.

"You need to elevate this now," he said, positioning her leg.

Well, he certainly knows his first aid, Marie thought as he unlocked the first-aid kit, tore open a cold compress, snapped it and gently but firmly pressed it around her ankle. Before she could even utter thanks, he had marched around the truck, bounded into the front seat and grabbed a clipboard in one hand and his radio mike in the other.

"Cruiser one to headquarters. Awaiting backup on Manning property. Advise medical examiner investigators should be through at the scene within the hour. Over."

A female voice crackled over the radio. "Ten-four, cruiser one. Cruiser two is three-tenths miles from scene. Over."

"Ten-four, headquarters. Cruiser one out."

He replaced the mike, turned to Marie in the back seat and said, "The backup deputy will be here soon, and then I'll transport you to the emergency room to have that ankle checked."

"Sheriff, if you don't mind, I'd rather go directly home. I'd like to reassure my children about this incident as soon as possible. In my judgment, the ankle can wait. I'm a nurse, after all."

He considered this, studying her face, then said, "Okay, I need to question your kids and this Honicker fellow anyway. And because the kids are minors, it would be better if you were present. When the deputy gets here, I'll take you home and question them at your house."

Question her children? Marie had not anticipated that. She did *not* want her children involved in this. "I don't know about questioning my children—"

"Mrs. Manning," he interrupted, "there's been a murder out here, and unless you want me to haul them all into town, I'll have to talk to your kids at your home." Without giving her a chance to respond, he turned and picked up the mike again. "Cruiser one to headquarters. Advise Cruiser three that I will proceed directly to Manning home with beginning mileage of 1-4-1-7-2. Over."

"Copy, cruiser one," the female voice responded, "Cruiser two should be on your road now. Out."

The rotating beacon of a sheriff's cruiser could be seen flashing around the bend of the rutted road, and without another word to the women, Whittington climbed out of his truck and went to speak with his deputy.

As he strode away, Marie gave his long legs and broad back a once-over. "Well, I swear," she fumed as she watched him gesturing orders to the deputy. "What we need out here is a *real man* to take charge.

Do you suppose he'll be this kind and considerate when he interrogates my children?''

"He is a bit gruff," Alice said. "But I think the sheriff will handle the kids okay."

"What makes you so sure?" Marie countered. "I understand he doesn't have any children of his own, has never even been married. Besides, I can't recall why exactly, but Carl never quite trusted the man."

Alice's mouth popped open to speak, but she looked down and bit her lip instead. Marie thought that was curious, Alice Croft suddenly resisting the urge to blurt out her opinion, but she realized why Alice had clammed up when the sheriff jerked the truck door open.

He hopped in and said, "Buckle up, ladies."

As he reached up to put the Bronco in gear, he added, almost as if it was incidental, "Oh! Did either of you ladies lose an earring when you came out here?"

"An earring? Don't wear 'em," Alice said.

He looked in the rearview mirror and locked eyes with Marie. "Mrs. Manning?"

His eyes, dark brown, narrowed slightly, and catching points of morning light, seemed to bore through her like lasers.

She reached up and touched each lobe, felt the emerald studs Carl had given her for her birthday two years ago—his last gift to her. "No," she mouthed, cleared her throat, repeated more confidently, "no."

He studied her reflected eyes a moment, then looked away, threw the Bronco into gear and went roaring down the road to Marie's house.

CHAPTER TWO

SITUATED ON the crest of a low rise, far back off the main road, the Manning place looked to Jim like something from another time.

So, this is where Marie Manning lives, he thought as he climbed out of the Bronco. Everything about the place said home, from the wind chimes singing in the October breeze, to the old Border collie barking near the back door.

Like everybody else in Deep Springs, Jim had heard stories about the vast Manning holdings, and he'd driven the perimeter of the land, but he'd never seen the house.

He was surprised when they entered the simple white plank gates with a Lone Star fashioned at their center. Still, as he drove around the last bend of the climbing narrow gravel driveway, he'd expected something enormous, a sort of Texas castle.

But here was merely a long and narrow one-story, huddled in among giant cedars, twisted live oaks and ancient pecan trees. The tall foundation, the six low pillars across the front porch and the towering chimneys at either end—all native limestone—hinted at some original grandiose design, but otherwise the house was modest and homey, and Jim liked it immediately.

Cheery, multipaned windows alternated with white siding, and the steep-pitched dark green roof looked almost black against the chalky limestone chimneys.

Marie Manning, he guessed, liked flowers. All around the place fading fall flowers lingered like aging ladies.

The valley below the house was bounded by an enormous outcropping of limestone from which Jim figured the stone for the main house had been quarried. To the west he saw the creek, which issued from Deep Springs, after which the county seat was named. To the east Big Pond and Little Pond glistened like mirrors. Local stories said the ponds had been engineered by the first resourceful Manning, Angus, early in the century.

Behind Jim, to the south, the winding highway and the Hill Country stretched as far as the eye could see.

Mrs. Croft was attempting to assist Marie out of the Bronco, and Jim sprinted around to help. When he grabbed Marie's elbow the Border collie charged forward, barking wildly.

"Bailey, hush!" Marie commanded.

Two little children, a boy and a girl, crashed out of the side door of the house and came running headlong toward the Bronco, their red hair gleaming in the morning sun.

Before they even reached Marie, the children started hollering: "Mom! Mom! Is old Cudd dead?"

"Jillian said that Alith found a dead body," the little girl lisped breathlessly as she ran up, her green eyes wide.

"And B.J. said it was old Cudd," the little boy

added as he came to a screeching halt in front of his mother, then pushed thick glasses up on his nose.

"We'll talk about that later, sweetheart," Marie said.

"But Mom—"

"Listen, your mother's hurt her ankle," Alice interrupted. "You kids go hold the door open so we can get her into the house."

Marie tried to bear some of her weight on her injured ankle but immediately gasped. Whittington pressed forward and slipped an arm around her waist, wondering if he shouldn't just scoop her up in his arms again.

The little girl took one look at her mother's pale face and ran toward the house to do as Alice asked, but the boy stood gawking up at Jim through bottle-thick glasses. He squinted at the county seal on the door of the Bronco and the light-bar on its roof. "Hey! You're the sheriff!" he informed Whittington.

"At the moment I am," Jim answered the child seriously as he secured Marie's arm over his shoulder. "You okay, ma'am?" he said softly.

Marie nodded and they started forward.

The youngster gave Jim a gap-toothed grin as he hopped alongside. "Yeah, election time, I geth."

Whittington stared down at the child, astonished. This kid couldn't be more than six or seven years old—how would he know about elections? But of course, he was a Manning, and everybody knew Mannings were too smart for their own good. "Would you do me a favor, partner?" Jim steadied Marie and tilted his head back in the direction of the truck.

"Grab my clipboard off the seat and bring it into the house while I help your mom."

"You bet, Sheriff!" The child dashed back and snatched the clipboard off the seat, slammed the Bronco door, then shot off toward the house.

Marie groaned. Jim glanced at her. Couldn't see much of her in those kids, unless it was the green eyes, and maybe her hair had been that red once. He eyed the cloak of rich auburn that partially covered her face. She had an amazing head of hair, and this close, he could smell some soft essence drifting up from it, like sandalwood, only cleaner.

She was gripping his shoulder, hanging on to Alice with the other hand, and to help her, so he told himself, he reached over with his free hand and gently gathered the heavy mane of hair, pushing it back out of her face, over her shoulder. It felt softer than silk; he was reluctant to release it.

She turned her head slightly and looked at him out of the corner of her eye, then she glanced down at her hair, still gathered in his large hand. "Thank you, Sheriff," she said, her cheeks blazing crimson—from the pain? or from something else?—and he released her hair in a wild tumble down her back.

She flipped an unruly strand off her forehead. "Could be I tripped on this mop in that ditch," she quipped.

Whittington smirked. Cute. He hadn't expected humor from her.

The kids, the dog and Alice got in the way much more than they helped, but Whittington maneuvered Marie up the short flight of porch steps and through the door in spite of everybody.

Once inside, they took a breather in a tiny mudroom. The shelves of a pantry, stocked to bursting, filled one wall. A mammoth freezer occupied the other. The smell of bleach drifted up from an old washing machine, chugging away companionably beside a whirring dryer.

A pass-through window opened to an airy kitchen beyond. Presently, a stout older man, in faded overalls and a crooked seed cap, filled the frame of the window. He wore an expression of total bewilderment on his blunt, ruddy features.

"Land sakes, Henry, Marie's hurt," Alice snapped. "Fix up a couple of chairs."

The man vanished from the window.

"Hand me my garden smock," Marie mumbled to Alice, indicating a heap of outdoor clothes piled on a coatrack.

Jim made a business of wiping his boots while Alice helped Marie cover the skintight leotard with a big denim tunic.

"This way," Marie said after a moment, and Whittington helped her up another short flight of steps and through a pair of louvered swinging doors to the kitchen. The two little kids were rinsing out cereal bowls at the sink. Without being told. Jim was impressed.

Henry had set two antique bentwood chairs facing each other and Marie crumpled into one awkwardly as Jim gently lifted her ankle onto the other.

"Thank you, Sheriff. And thank you, Henry," Marie said, exhaling a sigh.

"We'll need a fresh ice pack, Mrs. Croft," Jim said to Alice and she scurried to the freezer. His eye for detail picked up on a ladies' exercise video next to the small TV on the counter. That explained her funny clothes...and her great figure.

"Jillian and B.J.," Marie spoke to two older children who had been observing the activities with respectful silence, "this is Sheriff Whittington. He's going to ask you all a few questions."

The tall, lanky young man she'd called B.J. stepped forward, frowning. "Mom, what happened to your foot?"

"I just twisted my ankle a little. Jillian, honey, would you please get Mother a couple of Tylenol?"

The girl shot off down a narrow hallway, her long chestnut ponytail flying.

Alice brought a plastic bag full of ice and arranged it around Marie's ankle.

"All right, Sheriff, who's first?" Marie asked.

"Are you the oldest?" Jim asked the boy named B.J.

"Yes, sir. I'm fifteen."

Fifteen? How old was this woman when she had this kid? *Twelve?* Jim eyed Marie's flawless skin, her model's figure. Amazing.

"I'll question you first. Mrs. Manning, it'd be better if I questioned each child separately, so they don't influence one another."

"Fine, Sheriff." Marie winced and adjusted the ice pack.

She dispatched the two little ones down a short flight of steps to the basement to watch TV. Jillian arrived with the Tylenol, and then Alice spirited her away to the living room to practice piano. The Honicker fellow had apparently faded into the woodwork.

Jim removed his Stetson and seated himself at the round oak table with his clipboard and pen, endeavoring to collect his thoughts.

Outside, the dog recommenced barking; the old washer flew into a noisy spin; jerky, off-key piano pounding beat down the hall and mixed with zany cartoon music blaring up the stairs from the den.

He considered asking for a semblance of order appropriate to a murder investigation, but the attentive faces of Marie and B.J. indicated that everything was as normal as pie in the Manning household.

Resigning himself to the racket, he cleared his throat and proceeded to ask B.J. a series of routine questions.

B.J. was sober and manly in his answers, but on the last question, when Jim asked if he'd seen anything peculiar around Cudd's place lately, B.J. said *all* the people and activities at Cudd's place were peculiar. "Except my uncle Toots—he's not *peculiar*." B.J. grinned. "He's *unique*."

Jim knew B. J. Manning by reputation: a young man who had everything any Texas youth could dream of laid at his feet. Good looks, athletic prowess, brains, wealth, horses, this ranch. And yet the kid didn't seem spoiled or cocky. He smiled at Jim, his expression as open as the Texas sky.

"I'll have to meet your uncle Toots," Jim said. "He spent a lot of time with Mr. McCombs?"

"Well, not since my dad died," and then B.J.'s expression dimmed. "Since then he's mostly been over here, helping my mom."

There was one thing B.J. lacked. Jim glanced at

Marie. She was looking down into her lap, at her folded hands.

He thanked B.J., who shook his hand firmly, and sent the teenager into the living room to fetch his sister.

When the boy was gone, Jim said quietly, "Mrs. Manning, I'm sorry if this is difficult for you all, considering your recent loss, but a man has been murdered—"

"We're all right, Sheriff," she said without looking up. Then she straightened her shoulders. "We want to help in any way we can."

The daughter with the ponytail bounced into the kitchen.

He repeated the same questions to Jillian, softening his tone and reassuring her that any answer was correct, lest he intimidate this pretty little girl.

But before long, he realized that he had seriously misread this particular pretty little girl. There was no intimidating her. In fact, Jillian Manning seemed to relish her role in the murder investigation, and before long she was happily volunteering all kinds of surprising information.

She told him that when she'd turned twelve this past summer, her mother had given her permission to use the video camera, and, she confided, she had secretly videotaped Mr. McCombs about a month ago.

Marie's mouth dropped open at this news. "Jillian!" she said. "You didn't!"

"I did, Mom. And, Sheriff," she turned to Whittington, eyes shining, "I filmed him burying something out in his woods."

"Jillian!" Marie said again.

Jillian ignored her mother's reproach, and kept her attention on the sheriff. "Couldn't *that* have something to do with Cudd getting killed?"

"Possibly," Whittington said as he wrote on his clipboard.

Jillian's face broke into a satisfied smile, all braces. "I thought so!" she said.

"Jillian, really," Marie persisted. "Secretly video-taping a neighbor, and you have been strictly forbidden to go near the McCombs property—"

"Mom." Jillian seemed peeved at her mother for failing to appreciate the cleverness of what she had done. "I wasn't *secretly* videotaping anybody. I didn't even know I was in Cudd's woods. I was following Tyler while he stalked a squirrel—"

"Who's Tyler?" Jim broke in.

"Our cat," Jillian and Marie both answered.

Whittington frowned and rubbed his forehead, trying to absorb everything. It was a thrill a minute around here. Exactly how many animals, kids, relatives, farmhands, neighbors and general hangers-on did this woman have?

Marie gave him a worried look, then hollered down the stairs, "You kids turn down that TV! It's loud enough to wake the dead!" Then she blushed, apparently realizing her unfortunate choice of words.

Jim cleared his throat. "All right," he said. "I'll have to confiscate that videotape."

Marie turned to Jillian. "We'll discuss your manners later, young lady. Where is that tape?"

Jillian looked stuck. "How the hell should I know?" she said innocently. "I was filming on one of the family tapes."

Marie turned back toward Whittington, her face now many shades redder. "Sheriff, I'm afraid we'll have to review several tapes before we can give you anything."

Whittington made another note on his clipboard. "I can pick it up in a day or two." He looked up at Jillian. "I guess that's all for now. Thank you very much."

Jillian gave him a hundred-watt smile and bounced off.

"Excuse Jillian's language, Sheriff," Marie said when the child was out of earshot. "She is currently operating under the assertion that *hell* is not a curse word, it being a real place in the Bible and all. If I try to chastise her for using it, we only get into a pointless argument."

Jim wanted very much to laugh and assure her he'd heard slightly fouler language, even from twelve-year-olds, but she looked so thoroughly embarrassed that he only nodded sympathetically. "I'll see the two younger ones together, Mrs. Manning," he said. "They may feel more at ease that way. How old are they?"

"Six."

"Both six?"

"They're twins."

"I see," he said, and again he glanced at her figure. Amazing. "Well, with children that young, we usually can't use anything they say as evidence, but call them anyway."

"Mark and Mandy, turn off the TV and come up here, please," Marie called down to the den.

Jim changed tactics completely with the twins. He

adopted a relaxed, friendly attitude. "That looks like a good old dog you have out there, what's his name?"

"Bailey," the twins answered in unison.

"Does he ever bark at night?"

"All the *time*," the little girl assured Jim.

"He does *not*," her brother corrected her. "He only barks if something's up."

"Well, that's good, isn't it?" Jim said seriously. "He wouldn't be a very smart dog if he barked at every little blowing leaf, now, would he?"

The twins first nodded, then shook their heads.

Jim managed to suppress a grin.

"Did you guys hear old Bailey barking last night, or early this morning?"

The twins looked at each other, their little faces set in consternation. Then they turned to their mother as if she possessed the correct answer. Outside, Bailey started a fresh round of barking.

Marie smiled and rolled her eyes.

"I get the picture," Jim said. "Well, I guess neither of you heard anything *besides* Bailey's barking then?"

"Like what?" Mark asked, his green eyes huge behind his glasses.

"Oh, like a car engine, a shout, horses."

"Like a *gunshot?*" Mark said, eyes getting even bigger.

"Did you hear a gunshot?" Jim asked calmly.

"Heck, no, but I'd tell you if I did, Sheriff."

Little Mandy twirled her finger in a circle beside her ear. "That kid has a *very* big ee-magination," she said.

Jim smiled again. "Tell you what," he said. "If

either of you remember anything you think I should know about Cudd, you just tell your mother and she'll contact me. Okay?''

The twins nodded.

''Sheriff,'' Mark said, edging in close to Jim's shoulder. ''Do you want me to look around for you? I'm awful good at finding stuff.''

Jim looked up at Mark. His eager little face made Jim want to smile again but he knew better than to hurt the kid's feelings. Mark had lost his father recently, and Jim knew how that felt. Even though his own father hadn't died until Jim was twenty-five, he felt he'd actually lost his dad many times before that, to one alcoholic blackout after another. Jim had been a very sad, lonesome six-year-old.

''Well…let's see, Mark. This is a pretty big case, and to tell the truth, I *could* use help out here. Tell you what, have you got a notebook?''

''Yeth, sir.''

''Then you take that notebook and you write down your family's names and ages and all the neighbors' names and ages, and the names of your pets and anything else important.''

Mandy clamped her hand over her mouth and hid a giggle.

Mark shot his twin sister a hateful look, then his expression became crestfallen. ''I can't,'' he said to Jim.

''Mark is just learning to read and write,'' Marie explained diplomatically.

Now Whittington felt a red wash of embarrassment rise up *his* neck. Of course, a child of Mark's age couldn't keep a notebook. *If you aren't the clever one with kids,* he thought. "Oh, well," he said to Mark. "There's more important stuff than that to do in a murder investigation anyway. Such as...such as...let me think on it, and I promise if I need something, I'll call you. I appreciate your attitude, partner."

Jim offered Mark his hand, who startled him by high-fiving it instead of shaking it. Mortified by the whole awkward exchange, Jim glanced at Marie, but her green eyes twinkled and she smiled so warmly that his self-consciousness evaporated.

He took the little girl's hand lightly and said, "Thank you, Mandy, for your help."

He stood and put on his Stetson. "Mrs. Manning, I'd better take you to the emergency room now to have that ankle examined."

She looked up at him, still smiling faintly, but when she spoke, her tone sounded starchy. "Thank you, Sheriff, but I prefer to wait until my children are safely off to school. The ankle can wait. Alice will take me."

He looked down at her ankle. He knew from the swelling that it must be killing her, but evidently the pain wasn't going to come before her kids.

"Yes, ma'am. It's your ankle," he said. "In that case, I'll go ahead and question Mr. Honicker before I leave."

"Henry's probably in the barn, or out at the bunkhouse," she said. "B.J. can fetch him."

He raised a palm. "Not necessary. Your son needs to get to school. I can locate Mr. Honicker."

She smiled again but this time it only went as far as her lips. Her eyes looked...something. Guarded? Wary? *Now* what was she thinking?

"I think it would be better if you didn't wander around out there alone. Manning Ranch is a big place," she said.

A big place? Jim thought. And Carville County isn't? For some reason she doesn't want me out on her ranch alone, but she doesn't want to say so. "Oh, I'll be all right, ma'am," he said and returned her counterfeit smile.

He picked up his clipboard, tipped his hat and let himself out of the door, thinking, What's with this woman? Manning Ranch is a big place? What does she imagine I do all day? Sit around the office and drink coffee? No, she knows better.

As he walked down the hill to the barn and outbuildings and thought about it some more, he was convinced he was right. She didn't want him wandering around on her ranch alone. She didn't trust him. And when he turned to look back at the house, and glanced at the small kitchen window, he felt as if his instincts were confirmed. Despite her ankle, there she stood, her face framed in one of the wavy panes. There she stood. Watching him.

CHAPTER THREE

EVERYTHING WILL BE JUST FINE, Marie reassured herself—again—as she looked out her kitchen window—again—and thought of him—again.

This morning he'd turned around and, she felt certain, seen her standing at this window, watching him.

She stared out at the valley below and sipped a warmed-over cup of coffee, transfixed. What was it about him? Just thinking about him felt vaguely dangerous. Apprehension floated up, like a low fog, but she pushed it down.

Thank God the children would come bursting in from school soon, with their chatter, their schedules, their needs. Whittington had been careful with them. Why did that surprise her?

Again, she tried to recall the misgivings her late husband had expressed about the sheriff. She hadn't paid attention at the time, dismissing Carl's comments as "just politics," but now some far off warning sounded within her.

In the year since Carl had died, she'd managed to shrug off these feelings of apprehension over and over again, telling herself they were normal for a woman who'd recently lost her husband.

But today the foreboding was stronger, like the panic she'd felt once when, exhausted from caring for newborn twins, she'd awakened from a fitful nap to find the oven buzzer screaming and a scorched casserole smoking up the kitchen.

It was like that now, as if she were powerless to wake up, even as danger closed in.

Did this have anything to do with *him?* She hadn't been able to get him out of her mind all day.

Or was she suffering from some form of—what'd they call it?—post-traumatic stress disorder? Sprain your ankle and find a dead body in your backyard first thing in the morning. Guaranteed to make you start seeing everything as threatening.

She eyed the inflatable brace on her ankle, wondering if she could tolerate it the full four weeks. When Alice had finally got her to the hospital, the doctor had said it was a mild sprain and the air brace would permit her to walk. For that she was grateful. Immobility was not her style.

She limped to the counter and poured the coffee down the sink, and when she looked out the window, she welcomed the distraction of a familiar sight: Toots Daniels's shiny red pickup bouncing up her driveway. Feeling better, she started a fresh pot of coffee.

Toots went through the motion of rapping on the back door, then let himself in.

"Whittington came out and questioned me a while ago," he announced around his ever-present toothpick. "And he told me about your ankle, Missy." He pushed his standard Massey-Ferguson cap back off his forehead and gave Marie a stern look. Then he reached out and gave her a hug.

He smelled like a gust of crisp October air, and his

little squeeze was an immediate solace. "My ankle is no big deal," she said. "I'm just so sorry about Cudd."

Toots cleared his throat. "Cudd wasn't no angel, but he sure didn't deserve this."

"You knew each other a long time." She studied the beloved old face.

"Ever since The War." Toots gazed past her as he spoke. "Cudd wasn't always the way he turned out at the end." He fell silent.

Not knowing how to respond to this, Marie turned to do what she could to comfort Toots. She poured him a cup of coffee just the way he liked it—with a "notion" of sugar—and handed it to him. "What did Whittington have to say?" she asked.

"Not much. First time I ever met the boy. He seems kinda…guarded." Toots settled himself in his usual chair. "But I had a little tidbit that made his eyebrows shoot up."

"What was that?"

"Well, Cudd told me something the other day that didn't exactly add up. You know how Cudd was always—"

"Lying," Marie interjected.

"Now, Missy, don't speak ill of the dead. I've been known to embellish a story myself. Even if he did fib a little once in a while, Cudd had his good points."

"Oh, yeah, I forgot. He liked to drink, gamble and shoot." Marie stopped herself right there, but silently she added, *Or are you referring to the fact that he was forever trying to cheat somebody in a shady business deal?*

But she didn't want to upset Toots any further. He

harbored some kind of dogged loyalty to Cudd that
Marie couldn't fathom because Toots and Cudd were
definitely *not* birds of a feather. Unlike filthy old
Cudd, Toots's personal hygiene was impeccable, and
Toots would sooner take a beating than a tainted dol-
lar. "What'd you tell the sheriff?" she said.

"What Cudd told me." Toots took a swig of coffee, swallowed it tight-lipped. "Yessir. The sheriff
practically had a stroke when I told him."

Toots liked to make a drama out of everything.
Marie knew that the more curious she acted, the
longer he'd drag the game out.

She limped over to a cabinet, measured flour and
cornmeal into a crockery bowl, added milk and eggs
and started stirring.

"Yessir," Toots mumbled again into his coffee cup
while she stirred, "I believe our sheriff thought it was
mighty interesting, what Cudd told me."

"Uh-huh," Marie said absently as she reached into
the refrigerator for butter. Behind her, she heard him
tapping the handle of his coffee cup.

"Hoot damn, Missy! Ain't you even curious?"

Marie looked over her shoulder. "Should I be?"

"All right then!" Toots slapped his palm on the
table as if Marie had begged him to tell all. He leaned
forward as she put the butter in the microwave. "A
while back," he said in a low voice, though there was
no one but the old dog within miles of the house,
"Cudd told me he had come into a *lot* of money.
Wouldn't say how. Anyway, I told the sheriff I noticed Cudd going into Bud Weimer's building the
other day and I told him—the sheriff—as how I never
knew Cudd to have any dealings with the likes of Bud

Weimer before and didn't he think that was interesting and all, and right then, the sheriff, he went kinda white.''

Marie was puzzled. "Let me get this straight," she said. "You saw Cudd going into the Carville County Construction building—the good old Triple C—then he comes into a large sum of money, and you think those two things are connected. Well, what if they are? Couldn't Cudd have been selling off some of his land to Triple C? They've tried to buy me out a couple of times. Or Cudd could have been—" she made quotation marks with her fingers "—embellishing things again.''

Toots slapped his hat on his thigh. "Hoot damn, Missy! It ain't just the money or Cudd's visit to Weimer. It's the way *the sheriff* acted." He scratched his jaw. "Maybe Whittington's worried about his damn election getting fouled up.''

Now Marie was really confused. "What does this have to do with the sheriff's election?''

"*Bud Weimer* is one of Whittington's big campaign contributors..." The microwave squealed and Marie and Toots jumped.

Marie walked over to retrieve the melted butter and Toots continued. "Some say Weimer controls the sheriff's department. Hell, some say he controls the whole of Carville County. And now Whittington's got to go over to Triple C and ask some pretty touchy questions. Or maybe..." Toots paused for dramatic effect.

But Marie was too jittery to play games now. "Maybe *what?*''

"Maybe our sheriff has to help Weimer cover up

something. I tell you, that boy was damn uncomfortable. Right after Bud Weimer's name came up, he did a tricky two-step and got out of there.'' Toots finished off his coffee.

Marie considered all of this while she poured the butter into muffin tins.

Her own first impression of Whittington had been mixed. He was a little…something…and here was Toots, whom she trusted with her life, telling her that Whittington was beholden to a man like Bud Weimer. She poured the corn-bread batter into the tins, thinking as she did, money, murder—Weimer, Whittington. Wait. Suddenly she remembered something. Carl had called the pair Weasel Weimer and his Wonderdog Whittington.

She heard the school bus out on the highway, decelerating, then accelerating. She limped to the window and saw the twins walking up the driveway, dragging their backpacks and kicking up rocks and dust.

She turned to Toots.

''Well?'' he said.

She sighed. ''I guess there's something besides air under that seed cap of yours, after all,'' she said.

Toots nodded, ''Damn straight.''

''But we'll have to discuss this later. The twins are home. I don't want them upset about this.''

''How're they taking Cudd's murder?'' Toots asked.

''The whole thing frightened them a little, so I went by their school at lunch hour, while I was in town getting this checked—'' Marie pointed at her ankle ''—and they seemed okay. They were the center of attention when the other kids heard about the sheriff being at our house. Mark was still going on about the sheriff at lunch. I think a little hero worship has set in.''

"Let's hope it's justified," Toots said sarcastically. "And the big kids?"

"B.J. understands the gravity of the situation, I guess. And Jillian's got her usual morbid curiosity about everything. She thinks she has some sort of evidence on a videotape she made of Cudd burying something.''

Toots shot Marie a warning glance. "Did you all tell the sheriff that?" he asked.

"Well, yeah, of course," Marie said.

"Did you give him the tape?"

"Not yet."

"Don't. Not until I check out some of my theories.''

"Well, just keep your theories to yourself for now," Marie cautioned as the twins came into the mudroom.

The twins piled on top of their great-uncle Toots, pulling on his cap and blurting out their conflicting versions of the sheriff's visit.

As Marie watched, Toots reached up and adjusted his hearing aid—one could be stone-deaf and still hear the twins—while balancing both children on his lap, and she thought how dear Toots Daniels was.

"Want to stay for dinner?" she asked.

"Sounds right medicinal," he said. "But I'll only stay on the condition that me and these children do all the serving and such and you get off that ankle."

"Agreed," Marie said and sat down at the table with a colander of potatoes to peel.

Later, Jillian appeared off the junior-high bus, and Toots drove into town to pick up B.J. from football practice.

Henry, finished with the evening chores, poked his head in the door. "I was wondering if you needed any help, since you're hurt and all, Mrs. Manning." He said this bashfully, holding his hat in one hand and a basket overflowing with ripe tomatoes in the other.

Marie smiled. "Why, Henry, how you manage to get tomatoes out of that garden all the way into October is a wonder. Put them in the sink and Jillian will slice them for dinner. Why don't you eat with us?"

"Yes, ma'am." Henry ducked his head and went to the sink with the tomatoes.

Since Carl had died, Henry ate supper in the main house more and more often, but he would never do so without an invitation. That would be against his code, and Marie knew better than to ever ask Henry Honicker to step outside the boundaries of his code.

Then, just as they were putting the food on the table, Alice showed up with a large pan of hot apple crisp. "Well, I'll be. Looks like I'm just in time." She laughed. Alice needed no invitation.

As they crowded chairs around the old oak table and ate the ham and beans Marie had started early that morning—before the murder had materialized—Marie looked at the faces of Alice and Toots and Henry, laughing and smiling with her children.

Friends, God bless them. She could make it through

anything with friends at her side. And even as the vague apprehension welled up again, she was able to push it down. Everything is fine, she told herself. Everything is just fine.

And it was. At least for the night.

CHAPTER FOUR

THE NEXT MORNING Marie rose at dawn. "You had enough murder and mayhem yesterday," she mumbled into the mirror. She'd leave that stuff to the likes of Mr. Whittington and people who thrived on such messiness.

She opened the drapes to a beautiful, first-frost morning, and as she dressed, she made plans to work in her garden as soon as the children left for school. Bring in the last of the fall tomatoes. Enjoy a little peace and quiet.

She limped into the tiny dressing room that had originally been a long, narrow closet spanning one end of the bedroom before Carl had converted it into a private retreat for her. He'd even installed a bolt latch on the inside of the door so she could lock out little invaders if she needed solitude.

She skipped the makeup and slipped on a pair of snug, well-worn jeans, then a denim work smock over a hot-red turtleneck. She wanted to wear her cordovan cowboy boots that fit like a second skin, but the air cast forced her to settle for a pair of scuffed-up Nurse Mates oxfords instead. *No one will see me today anyway,* she thought.

As she tied the oxfords, Marie surveyed her surroundings. She loved this room—the roses and lilac wallpaper, the elegant chintz fabrics, the antique furnishings that all said "only the finest."

The ceilings in the old house were all ten feet high and every door had an old-fashioned transom above. Marie had installed one of her own stained-glass creations in the transom above the closet door, and as she sat and brushed her long, wavy hair up into a high ponytail, the morning sun gleamed through the stained glass, making jewel-colored patches on the snowy-white dresser cloth. And suddenly, as she splayed her hand over the pattern of colored light, staring at the rose and gold hues, a disturbing memory surfaced.

Goodness. Why was she remembering *that* now? Maybe because it had been a sunny morning like this. At Big Pond.

Big Pond had a meandering shoreline, indistinguishable in places from its source—the wide, slow-moving creek that rose from Deep Springs and ultimately fed into the Llano River.

At the narrowest point, the pond was traversed by a quaint limestone and timber bridge, engineered by Carl Manning himself with what he termed "innate Manning knowledge and skill." He'd built the bridge so the children could fish and play, but they preferred the tree house, or the barn loft, or the deep vee in the old black oak with the twin trunks, and the bridge ended up being Marie's other private spot. Seeing her from a distance, with her legs dangling off its side, no one ever disturbed her at Big Pond bridge.

That's why it had unsettled her to see Carl striding out of the woods toward her that morning with a troubled expression on his face.

She'd stood and met him in the center of the bridge.

He started right in. "Marie, I'm going to Austin today," he said, "to see Mike Garrett, the legal counsel at the highway commission. You remember Garrett?"

Marie shook her head. How was she supposed to remember all of these political types Carl associated with?

"You met him at the Bluebonnet Banquet last year."

Marie shook her head again, getting impatient. Something was wrong, and she wanted to know what. "I don't remember him. What's going on?"

Carl sighed. "Lately I've been working on something…well, I'm not sure how much to tell you."

Then he had grasped her firmly by the shoulders, a gesture so unlike Carl that Marie felt truly alarmed.

"Listen, Marie," he said. "For a while I'm going be in Austin a great deal of the time. I may have to spend more time there than here in Deep Springs. Do you understand?"

Immediately, resentment boiled up and replaced her anxiety. *It's always more and more time in Austin,* she remembered thinking.

"Can't you tell me what this is about?" she insisted.

"No, it's best if you don't know anything. It'll all come out in the wash soon enough. But the point is—" he dug around for something in his jacket pocket "—I stopped in San Saba yesterday and got this."

Marie was stunned to see him produce a small dull-bluish-gray handgun. She stared at it as if it were a rattlesnake.

"What is this?" she breathed.

"A Smith & Wesson .22 automatic," Carl said distractedly, mistaking her meaning. "I want you to learn to use it," he continued. "Toots'll teach you."

Still staring at the gun, Marie took a step backward. "I am not using any gun, Carl. You know how I feel about guns. Besides..." She scrambled to bolster her argument. "Besides, Henry is always out here on the ranch with us."

"Henry is scared of his own shadow. I don't have time for arguments, Marie. You must learn to shoot this gun."

He took her hand and pressed her fingers around the weapon.

She remembered how compact and cold the thing felt, how she wanted to fling it into the pond. She remembered how her hand shook as she stared at it and swallowed hard. And she remembered how angry she felt. How abandoned. Carl was leaving her out on his isolated ranch, with four kids and a simpleton ranch hand, so he could chase after yet another political tempest in a teapot.

Months later, when Carl died, and her secure little world had come apart, she had been too shocked and overwhelmed with everyday survival to remember that morning at Big Pond.

Until now.

She was astounded that she had never thought beyond her own petty resentment at Carl's absences and asked herself the questions that were suddenly vexing her now.

What was the "something big" Carl had referred to?

Why had he suddenly decided that she needed a gun for protection?

Protection from what? From *whom?*

And now there was Cudd's murder. Was there any connection?

And Carl's death? Was it really an accidental drowning?

She could no longer avoid these questions. She no longer wanted to.

She stood up.

She wasn't going to pick any stupid tomatoes this morning. She was going to retrieve that gun and learn to use it. She was going to look at that videotape. She was going to get some answers to those questions.

TOOTS WAS HAPPY to oblige with the firearm lessons.

"You should have learned to shoot this thing when Carl bought it for you, instead of making all those goll-darned excuses," he admonished.

"Never mind that," Marie said. "Just get on with it."

The morning sun was in her eyes, the dew was soaking through her old nursing shoes, a morass of work waited inside, and Marie hated it when Toots was like this, all bossy ex-marine. She was beginning to regret her decision to master the weapon.

Her eyes involuntarily squeezed shut every time she pulled the trigger. How she loathed guns!

"Now," Toots said, "brace yourself and look at that target. Use the gun like it was an extension of your eyes and hands. Squeeze the trigger steady-like.''

''Go on.'' Toots pointed at a feed sack, as big as the side of a cow, which Henry had leaned against the fence. Beyond it was an empty two-acre field, freshly plowed and fallow thanks to Henry's forgetting to load the seeder. ''Seed?'' he'd said, looking sideways from under the brim of his cap.

Marie fired at the sack, missed by a mile.

A brisk breeze had picked up and her fingers ached in spite of her snug leather hunting gloves. ''Tell you what,'' she said. ''Let's go inside and warm up that leftover apple crisp and have a nice big mug of hot coffee.''

''Nothing sounds better, and we'll do that, as soon as you learn to fire this pistol with no hesitation whatsoever.'' Toots turned her by the shoulders and carefully raised the hand in which she held the gun. ''Now, shoot!''

Tired of being bossed around, tired of being cold, tired of missing the target, she fired three times, blinking violently each time the gun cracked. When she opened her eyes, she was amazed to see one neat hole oozing grain from the sack.

''Hey, I hit it!'' she said, looking from the sack to Toots with a self-satisfied expression, but he was frowning at something in the distance.

''Company's coming,'' he said.

She recognized the Bronco immediately. ''Wonder what he wants,'' she said.

''The tape,'' Toots answered.

She flicked up the safety on the gun, and handed it to Toots. She hastily undid, tidied up and reclipped her hair. Then she limped out to the edge of the driveway, muttering, "Law or not, he should have called."

He brought the Bronco to a halt, jumped out, slammed the door, strode up to Marie and without exchanging amenities, said, "Mrs. Manning, my deputy observed you out riding a horse on the McCombs property just after sunup. I must caution you against that kind of thing for the time being."

It irked Marie that he had marched up to her and issued his "caution" without so much as a hello. "Sheriff, I would think you and your deputy would be too busy investigating a murder to be concerned about my personal comings and goings," she said.

His eyes narrowed briefly, looking her up and down, assessing her inelegant appearance. She felt strangely vulnerable standing there, devoid of makeup, in her stupid oxfords. Then he pushed his hat back on his head and massaged his forehead.

Very quietly he said, "Mrs. Manning, my deputy was out searching for evidence at first light. You'll recall, I told you there would be deputies about for the next few days. I'm just asking you not to wander around out there by yourself—for now."

Marie felt a telltale flush climbing up her face. She mumbled "Of course," because what else could she say? She sure didn't want him to know she'd been looking around Cudd's woods because of what she'd seen on that videotape.

"Be careful, ma'am. Mr. Daniels." He tipped his Stetson and turned to leave, then turned and said, "Oh! Have you had time to find that videotape?"

"Not yet," she lied. What she meant was, she and Toots hadn't made a copy yet.

"Would it be all right if I pick it up later today?"

"Of course."

He touched the brim of his hat again and turned back to the Bronco. Then he stopped and pointed to the pistol. "By the way, I saw your target practice. When you take the clip out, don't forget you've still got one in the chamber."

Marie flushed higher. Had he seen her preening too?

"Of course," she repeated. She pointed at the feed sack. "You'd better tell your men to check in with me if they're going to be anywhere on my property."

He squinted over his shoulder at the sack with its one lonesome hole, then looked at Marie. "Right. I'll tell the deputies to check in with you." He tipped his hat again and climbed into the truck.

As they watched the Bronco pull away, Toots said, "That sure is a hat-tippin' varmint."

"What on earth do you mean by that?"

"I mean, you make him mighty nervous, Missy."

"I doubt anything makes him *mighty nervous,* unless maybe it's the Manning name," Marie said, fiddling with her hair again.

"Well, that, maybe. But I'm talking about *you,* Missy. And him. You bother him in an entirely different way."

She turned her burning face away from him and jerked off her hunting gloves.

"Toots, I've had enough target practice. I'm going back over to Cudd's to have another look around. If the sheriff comes back for that tape, make up some excuse, but don't give it to him, and *don't* let him know where I am. He seems to think I should just cower in my house like a scared rabbit while people are stabbing each other right under my nose."

"Now, Marie." Toots followed her as she limped off to the house. "What did the sheriff just tell you? And what about that ankle? And I don't think you need to be digging around Cudd's dingy dugout. It ain't…it ain't no place for a lady…" Toots stopped.

He looked genuinely embarrassed, but she didn't have time to worry about proprieties. Toots also apparently thought she should stay in her house with her hands folded in her lap.

"My ankle's fine. And after what I remembered this morning—" she snatched the gun from him "—I realize that I can't leave unpleasant or messy things up to other people." She fumbled to remove the clip. "This is *my* life and *my* home and I am going to check things out for *my*self."

"You just be careful, Missy, when you go checking things out."

"I know what I want to do," Marie said as she handed him the unloaded gun.

"That is exactly what worries me," Toots muttered.

MARIE DROVE the Jeep near to the spot in Cudd's woods where she thought the video had been filmed. She climbed out and walked the area, so she could examine the grounds more closely. Again, she found nothing. Not even a patch of disturbed earth. The air cast was working remarkably well, so she kept going, taking a shortcut through the woods to Cudd's trailer.

Which was indeed a dingy dugout.

It was locked, and Marie slapped her forehead for

forgetting to get the key from Toots. But peering in the windows and seeing the conditions outside the trailer—rotting potato peels, grease poured outside the kitchen window—was enough to make Marie want to "retch," as Alice had put it.

She looked into all the windows of the rusty car bodies littering the yard. Then she moved on to the equally rusty metal shed behind the trailer.

The shed proved too crowded with junk to permit entry. Still not having the faintest idea what she was searching for, Marie moved to the barn.

Cudd's barn was as dissimilar to Marie's as two barns could be. Hers was maintained with several flawless coats of deep red—at least Henry could paint with competence; Cudd's had no fleck of paint left on its warped gray exterior. Her doors glided open levelly at the slightest tug; it took all of her might to pry Cudd's open a few inches.

The inside was cavelike in its darkness, even on this brilliantly sunny morning. All portals that might admit sunlight and fresh air had been blocked long ago and Marie feared for her health as she breathed the stale, mote-filled air. She pried the door open as far as she could.

The stench was like that of the shed: rust, machine oil, rotting paper, ancient dust. No hint of healthy animals or fresh vegetation, unless one counted the wild grapevine that had forced its way through the cracks in the siding. Wishing she'd brought a flashlight, she stepped into the filthy cavern, slapping away cobwebs just inside the door.

Strange things here, she thought as her eyes adjusted to the gloom. Old farm implements and car parts, stacks and stacks of rotting newspapers and magazines, boxes overflowing with faded plastic flowers—Thelma's?—parts of shelves, chairs and tables, a pile of old boots and shoes in a corner, and more cans and bottles and jars than Marie thought possible to accumulate in one lifetime. All of it giving mute testimony to one certainty: Cudd McCombs owned nothing worth being killed for.

Against a far wall stood the one valuable item in the whole mess, a massive antique highboy. With a mixture of fascination and disgust, Marie peeked into its creaky drawers one by one and found old photographs, neatly folded yellowing linens. She was delicately lifting the old lace tablecloths in the bottom drawer when she found it.

Money.

Marie heard her own short gasp and felt her heart race as she uncovered the neat stacks of brand-new hundred-dollar bills. A lot of money.

She slid out one package of bills and became so absorbed in counting them that she didn't notice the change in the lighting as a shadow stole across the floor.

"Find anything?" a deep voice asked from behind her.

Marie screamed and stumbled backward against a pile of tattered quilts.

Jim Whittington stood above her, calmly looking down from under the brim of his Stetson. He extended a gentlemanly hand to help her up, but she kept one palm over her heart and the other fist under her hip, clutching the money.

She gulped for air—it took her a minute to speak. "Are you trying to scare me to death, Sheriff?"

"No, but maybe I could scare a little sense into you," he said and put his hand out again.

Marie lifted her hand from her heart and accepted his with dignified aloofness, but he jerked her rather roughly to her feet and she lost her balance. He steadied her against him. She stiffened and stepped back, folding her arms under her bosom tightly, hiding the money, and thoroughly shaken by their contact.

"What are *you* doing here?" they both said at once.

Whittington's mouth puckered in a sarcastic expression that indicated his reasons for being there were quite obvious, and he waited for her answer.

Marie looked around the floor of the barn as if she would find a plausible lie among the debris, but when she met his steady gaze, she doubted her ability to dupe this man.

"I'm nosying around," she stated bluntly.

"Well, you're nosying around in something out of your league, Mrs. Manning. I'll take you home now." He looked down at her ankle and took her by the elbow. "I've got a horse."

"A horse?"

"I've been checking out parts of the McCombs property inaccessible in the Bronco." He gave her elbow another tug.

That's why she hadn't heard him drive up.

The tablecloths in the drawer had fallen back over the money, but Marie feared he would discover the wad she had hidden in the folds of her smock and she jerked her elbow free. "Thank you, but the doctor said I could walk as long as it doesn't hurt. I'll go back to my Jeep. Besides, I'm not through looking around yet.''

''Yes, you *are* through looking around. I suggest you go home, and learn to *really* use that gun.''

Marie wanted to ask what the devil he meant by that. But she decided she'd better get out of there while she had the chance, before he discovered the money.

''Yes, I guess you're right, Sheriff. I'm not really a very good marksman at all. That was just a lucky shot this morning.''

Marie looked up into his eyes meekly, but he returned her gaze with one of cool appraisal.

''I know that,'' he said. ''Now, will you please leave the investigating to law enforcement?''

''All right, I'll go.'' Marie pretended to capitulate. ''But you will let me know if you find anything out here, won't you?''

''Depends on what I find.''

''Yes. Sensitive evidence and all, I guess. Well, goodbye.''

Marie limped out of the barn quickly. She could feel him watching her until she got around the curve in the weedy driveway.

When she was sure she was out of his view, she circled back through the woods and found a place where she could hide and spy on him.

She watched him progress from barn to shed to trailer and was surprised to see that he had a key to the trailer. He remained in there a long time. When he came out, he began walking straight in Marie's direction, moving fast, whistling loudly.

Marie started to run for better cover, but her ankle immediately reminded her how futile that effort was. She whirled around, looking for a better place to hide. The whistling was getting louder. In desperation she climbed a gnarly old live oak that hung low to the ground.

She had the money tucked in the pocket of her smock, so that both arms were free, and she wrapped herself around a fat limb. She put her cheek against the rough bark and bit her lip because now her ankle was really smarting. Walking around with the air cast was one thing—tree climbing was another.

Whittington slowed down when he got into the woods. She heard his boots crunch on the underbrush and halt a few times.

Then, to her horror, he came to a stop under the very tree where she hung so precariously. He leaned against the trunk and fished a cigar out of his jean jacket. He bit off the tip, spit it out and struck a match on his boot. Soon Marie saw a thin trail of smoke coming from under the brim of his Stetson.

She was so tense her ears were ringing. She wanted to scream, but instead she bit her lip and held her breath.

Whittington continued to smoke for what seemed an eternity. His posture was relaxed and perfectly still. The breeze whispered through the leaves as Marie controlled her breathing in soundless little puffs.

He coughed a short bark and Marie almost slipped off her limb.

"Mrs. Manning," he said quietly from under the hat, "I think you can help me. Want to come down?"

Marie felt herself blush fire red as he slowly looked

up. From under the brim of his hat, his face gave no hint of mockery; his eyes only regarded her with solemn inquiry.

Marie had never felt so humiliated as she tried to descend from the tree gracefully. He stood directly below her, and kept his eyes on her the whole time, possibly to catch her if she slipped, but his penetrating observation of her awkward climb down added to Marie's discomfort. Vanity pricked at her as she remembered the little hole in the seat of her jeans and thought again of how totally oddball her worn-out white nurse's oxfords must look.

When she got within his reach, he propped the cigar in the vee of a low limb and encircled the back of one of her slender thighs with his large hand. He steadied her at the waist with the other hand and lowered her to the ground as protectively as if she were a child. She touched her feet down as softly as a feather, facing him, so close that she could feel the heat from his chest and she could smell that wonderful enigmatic scent of his.

He stood there, and Marie was acutely aware that, for the third time in two days, this man had his hands on her, which was more than any man had touched her in the last year and four months. And furthermore, she realized with a shock, she liked it. She liked it way too much.

"Now," he said, jamming one hand into his jeans' pocket and retrieving the cigar with the other, "I suppose you just stopped to rest up in that tree on the way to your Jeep?"

Marie felt a jet of defensive anger.

"I was spying on *you*," she responded.

He feigned a look of shock. Then his face clouded over with genuine exasperation. He stuck the cigar in the corner of his mouth and talked around it. "Mrs. Manning, I was led to believe you are a woman of good sense. Don't you understand that this is not a game?"

Marie couldn't think of a comeback, and with absolutely no warning, tears popped up in her eyes. She turned her face away. He thought she was just a nosy woman, a silly woman, running around in a pair of crappy old nursing shoes. How could he understand the anxiety that had reared its head since they'd discovered Cudd's body? How could he understand the doubts raised by her memories this morning? How could he understand the dire need to *do* something—anything—that had driven her over here? A miserable whimper escaped her throat and her shoulders heaved.

He took the cigar from his mouth and cleared his throat. She sensed his discomfort, but she didn't care.

"I don't think I handled this very well," he said. "Let's…let's just pretend this whole little deal in the tree never happened. Okay?"

How could he understand that when he spoke kindly to her, it made her want to trust him, to tell him everything about that morning at Big Pond? How could he understand that she couldn't trust anyone now, at least not until she talked to Mike Garrett, the Highway Commission Council?

"Mrs. Manning?" he said as he came around and tried to look her in the face, "I didn't mean to embarrass you. Does…does your ankle hurt?"

Marie shook her head. She held her hand over her mouth and hiccuped violently.

"Won't you let me take you home now?" he asked quietly.

When she shook her head again, he straightened up and pushed his hat back, frowning.

"Mrs. Manning, I really did mean what I said, about your being able to help me. If I take you on the horse, could you show me the shortest route through the woods to the place where McCombs was murdered?"

Marie calmed down and stopped hiccuping while she considered his request, then she remembered the money in her pocket. That could get her in a lot of trouble; she'd be better off going home on her own. But she couldn't think of any excuse not to cooperate with him.

She nodded her consent and wiped her eyes with the back of her hand. She looked up at him and it struck her that he had the kindest pair of dark brown eyes she had ever seen.

"You know what?" he said with a gentle smile. "I have to admit, I admire a woman who takes action, even if she does find herself—" he looked up "—up a tree." He grinned at his own corny joke.

Marie returned his grin with a sheepish one of her own.

"Now," he said, taking her elbow lightly, "let's go get my horse and see what we find."

When they got to the horse, his hands were on her again as he assisted her into the saddle. The air cast would not fit in the stirrup, which made her ascent awkward. And arousing.

But not nearly as arousing as riding around the two ranches with him behind her. He wrapped his long arms around her to handle the reins, and a couple of times he steadied her at the hips. She was aware the whole time, all too aware, of his body heat, his wonderful scent, the rumble of his deep-voiced commands to the horse.

All too aware.

CHAPTER FIVE

"I WENT OVER to the Swing Door last night, for a little tipple, and I overheard one of the regulars talking about you and the sheriff."

Toots had popped in for morning coffee before he helped Henry haul a couple of steers off to the packers. Marie was hurrying through her morning routine so she could make her call to Mike Garrett, as soon as the kids were gone, and she'd been basically ignoring him. Now she turned on him, aiming a spatula as if it were a microphone. "You overheard *what?*" she said.

"You heard me. Russel Garms was blabbering to everybody in the Swing Door about how Carl Manning's widow and the sheriff were trotting all over the Manning property together yesterday."

Marie stood frozen, spatula suspended. "The Swing Door *bar?*" she said. For crying out loud. They were gossiping about her in that godforsaken hole?

The Swing Door—named for its metal freight door that swung both ways for the convenience of all the regulars and the beer deliveries—had a dim reputation.

Marie, like all the other women in Deep Springs, knew the story about the time Dickey Wayne Bauer's pesky girlfriend came busting through the swing door to hunt Dickey Wayne down and accidently surprised poor old Henry Honicker while he was in the doorless rest room. Henry, though flustered, had tipped his hat politely enough, but the poor girl never lived it down. Marie had never had any desire to set so much as a toe inside the Swing Door, and she would certainly have preferred not to have her name mentioned there.

But Toots seemed annoyed at *her*. "What were you thinking, Missy, running around on your hurt ankle like that?"

"We were on a horse." Marie waved the spatula.

"*A* horse? *One* horse?" Toots tapped the handle of his coffee mug.

Marie's cheeks flamed and she turned back to flipping pancakes. "What, exactly, did Garms have to say about me?" She tossed the pancakes onto a plate.

"He was telling some fellas in the next booth how Whittington was sure spending a lot of time out on the Manning place, and he was wondering out loud, mighty loud, why Whittington was being such a bulldog about a rotten old drunk getting stabbed or if Whittington was maybe sniffing around that classy-looking Manning broad—his words, Marie, not mine—"

"Who is this Garms person?" Marie interrupted.

"Russell? He's a no-account punk. Hangs around Bud Weimer like some whipped pup looking for scraps."

Marie slammed the spatula down. "What I do on my own ranch should not be the subject of scurrilous, speculative gossip by a bunch of drunks at the Swing—"

"Eww, gross! A mutant!" Mark said, holding up a lump of fused Cheerios, reminding Toots and Marie that they were having this conversation in the presence of the children.

Marie gave Toots a "that's enough" look and his mouth formed a tight line, then he drained his coffee cup.

"Jillian, finish your pancakes and help the twins into their rain slickers, please. It looks like it's getting ready to storm," Marie said.

Jillian wiped her hands on her napkin, then reached for the raincoats. "To hell with that Garms guy, Mom. If you ask me, Sheriff Whittington is doing a hell of a good job."

Marie ignored Jillian's "hells" and thought that if Toots hadn't already ducked out the door, she'd bean him. She wished she'd never heard of Cudd McCombs, and as for Sheriff Whittington—somehow he had to be responsible for this Russel Garms character knowing about their horseback ride yesterday.

She had half a mind to drive into town and confront the sheriff, but she couldn't afford the time. She had to uncover the truth about what happened to her husband. And the first thing she needed to do was call Mike Garrett.

There was also the videotape to deal with. Disturbing. Cudd digging—burying?—something out in the woods.

Thunder boomed in the distance. Maybe she'd better look for that spot in the woods again before the ranch roads became impassable.

NAVIGATING THE JEEP in the rain, on the rutted ranch road, was nerve-racking enough, but with Toots Daniels as a back-seat driver... Shoot, Marie thought, it'd be easier to drive the Indy 500 with a screaming Brownie troop packed in the back.

When he hissed and stamped his foot into the floorboard as if to brake, Marie'd had enough. "Kindly cut it out," she said.

"Then you kindly slow it down. You shouldn't even be driving with that ankle."

"It's my *left* ankle and if you don't like my driving, you shouldn't have insisted on tagging along."

"Tagging along? Lady, I was shanghaied." Toots set his cap at a rakish angle, turned his face to the window, and a punitive silence ensued.

When the rain had started, Henry had come into the mudroom and said, "Tomorrow's as good as today. That beef ain't gonna rot on the hoof." Then he'd plodded off to sit on the porch, whittle and count raindrops.

That's when Marie talked Toots into investigating Cudd's property with her; she didn't want to get stuck out on some muddy road with a bad ankle. And besides, Toots could be a very wise sounding board, when he wasn't sucking in his breath every two seconds and emitting muffled hooting noises like some kind of uptight owl.

She glanced over and said mildly, "Tell you what, Toots, I'll just steer and you drive, okay?"

Toots grinned. "That's more like it, Missy."

"I'm sorry if I've been acting a little touchy. Mind if I tell you what's bothering me?"

"It'd be a lot better than running around acting one biscuit shy of a dozen."

"Is that how I've been acting?"

"Nah." Toots waved his hand at her. "You just haven't been yourself. What's eating you?"

Marie gripped the steering wheel and watched the wipers slap back and forth a few times. If she could trust anyone with this nonsense, it was Toots Daniels. "A whole bunch of things that don't add up. I started remembering things that Carl did right before he died—"

"Like the gun?"

"Yeah. And other things that seem sort of odd to me now, looking back. I'm starting to think I was blind. I don't think I saw the warning signs."

"The warning signs?" Toots said, and cranked up his hearing aid.

"Signs that Carl was involved in something dangerous, signs that he was extraordinarily stressed. Like one morning after he gave me the gun, I looked out the kitchen window and saw him loading some paper boxes into his car and, without coming into the house to say goodbye or anything, he just drove off. Like a bat out of hell. I remember running out the door and standing in a cloud of gravel dust, watching his car disappear onto the highway toward Austin, and being overcome with a wave of sadness. Maybe it was a premonition. I guess this does sounds crazy to you."

Toots reached up and patted Marie's shoulder. "Listen here, Missy. This is old Toots you're talking to."

Marie nodded. "And there were other things. Carl became really secretive about his office at home. And he was irritable with the children. That wasn't like Carl.''

Marie jerked the Jeep around a big puddle, then continued. ''Suddenly, I'm seeing things I didn't see before. Seeing connections. Remember when you told me you saw Cudd going into the Triple C building?''

Toots nodded.

''Well, I'm ashamed to admit it, but during all those weeks when Carl was acting so distant and strange, one day I was cleaning his office and I kind of…kind of peeked…at some of the stuff lying on his desk—''

Toots shrugged.

''And one of the files said, Carville County Bidding Practices and Triple C was listed in that file over and over. At the time, I just passed it over. It looked like ordinary highway commissioner business to me. But that was a big file, Toots, a big accordion file, and when I cleaned up his office after he died, I realize now, that file was gone. Back then, I didn't think a thing about it, but now I wonder.''

''Because I saw Cudd hanging around Triple C?''

''Yes. And also because you said Cudd claimed he'd come into a large sum of money…and guess what, Toots?'' The wipers slapped back and forth a beat while Marie hesitated. ''For once, Cudd wasn't lying.''

The wipers whacked again and Toots turned to her.

''I found that money, or at least a big chunk of it.''

Toots looked dumbfounded. ''You found Cudd's money?''

"Yes. Stacks of hundred-dollar bills. Hidden in an old dresser in his barn."

"I'll be damned," Toots breathed.

"The sheriff showed up right when I found it, but I managed to hide it. I secretly watched him search Cudd's place and it didn't look like he discovered the money, but of course, it's just a matter of time—"

"Marie, have you gone loco?" Toots interrupted. "You found a load of cash in a murdered man's barn and you didn't report it to the sheriff?"

"Now hold on a minute. You're the one who told me that Bud Weimer is one of Whittington's big campaign contributors. Let's suppose Cudd *did* get the money from Weimer, and for some reason Weimer doesn't want anybody to know that? What if the sheriff owes Mr. Weimer a favor in return for the campaign contributions?"

"I get it. Like maybe Weimer told the sheriff to get ahold of that money before anybody else finds out about it? That would explain the sheriff's being so het up when I mentioned Cudd's money and Triple C in the same breath."

"That's right," Marie said. "And here's something else. Whittington had a key to Cudd's trailer. Did you know anybody else had a key besides you?"

"Nope. Cudd didn't have any kin or anything."

"And when were you planning to begin to dispose of Cudd's worldly goods?"

"Well, not until after the funeral. The sheriff asked me to wait a few days, until they got through with their investigation."

"Exactly," Marie said, jabbing her finger at Toots, then she clutched the wheel when she hit a mud hole.

"They've got to *find* something all right—an obscene amount of money."

"You don't think he found the money yet?"

"Not yesterday, he didn't. Not as far as I could tell, but—"

"I'll go over there and pick it up as soon as we get back. You shoulda told me about this sooner, Missy."

"I *told* you I was distracted," she defended.

Thunder boomed overhead. Toots took a toothpick from his pocket and chewed it.

"So, what the hell are we doing out here?" he asked.

"Well, I'm guessing again, but I think maybe Cudd was burying something—more money maybe—or…"

"You want to see what Cudd was burying when Jillian taped him?"

"Yes. But so far I haven't found anything in these woods. They're so dense, and the tape's not at all clear."

"No, I couldn't tell much from watching it. Did you give the tape to the sheriff yet?"

"No. He never came back yesterday."

Toots set his hat straight and chewed on his toothpick again, thinking.

God bless Toots, Marie thought as she glanced over at his serious expression. *He doesn't think I'm crazy.*

"Do you think all this could have something to do with—" Marie stopped and the wipers slapped back and forth a beat.

"With what?" Toots said.

"With Carl's death."

There was a long silence then. The whir of the tires

on the muddy road, the *slip-slap* of the wipers, the drumming raindrops, all seemed amplified inside the Jeep as Marie felt Toots examining her profile. Now *he thinks I'm crazy,* she thought.

She glanced at him. His old blue eyes were bright with something—pity? understanding? disbelief?

"Well, my stars, Missy, if that's what you've been thinking, then I can see why you've been acting a little strange," he said quietly.

"That's exactly what I've been thinking." She felt a rush of relief to be admitting it out loud.

"Well, then, I reckon nothing will set your mind at ease but to know the whole truth," Toots said. "And I'm here to help you, every step of the way."

Marie felt sudden tears sting her eyes. Was there anybody in the whole wide world like Toots Daniels?

"Toots, you know what?" she said. "You're one in a million."

"Nah." Toots waved his hand at her. "Maybe one in nine hundred thousand."

Marie laughed through her tears.

Suddenly she slammed on the brakes on a rocky spot and turned to Toots. "Listen, we aren't going to find anything in this rain. If you really want to help me, could I drop you at my place so you could be there when the kids get home from school? I need to go into town."

"Sure, but first I gotta get that money. And I won't cook for 'em. Your kids are too spoiled by Mama's cooking."

Marie had seen some of the hideous concoctions Toots called food and decided her kids had good survival instincts. "Okay," she said. "No cooking. If I'm not home by suppertime, I'll call Alice."

"It's a deal. But why the sudden need to run into town?"

"I just realized there's one vital record I need to get my hands on and the fastest way to get it may be through the sheriff."

Marie saw one gray eyebrow shoot up.

"I'm going to see the sheriff, Toots. That's final. I don't care *what* the fools at the Swing Door say."

CHAPTER SIX

A LIGHT DRIZZLE was still falling and the October sky hovered at dusk by the time Marie arrived in Deep Springs. Several attempts to get through to Mike Garrett had taken much longer than she anticipated. Was Garrett's receptionist a complete biddy or what?

As she limped up the long flight of limestone steps to the courthouse portico, she suddenly realized how drained she felt, how much her ankle hurt.

She stopped to catch her breath. Dead leaves swirled around the marble pillars, making the monstrous old building seem abandoned. She looked back out over the square and saw only a half-dozen cars. Main Street looked deserted, and the clock on the First Texas Bank read 5:48. Maybe she should just dash over to the music store for Jillian's orchestra book and forget about seeing the sheriff until tomorrow.

As she turned to make her way down the steps, she noticed a lone figure crossing the courthouse square. He looked vaguely familiar and his behavior struck Marie as odd. Furtive. She stopped to watch.

The short, paunchy, balding man jumped the low hedge beside the sidewalk, cut across the courthouse lawn and climbed over a low retaining wall along the west wing, disappearing from sight.

Marie limped to the west end of the portico and peered over the railing. Where had the man gone? She could see a row of windows in a basement just behind the low wall where a short flight of stairs led down to a door. He must have gone in there.

She was turning to leave when the door cracked open and a beam of light bled up the side of the courthouse, throwing the stonework into sharp relief. Marie jerked back into the shadows as two men came partway up the stairs, talking.

It was the pudgy little man—with Jim Whittington. Standing in the damp evening air, Whittington looked naked without his Stetson. He ran his hand through his thick dark hair repeatedly while the little man shouted and jabbed a finger at him.

Even in the dusky light, she could see how florid the man's face was becoming, but from this distance, she couldn't make out his words. She heard Whittington reply in low tones.

The man shouted again and Marie saw Whittington bring one hand down in a chopping motion that seemed to end the conversation. The man turned without another word and walked up the steps and around the corner, disappearing somewhere to the back of the courthouse.

Whittington turned and stomped inside. The heavy metal door drubbed closed.

Marie leaned against the limestone railing of the portico and fought the urge to scurry back to her car. Now that she knew Whittington was in the courthouse, she intended to get what she wanted. She limped around the portico and went inside.

She ducked into the ladies' room and checked herself out in the mirror. She looked drawn, severe. She reached up and touched the emeralds on her ears. A peace offering after one of Carl's long absences.

She pawed through her purse for a lipstick and her fingers came across the prescription painkillers the doctor had given her yesterday for her injured ankle. *Boy, do I need these now,* she thought, and downed two. Then she applied the lipstick and tried to tame her hair. *Why was she being so picky about her appearance?*

She told herself to keep her mind on business and went out to find a wall chart, which showed the sheriff's office to be in the basement.

Descending the dimly lit stairs Marie caught a whiff of stale urine drifting from a narrow corridor that had Holding Cells stenciled on the wall above. A shiver coursed through her. Down the hall, a square of light filtered through the frosted glass on a door that had Carville County Sheriff's Office stenciled on it. Behind it, Marie could hear phones ringing and muffled voices.

Just as she placed her hand on the doorknob, a deep voice behind her said, "Need something?"

She jumped and looked up at a muscular young man in a too-tight deputy's uniform, standing with his hands on his hips and his pelvis thrust forward. He pushed a toothpick around with his tongue. He was not smiling.

"I…yes, I need to see the sheriff," Marie said.

The deputy did not remove his reflective sunglasses, his hat or the toothpick. "Sheriff's not here," he said. Then he reached in front of Marie, threw the door open and stepped in front of her into the office.

He didn't close the door behind him so Marie followed. A young woman—a dispatcher?—and two older deputies were sitting on the corners of their desks, talking and laughing, but they fell silent when they saw Marie.

"I need to see the sheriff," she announced.

There was a cough from one of the older deputies. Marie noted the scattering of Whittington-for-Sheriff campaign paraphernalia at the back of the room. What would Carl have said about that? Campaign materials being distributed from a county office? She gave them all a scathing look and the two older deputies slid off their desks and retreated to the coffee station at the back. The muscle-bound deputy slumped in a desk chair.

"I thought I saw the sheriff coming in just now." Marie directed this inquiry to the young woman.

The girl seemed to want to be more helpful. "He was here, Mrs. Manning," she said, "But he left for home about two minutes ago. He has some big political thing tonight."

Marie noted with a shock that the girl knew exactly who she was. For some reason, that increased her discomfort, but she refused to be put off. "Then I need to know where he lives," she said.

The girl looked taken aback. "Why, ma'am, I can't tell you that," she said. "The sheriff isn't even listed in the phone book. For security reasons—"

"Look—" Marie took a step forward and pointed at the girl "—I am a citizen of this county, and as you all know—" her finger swept over the others "—a murder has occurred right on my property. Now, I have urgent business with the sheriff and I do *not* want to wait until he's through playing politics. *Where does he live?''*

The dispatcher shot a distraught glance at the sullen deputy, whose expression was inscrutable behind the dark glasses. Without budging from his slouched position, he said, ''Well, ma'am, I'm the officer on duty. You'll have to take up your urgent business with me.''

Marie marched over to his desk and read his name tag. ''Deputy Pruitt,'' she shouted, ''my business is with the sheriff, not with you. I demand to see Sheriff Whittington *tonight.''*

Marie, who never raised her voice, thought, *It must be those painkillers* and made a mental note not to take any more of the stuff.

Pruitt gave an imperceptible nod to the dispatcher.

The dispatcher nervously scribbled down Whittington's address.

JIM ARRIVED at his front door on the run. He tossed aside the wrapper from the cheeseburger he'd inhaled on the drive home and sprinted to the shower.

While he scrubbed himself, his mind whirred. Did he have any clean shirts left? How could he have almost forgotten this forum at the library tonight? Should he spend the night in Austin on Monday? When was he going to find time to get back out to Marie Manning's and get that videotape? He could always send Pruitt, but he had to admit that he wanted to go himself—he wanted to see her again. He thought of her awkward descent from the tree and chuckled. Then he thought, *Keep your mind on your*

*business, boy. No one else is going to win this election
for you.*

He wished again for a professional campaign man-
ager, or at least someone to look after his calendar
and keep track of the money. The money. The money.
The money. He was sick to death of worrying about
the next campaign dollar. Not only had Weimer failed
to come through with volunteers, now he was threatening to dry up financially. This evening had been a
good example of Weimer's kind of "help." *I'd be on
time right now if Weimer hadn't come by to tell me
how to run that murder investigation.*

He despised Weimer and all of his ilk. Weaselly
little bastard. First it was the helicopter. "Sure, the
county can afford it!" Weimer had said and promptly
delivered the commissioners' votes to fund it. Then
he'd proceeded to tell Jim how to use the thing.
Inappropriately. Manipulatively. Shamelessly. It
reached the point where Jim felt queasy every time
he had to walk around it in the south lot.

Weimer had been right about all the publicity the
chopper generated, but lately, the man used it like a
weapon, as if agreeing to that silly helicopter had
made Jim a part of Weimer's little clique. Jim told
himself he had to play this game to get elected, but
right now he couldn't tell if he'd wolfed down that
cheeseburger too fast, or if the knot in his stomach
was from facing the truth about what was happening
to him.

Only when he turned off the water did he hear the
doorbell. Damn! Now what? He grabbed his bathrobe
and rubbed his hair with a towel as he padded to the
front door.

He peeked around the drapes and saw Marie Manning, of all people, standing on the front porch. He felt a split second of irrational panic, then renewed irritation. This was just beautiful.

He took a deep breath and opened the door a crack.

"Mrs. Manning!" he said, standing with as much of his bulk behind the door as possible. He dabbed at his dripping hair awkwardly with the towel.

"Sheriff, I need to see you," she said, seeming not to notice that he was wet.

"Now?"

"If you don't mind."

The tip of her nose was red and the corners of her mouth turned down slightly. The wind whipped little tendrils of hair into her face. For a second, she reminded him of a little girl about to cry, but when he looked closer, he could see that she was, in fact, a determined woman. Deciding it might be easier to deal with her inside, he opened the door wider and said, "Okay. Come in."

She stepped inside, and he closed the door.

Her eyes widened a fraction as she took in the sight of him in the bathrobe.

"Pardon me," he said self-consciously. "You caught me in the shower."

She looked away. "I'm sorry. I can wait if you want to get dressed."

Jim cinched the belt on his robe, drew a nervous breath and exhaled with puffed cheeks. "Mrs. Manning, I don't mean to be rude, but is this going to take long? I've got an important meeting at the library in about half an hour. I'll be happy to see you in my office tomorrow, unless there's some kind of emergency."

"No emergency, Sheriff. I understand about your important meeting—I've done some politicking myself—but I think your *current duties* are as important as your *future ambitions,* don't you? No, this won't take long."

Did this woman have a little lecture rehearsed for every occasion? he wondered as he watched her limp across the room, sit down in his antique rocker and cross her legs. She folded her hands on her knee and the corners of her mouth stayed firmly down.

He could tell she was not going to leave any time soon. Just what he needed—more pressure.

"Make yourself comfortable. I'll be right out." He exited down a brightly lit hallway.

While he was dressing, Marie surveyed his living quarters with reluctant curiosity.

An interesting antique barber's chair looked as if he actually sat in it, absorbed in that giant TV, no doubt. She read some of the titles on the stacks of videotapes on the floor next to the television. Old westerns. War sagas.

Predictably, there was a locked gun cabinet chockfull of various and sundry firearms, next to an antique coatrack festooned with an assortment of cowboy and baseball hats.

A comfortable-looking black couch—real leather?—was draped with an impressive, rich-colored Navajo blanket and padded by several natural-fiber throw pillows. An old library table, cut down to coffee-table height, was littered with hunting-and-fishing magazines and a dismaying accumulation of mail, political flyers, county newspapers and dirty cups and glasses.

Next to the fireplace a massive oak wall cabinet housed cases and cases of cassette tapes and CD's, and a sound system that could probably kill small rodents. Native American art graced the walls.

But the most intriguing thing about the room were the bookcases. They filled one entire wall. It was an amazing collection.

She wanted very much to go over and examine the titles, but she decided that would be too nosy. After the tree incident, she didn't want to reinforce the idea that she was a snoop. Besides, she was here on a mission, not to find out more about the enigmatic Sheriff Whittington. She rearranged her ankle for comfort and tried to regulate her unsteady breathing.

An elderly-looking black Labrador retriever sauntered into the room and laid himself at Marie's feet. He lowered his muzzle onto his paws and regarded Marie with solemn red-rimmed eyes.

"Hello, old fella," Marie said.

With that small encouragement, the dog inched forward and laid his head on Marie's foot.

"Amos." Whittington's voice startled them both. "Leave the lady alone. Out." He pointed in the direction of the kitchen.

The dog raised his head and looked over his shoulder at Whittington, turned, regarded Marie and laid his head back on her foot.

Whittington rolled his eyes. "That dog always did obey real well."

"You're a good old boy, aren't you, Amos?" Marie reached down and stroked the dog's head.

Whittington seated himself on the couch facing Marie. "Now, what can I do for you, Mrs. Manning?" he said.

Marie stared at him for a moment as he draped his tie and jacket over the arm of the couch. She had never seen him in anything but rugged western clothing. In his freshly starched pin-striped shirt and expensive-looking navy worsted-wool suit, he looked like a different man. Freshly shaven, his planed cheeks and square jaw stood out against his dark eyes, thick lashes and jet-black eyebrows. His hair was combed neatly back. His rich aftershave filled the air. Marie suddenly felt pale and plain next to his overwhelmingly polished masculinity.

"Mrs. Manning? What can I do for you?" he repeated.

Marie looked down at her hands. Now that she was here with him, she didn't know what to say. It seemed dumb to have rushed over here as if this were some emergency, but she had no choice but to tell him.

"I'm not sure you can help me, Sheriff. I want…that is I *need* some information about Carl's death."

"*Carl's* death?" Whittington looked confused.

"Yes. Carl…my late husband. When he died, I only received copies of his death certificate, but now I want to look at the entire accident report, and the autopsy."

He frowned. "That investigation was done by the Dulane County Sheriff's Office. I didn't have anything to do with it. An accidental death is investigated where the accident takes place, not where the victim lives."

"Oh, I know that, Sheriff," Marie said. "I was just hoping you could help me obtain the records from the Dulane County sheriff, and from the medical examiner."

Whittington's puzzled frown deepened. He'd been trying to get his hands on that report for months. His gut told him there was an answer buried in there somewhere. But her meddling would only complicate things. He shook his head slowly. "Mrs. Manning, why this sudden interest in your husband's accident? Wasn't it all explained to your satisfaction at the time?"

"I *thought* it was—" Marie began to rub her forehead "—but now I...I just don't think I got it all straight at the time."

Whittington studied her for a moment and his voice became quiet. "I suppose I could have a look at the records. Call my office in the next few days and we'll see what we can do." He checked his watch, then stood up and crossed over to Marie. "But right now, you'll have to excuse me." He took her elbow and raised her out of her chair.

Marie swayed a little when she stood up. The pain medicine was actively buzzing through her now. She couldn't seem to focus her thinking, and somehow she felt he didn't understand that she wanted copies of the records *for herself*. She pulled her elbow away and looked up into his face. "Sheriff, I want—" She put her hand to her temple and squeezed her eyes shut. "I want—" Her hand slid to her throat and she swayed again. She could barely hear Whittington's voice above the buzzing in her ears.

"Mrs. Manning? You'd better sit back down. Mrs. Manning!"

The buzzing grew to a roar and everything went black.

MARIE OPENED her eyes.

Jim bent over her, peered into her face and placed a cold cloth on her forehead. "Mrs. Manning," he said. "Are you okay?"

Her eyes slid open and then drifted closed again.

He switched on the antique hansom lamp behind the couch he'd placed her on and studied her face. She was very pale, but even so, he thought, extremely beautiful. She was maybe a little too slender—almost thin, he thought, glancing at her body. She had long legs, delicate feet. Had she fainted because of some problem with her ankle? He looked back up at her face, and felt a stab of worry. The dark circles under her eyes and the tiny beads of perspiration on her temples were not reassuring. "Mrs. Manning, wouldn't you like me to take you to the hospital?"

She smiled feebly, eyes still closed. "Sheriff, you are forever trying to haul me off to the hospital. I'm sure I've only fainted out of my own stupidity. I haven't eaten anything today, except a couple of pancakes this morning, and I took two pain pills, which were probably much too strong for me."

He nodded. "Well then, first things first. You just stay right here. Try to sip a little bit of this water while I'm gone." Then he disappeared into the kitchen.

Something to eat. She needs something to eat. He jerked open the refrigerator door. Three eggs, a tub of margarine, a bottle of salsa, four beers and a half-eaten Snickers bar stared back at him.

"Damn," he said under his breath.

"What?" she called out weakly from the living room.

"I said, 'That's it!' I found something to feed you," he lied.

He took the eggs and margarine out and set them on the cabinet. He clanged around among his pans, but couldn't find the skillet. "Damn," he said again, this time soundlessly.

He decided to microwave some scrambled eggs, then cast around for something to serve with them. He lurched across the room and threw open the door on his small pantry. *Something nourishing, something a lady would like.*

Amos padded into the kitchen and looked up at Jim expectantly.

"Amos, old buddy," he mumbled. "We've got us some high-class company out there. Now what in tarnation are we gonna feed her?"

MARIE SAT UP as he placed a tray on the low library table in front of her.

She looked down at the food, blinked and then struggled to keep a straight face. On a thick pottery plate lay a grotesque mountain of scrambled eggs laced with hot sauce, two toasted hamburger buns and a dainty pile of raisins. Next to that was a hefty mug of steaming tea. The place setting consisted of a paper towel folded like a napkin and a single fork.

"Sheriff, I really appreciate this," she said.

"No problem. Maybe this'll put some color back in your cheeks."

"No doubt." Marie smiled bravely.

"So, dig in."

Whittington sat across from her, watching her eat while he slowly peeled a Granny Smith apple with his pocketknife. Marie felt as if he was counting every bite the way her father had when she was little, but she was surprised at how delicious the eggs tasted. Either she was hungrier than she thought or he could whip up some pretty tasty huevos rancheros.

"So," he said after she'd had a few bites, "why this sudden concern about your husband's accident?"

Marie thought about how to answer his question. How could she explain it to him? What would he say if she told him her suspicions about Triple C Construction?

She hadn't touched the raisins, and he offered her a slice of the apple. "Dessert," he said, then cut himself a thick slice and popped it into his mouth. When he finished chewing, he said, "Does it have something to do with the McCombs murder?"

Marie stopped chewing and swallowed hard, as she realized that the man she'd seen with Whittington outside the courthouse this evening was Bud Weimer. She'd met him in the crowd at a barbecue fund-raiser in the county-fair barn last year.

Marie put the apple slice down and dabbed at her mouth with the paper towel. She looked at her watch.

"Oh, gosh!" she said. "I completely forgot about your meeting at the library. It was so rude of me to keep you this long, Sheriff." She stacked up her dishes and started to carry the tray into the kitchen.

He came around the table and cut her off. "Don't mess with those dishes." He took the tray and set it back down on the table. "They'll blend in just fine with all the others."

Marie nodded and turned to walk in the direction of the rocker to get her purse, but he grabbed her upper arms and turned her back toward him.

"Is there something about your husband's death I should know, Mrs. Manning?" he asked, searching her face.

She tried to avoid meeting his eyes, but his hands seemed to burn through the sleeves of her sweater. "No," she said, and she wasn't lying. She wasn't so sure he *should* know. "I just decided my records would be incomplete without the accident and autopsy report. And...and the life insurance company's being so slow—"

"And so you had to come over here and see about getting them *tonight?*"

She twisted free. "I was in town, that's all. I meant to bring you Jillian's videotape as well, but I forgot it. To tell the truth, I don't think I'm managing things too well lately."

He folded his arms across his chest, as if waiting for her to say more.

But she hid behind the amenities.

"I'm really sorry for the inconvenience, Sheriff. Thank you for feeding me. It was very kind of you. I'm sorry I made you late for your meeting."

He unfolded his arms. "It seemed like you needed me more than the voters of Carville County. They just want to pick my bones anyway." Then his voice was gentle. "I wish you'd tell me what's really on your mind."

Their eyes met, and Marie felt an intense wave of longing. She wanted to trust this man so badly. But the vision of him talking to Bud Weimer outside the courthouse rose between them. What if Toots was right about Whittington's connection to Weimer?

She turned and gathered up her purse and jacket from the rocker.

He picked up his jacket and tie and a folder from among the morass of papers on the table. "Are you sure you're able to drive home safely?" he asked.

"Yes. I feel fine now." She smiled. "Thanks to your cooking."

"I've saved many a soul from the jaws of death with those eggs," he said, then looked uncomfortable as if he wished he hadn't made a joke about death.

He draped the tie around his neck, went to the door and held it open for her.

Then as she started to pass, he put his arm across the doorway, blocking her. "Mrs. Manning—"

She stopped within inches of his arm, stared at it briefly, then looked down.

"Would you do me a favor?" he said.

He was so near that his deep bass voice seemed to resonate through her, and she could hear his controlled breathing while he waited for her answer. She couldn't bring herself to look into his face.

"I...I don't know," she said. "What do you want?"

"Would you just concentrate on taking care of those four great kids of yours, and leave this murder investigation to me?" he said quietly.

Marie's mouth tightened into a firm line and her head snapped up. She looked him directly in the eyes. "You are not the one to be giving me advice about my children, Sheriff."

He dropped his arm. "What is that supposed to mean?"

"I don't see any children running around here."

"And what is *that* supposed to mean?"

"It means, you do your job, Sheriff, and I'll do mine."

"Exactly. That's what I said. I'll worry about the law enforcement and you do what you're supposed to do." He splayed his other hand on his chest. "I wasn't prying or trying to tell you how to be a parent. I just meant, it seems like your big concern now would be taking care of those four kids, instead of running around looking up old accident reports and digging around in Cudd's barn and the like. Kids can't fend for themselves—it's got to be hard on them, getting along without their daddy..." His voice trailed off. Then he said, "You're right. This is none of my business," and straightened to let her pass.

Marie went through the door, then stopped. Without turning around to look at him again, she said, "I would appreciate a copy of that report and autopsy as promptly as possible, Sheriff."

Whittington said, "Sure." And when she glanced back at him, something about his eyes looked both offended and concerned.

He nodded.

She left.

CHAPTER SEVEN

AS MARIE DROVE the long winding highway back to Manning Ranch, she had plenty of time to think.

The drizzle had stopped and the clouds had cleared, giving way to a full October moon rising in the east as mist gathered between the low hills and in the hollows along the roadside. The highway dipped where a low-water bridge crossed a narrow creek. The hours of rain—unusual in the Hill Country—had caused the creek to rise and Marie heard the *shush-shush* of water against her tires.

She braked the Jeep and watched the moon glisten off the rocky little creek. She rolled down the window, breathed in the cool night air and listened to the soothing rhythm of the water as it gurgled past the tires. Out here, in the hills, she always felt calmer.

She thought of the artless meal the sheriff had fixed for her. It was funny how being fed, eating under his watchful eye, had soothed her. A pile of raisins! Marie smiled at that. She remembered the sounds he made, banging around in his kitchen.

She remembered the way he had looked at her: with such concern, such *interest*. Maybe she was just being a silly widow, starved for male attention. Why would a man like that be interested in her? A man like that—so good-looking, so virile—probably had women dripping off him all the time. He was only being kind to her.

Her cheeks grew hot, thinking about fainting in his living room like that. But the memory of his eagerness to help caused her embarrassment to vanish in a soft smile.

She put the Jeep in gear and drove on, past fences, mailboxes, huge old trees that stood serenely soaking up the moonlight, unchanged since her childhood.

When she was little, her father used to play a game to alleviate the boredom of the long drive into town. "Cooper's mailbox," he'd sing out as they drove past, and Marie would echo, "Cooper's mailbox." Big Blue Barn, Flat Rock, Surprise Creek, the list of landmarks went on and on. Marie could name them all by the time she was five.

Suddenly she ached for her father. He could help her sort out this confusion. He could point out her real priorities. Maybe Whittington was right. Maybe she should go back to raising her little family and leave everything else up to the Law. Then again, what about the sheriff's connections to Weimer? Her father would know the answers, she felt sure.

"Jeb was a good old boy," Toots always said of her dad, and Marie knew that, from Toots Daniels, those words were the highest praise.

Marie's mother uprooted herself after Jeb died, moving to Dallas and a real-estate job. She said that with Jeb gone, wild horses couldn't keep her in the Hill Country. But wild horses couldn't drag Marie away, and even though she was only nineteen when her father died, she had stayed in the Hill Country, married Carl Manning and put down *her* roots in the rocky soil of Manning Ranch.

On impulse, she turned the Jeep off the main highway, onto the narrow gravel road that climbed Stranger Hill.

Nobody in Carville County knew exactly how Stranger Hill got its name, but most said in the days when German settlers passed by in the 1870s and 1880s the "strangers" had climbed its summit to survey their new land.

Marie pulled the Jeep into a small clearing at the top. She got out, wrapped her jacket tight around herself and walked over to sit on one of the boulders that rimmed the clearing.

The moon, suspended like a golden wafer in a velvety black sky, illuminated Manning Ranch across the highway, shimmering softly off Big Pond and Little Pond. A few lights twinkled from the house and barn, contrasting with the dark woods and low hills surrounding them.

Above her, stars were beginning to show.

For a second, Marie thought she could hear something on the wind. She looked around, half expecting to see someone. But only the motionless moon and the silent stars answered her.

She looked again toward Manning Ranch where the lights of the house glowed. Her home looked like a speck floating in a vast universe.

Her life with Carl seemed so distant, as if it had been a hundred years ago.

It felt as if she had been living in some sort of suspended state since Carl had died and now for some reason the spell was broken. It felt as if at last she was going to have to face something. Something she did not want to face, not now, not ever.

But there was no point in hiding anything from herself anymore. Carl was gone. Their relationship, with all its shortcomings and all its strengths, was gone. She did not have to be Carl's "good wife" anymore. She could be herself in all things.

That realization made her euphoric and fearful at the same time. She could be herself, but who was she, really? She had, for so many years, allowed herself to be overshadowed by Carl and his life that she hardly had a clue about the real Marie Manning.

Sitting alone atop a limestone rock on Stranger Hill in the autumn moonlight, Marie made a decision. It didn't matter what anyone else thought, not Carl, not the people in this county, not even her own children. What mattered was what *she* thought. What mattered was that she would go forward with courage.

A gust of wind blew her hair around, over her lips, and Jim Whittington's face suddenly popped into her mind. She saw his brown eyes clearly as he smoothed her hair back off her forehead and placed a cool cloth there. She imagined him leaning forward and kissing her. Goose bumps erupted all over her.

Don't be dumb, she commanded herself and stood up abruptly. She limped hurriedly back to her Jeep. What on earth brought that on? Oh, the joys of widowhood—fantasies about inappropriate men.

She started the Jeep and gunned the engine fiercely. She had no time for such nonsense. She was going to find out what was going on in this county, with Bud Weimer *and* with Jim Whittington. And she was going to find out what had happened to Carl. That was what was really important, because she couldn't have real peace, she couldn't go on with her life, until she had answered all her questions about her husband's death.

and it was really rough just because she couldn't drive
and pass the exams...go on with her life until she
was restored to her old home from her former self-
confidence...

CHAPTER EIGHT

THE FIRST THING Marie heard when she arrived at her
back door was the reassuring sound of Jillian banging
on the piano, and then the not-so-reassuring sound of
the boys having a fight. She walked into the kitchen
where Alice stood at the sink, finishing up the supper
dishes.

"Hi." Alice smiled over her shoulder.

Marie gave Alice a quick squeeze. A door slammed
in Mark's bedroom off the den, followed by considerable pounding and yelling.

"Should we call 911?" Alice asked.

Marie laid her head on Alice's shoulder and whimpered, "Can't we just make 'em go live in the barn?"

"Are you okay, honey?" Alice turned, pulling her
glasses down with sudsy fingers to give Marie a close-
up examination.

Marie smiled. "I'm fine. Better than I've been in
days...in *months,* in fact."

"Well, you look a little pale. Do you want some
supper?"

"No. Jim Whittington fed me." Marie slipped her
jacket off and went back out to the mudroom to hang
it on a coathook.

Alice followed, hands dripping. She looked incred-
ulous. "*Did what? Jim Whittington* fed you supper?"

"Yes. He made me as nice a meal as one could expect on a moment's notice—considering that he's a bachelor type."

"I *know* he's a bachelor type," Alice said, seeming suddenly peeved. "He cooked you dinner *himself?* Where on earth did he cook you this dinner? I hope you weren't alone with that man. He has a reputation as a real womanizer." Alice dried her hands on her apron and waited, as if she expected a full explanation.

Marie smiled. Alice could be such a biddy about men. She wondered what exactly constituted "a reputation as a real womanizer" in Alice's mind. Marie squeezed past her and went back into the kitchen.

Alice followed, still clutching her apron in a wad, waiting for the explanation.

"Alice, the man just fixed me some eggs, for crying out loud. I wasn't, uh, feeling well and he was kind enough to feed me." Marie decided to omit the part about fainting. Nurse Croft would whiz her off to the hospital tonight over that one, and Marie had more important things to do. "Where is Mandy?" she asked by way of diversion.

"Back there." Alice jerked her head in the direction of the bedrooms. "Learning how to fight dirty by watching her brothers. Fixed you some eggs? Where? His house? What were you doing at the sheriff's house?"

The voices in Mark's room were getting louder. "I'd better go referee before physical warfare erupts." Marie pecked Alice on the cheek. "We'll talk after the kids are in bed."

As she walked through the den she overheard B.J.

saying, "Mark, don't you ever have trouble *finding* stuff in this pigsty?"

"Only if I'm looking for thomething," she heard Mark's defensive six-year-old voice.

"Hi, fellas," Marie said as she leaned against the doorjamb.

"Mom! You're home!" Mark yelled. He ran to her and put his chubby little arms around her waist.

Marie tousled his hair. "Were you a good boy while I was in town?"

"I sure was." His voice was whiny. "But B.J.'s being mean—"

"Mom," B.J. interrupted impatiently, "Mark lost one of my floppy disks again. Somewhere in this pit."

Marie looked down at Mark. "Did you get into B.J.'s computer stuff again?"

Mark pushed his glasses up on his nose and nodded solemnly.

Marie put a palm on Mark's head while she surveyed the room and felt a terrible wave of guilt. She needed to help Mark clean up and get organized. For the thousandth time in recent months, she wished for more hours in the day.

"Mom, I need my disk. The school newsletter's on it."

"Mark, do you have any idea where it could be?"

The little boy shook his head and shot B.J. a dirty look.

"Well, we'll all just have to look until we find it. Everybody help. Straighten as you look."

She bent down and picked up a filthy shirt and jeans and shook them. Mandy slid off the bed and started to arrange plastic dinosaurs in a neat row on the windowsill. Mark and B.J. began to pick through the mélange in grudging silence.

Marie knew where Mark crammed most of the things he wanted to hide. She got down on her knees to brave a look under the bed.

Mark dashed across the room and hopped on the bed, dangling his legs in her way. "It's not under there, Mom."

"It's not?" Marie said, pulling out tennis shoes, dirty socks, a baseball cap, a stuffed dinosaur. "How can you be so sure?"

"It's just *not*, okay?" Mark's voice sounded a little frenzied. Marie pulled her head out from under the bed and looked at him. His face was red and his eyes were wild.

"Mark," she said evenly, "I think we'd better see what's under this bed, don't you?"

Mark bit his lip, then nodded in resignation.

He got down on his knees and began to pull out all manner of debris. B.J. and Mandy gathered around to watch.

At first the child produced normal little-boy stuff— cars and trucks, toy guns and crayons, books and rocks, but when he slowly withdrew a length of multicolored fabric, Marie understood the trouble.

"Hey! That's my Mo'Betta shirt!" B.J. cried and lunged forward to snatch the cowboy shirt. "You little twerp! What else of mine have you got hidden under there?" He fell to his knees and started dragging paraphernalia from under the bed.

"B.J., don't call your brother a twerp," Marie said. She was about to insist that he let Mark retrieve his own stuff when B.J. dragged out a long white bone.

Marie's heart almost stopped.

She reached out and took it from B.J. "Mark, what in the world is this?" she said.

Mark looked doubly guilty. He reached under the bed and pulled out more bones of every size and shape.

"Mark, what's all this stuff?" she demanded.

"I'm not sure, Mom," Mark answered solemnly, "but I think it's some kind of dinosaur."

Marie stared at the bones, mouth agape, heart pounding.

B.J. let out a chuckle, bent from the waist, pawed under the bed, and pulled a bovine skull out.

"It's a dang *cow* skeleton," he said.

Marie let out a huge breath. Of course, it was a cow skeleton. Whatever was she thinking?

Mark looked humiliated. "How the heck was I supposed to know that?" he yelled.

Suddenly, Marie felt very weary.

"B.J.," she said, "why don't you take Mandy to Alice so she can get her ready for bed. I promise I'll wash and iron your shirt and find your disk later."

When B.J. and Mandy were gone, Marie sat back on her haunches surveying the bones and preparing to give Mark a lecture on the unsanitariness of harboring a cow skeleton under his bed.

Then she saw it.

It had been a long time since Marie had suffered through one of Dr. Wilkerson's anatomy labs with those geeky premed students, but she still knew a human phalange bone when she saw one. As she stared at this one, her heart pounded again. Maybe she was wrong. But, no—it was round dorsally, flat ventrally, slightly concave lengthwise. A finger bone.

"What is it, Mom?" Mark asked.

Her eyes traveled from the bone to Mark's face. The poor child had no idea what he had dragged home. "Nothing, honey," she said.

She slipped the bone into the pocket of her skirt, sat down on the bed and pulled Mark onto her lap. She held him snugly for a moment, deciding how to proceed.

Then she said, "You know what? This *could* have been a dinosaur. They've found them in Texas, you know."

"That's right, Mom. B.J. doesn't know everything."

"No, he sure doesn't. Tell me, honey, how long have you had these bones under your bed?"

"Not too long. A couple of weeks."

"Where did you get them?"

"I found them."

"Well, I figured that, but *where* did you find them?"

Mark looked guilty.

"Mark? Where did you find them?"

"In the ground. I digged them up."

"Where did you dig them up?"

"In Cudd's woods."

Marie took a heartbeat to absorb this. Mark had dug up a human finger bone in Cudd's woods. She struggled to keep her voice even as she continued her questioning.

"Really? You were in Cudd's woods?"

"Yes, ma'am."

"How did you happen to be in Cudd's woods and stumble on a cow skeleton?"

"Jillian told me she saw Cudd burying stuff out there and..."

"And what, Mark?"

"And I wanted to see what he was burying."

Suddenly Marie remembered Mark telling Whittington that he was "awful good at finding things" when the sheriff had interviewed the children the morning of Cudd's murder. It never occurred to her that Mark was talking about finding *bones*.

"Did you find anything else?"

"Like what?"

"Anything, Mark...other bones." She had to know.

"No. I found another place where there was fresh dirt—it looked like Cudd'd been digging there—but I never got to go back before Cudd got...you know...killed, and now I'm ascared to go back."

Marie hugged her little boy tightly. "You were right to want to stay away from Cudd's place after what happened there," she said. "There's nothing to be afraid of on our place, sweetheart, but it was wrong to play on Cudd's property. You know that, don't you?"

Mark nodded.

"Then I'm going to ground you for a while. I'm also grounding you for getting into B.J.'s things. Understand?"

Mark nodded again. "How long am I grounded for?" he asked.

"Three days," Marie answered. "No horseback

riding, no bike riding, no TV, no video games, no friends over to play. Okay?''

''Okay,'' Mark answered glumly, but he looked relieved.

''All's well that ends well,'' Marie said. ''Time for bed. Go brush those choppers, what's left of 'em.''

Mark gave her a gap-toothed grin and skipped off to the bathroom.

While he was gone, Marie gathered the bones into a garbage bag and put them out of sight in her bedroom, deciding to give them a closer look when the kids were asleep.

Later, when she was tucking Mark in, she said, ''Do you think you could remember where it was—the place where Cudd had been digging?''

Mark wrinkled his freckled nose, considering. ''Yeah, I think so.''

''And could you remember where you found the cow skeleton?''

''Maybe.''

''Well, then, I want you to show me, okay?''

''Okay.''

She got up and went to turn off the light.

''I love you, Mom,'' Mark said when she got to the door.

''I love you too, honey, more than you'll ever know. And you know what, Mark? I wish it *had* been a dinosaur skeleton.''

She meant that literally.

SATURDAY DAWNED cloudy, threatening rain again, and Marie didn't want to get up. She hadn't slept well. Yearnings had invaded her sleep like an unslakable thirst.

She threw back the covers, climbed slowly out of bed and opened the drapes. In the valley below, she saw Toots, Henry and B.J. loading the steers to go to the packers.

It occurred to her that the time might come when she could no longer afford Henry's modest salary, and again she worried about the delay in settling Carl's life insurance.

She showered and dressed quickly in jeans and a denim shirt. She pulled on one soft cordovan boot, then gingerly tested the other over her sore ankle. The boot actually felt better than the air cast. She cinched the matching cordovan belt at her waist, put her hair up in a neat, thick French braid and went to the kitchen. Alice had made fresh coffee before leaving for her walk. Marie poured a mug and went straight to Carl's office to find anything that had to do with Triple C Construction.

She'd forgotten how many boxes of papers there were, and the desk was packed, too. And that neat stack of floppy disks might as well be the national archives.

She seated herself in Carl's oak desk chair and pulled the trash can near, longing to sweep the whole mess in. But she had no notion of what was significant and what was not. All of Carl's official papers were in Austin, subsumed by the new highway commissioner—what was his name? Thornton?—but there was still so *much*...

She took a long, thoughtful sip of coffee and went to work.

She made piles: political-party business, unanswered letters, phone messages, notes on legal pads. Any of this could be relevant in her search for the truth.

She found maps, survey results, photos of an old trestle bridge. Another pile.

She worked steadily for an hour until Alice came to the door and said, "Do you want some breakfast? The kids are starting to get up."

"Sounds wonderful. It's going to take all the stamina I've got to plow through this."

Alice surveyed the office and bit her lip. "I can't say I blame you for putting this off for so long. Carl sure was a papermonger, wasn't he?"

Marie nodded and closed her eyes.

Alice tsked. "Would it help if I took Jillian and the twins over to my place and then to a movie tonight? After the men take the steers in, B.J.'s going to his friend Eric's to spend the night. This'll go faster if there's no one to bother you."

Marie's eyes popped open. "Alice, bless you."

Alice winked. "I'll get the kids packed right after breakfast."

BY EVENING, the rain was pouring and Marie was surrounded by stacks and stacks of paper, still with no answers.

She stopped when she found a photograph Carl had tucked away. A picture of the family on a snowy mountainside in Ruidoso, all standing on skis, snug in bright parkas. Carl had been so proud of his family.

Marie closed her eyes, suddenly miserable. Outside, thunder boomed. She blinked back the tears and decided a rainy evening might not be the best time to go through Carl's old papers.

Henry would be somewhere about the place doing the evening chores but then he would join Toots for their usual Saturday-night venison stew and dominoes, and she would be truly alone.

She went into the kitchen, seeking food, but on impulse dug the bottle of blush wine out of the back of the fridge. It might be nice, with no one to interrupt her, to relax with some wine and a comforting book.

She took a glass of wine into the office and pulled down a worn copy of her favorite romance novel. She switched on the brass floor lamp, and curled up among the throw pillows on the leather love seat.

After sipping the wine and reading a few pages, Marie began to feel warm and relaxed. Her mind seemed to finish the passages for her, as if she weren't actually reading the words, as if she were dreaming them.

Dreaming.

The grandmother in the story was talking nonstop. No, not the grandmother—Alice. They were in the ravine, she and Alice, and Whittington stood above them on the ridge, with the sun to his back so that she could not read the expression on his face.

"You think you represent the Law?" Alice was shouting at Whittington. "We know what you really are. We know what kind of folks you come from.

You're common, that's what you are. Common! Common! Common!''

Turning, Marie could see Whittington's eyes glittering brilliantly in the shadows of his face. He seemed to want to tell her something. But he did not speak. He did nothing to defend himself against Alice's hateful diatribe.

''You can get yourself reelected by this means and that,'' Alice ranted, ''but you'll never be anything in this county. You'll never be any Carl Manning.''

Whittington tore his gaze away from Marie, turning toward something behind him.

From the woods above the ravine, a shadow emerged. Marie gasped. What was Bud Weimer doing out here?

From somewhere in his clothes, the red-faced little man produced the very gun Carl had given Marie at Big Pond. Whittington lunged at Weimer, his mouth forming a warning. But there was no warning and no pistol report as Marie felt the impact of the bullet and awoke with a jolt.

In a daze, Marie slowly reached up and brushed tiny beads of perspiration from her temple. The brass floor lamp radiated quietly over her shoulder. Beyond its circle of yellow light, the rest of the house was utterly still. Outside, it was completely dark now, still raining. The book lay open on her lap. How long had she slept? She shivered violently.

First the fainting and now bizarre nightmares, she thought. She really was coming apart at the seams. The evening loomed long before her. She decided to go back to the kitchen and get something to eat.

She went into the mudroom to the freezer and pulled out the last of this year's steak, some frozen asparagus and a package of her refrigerator-roll mix.

As she lowered the lid of the freezer, she saw headlights coming up the driveway.

By now, she was able to recognize the sheriff's Bronco from quite a distance, even in the dark.

CHAPTER NINE

As she watched Whittington get out of the Bronco, pull his hat brim down and his slicker collar up, then step around the puddles in the driveway, Marie had mixed feelings. Part of her dreaded an encounter with him, but part of her was thrilled by the sight of him.

She laid the frozen food on top of the freezer, switched on the outside light and opened the back door just as he raised his hand to knock.

She stared at him through the wet screen. Seeing him in the flesh after her chilling dream was unnerving. Even looking down on him as Marie did now, even with the rain dripping off the brim of his Stetson, there was something imposing about the man.

His breath came out in cold puffs when he spoke. "Mrs. Manning, I hope I'm not intruding, but I happened to be out this way, and I was wondering if I could get that videotape, if it's not too much trouble."

"Oh...oh, of course, Sheriff," Marie said, shaking off her trance. "Please, come in out of the rain."

Whittington gave his slicker a powerful shake and came up the porch steps and through the door. He removed his Stetson and held it in both hands, waiting politely as it dripped on the mudroom floor.

"Let me just get this food—" As Marie turned to gather the frozen packages, an idea struck her. Perhaps she could do a little information gathering of her own.

"What brings you out here in this awful rain, Sheriff?" Marie asked as she stacked the packages in her arms.

"This awful rain," he replied, then smiled at her puzzled frown. "The sheriff's department checks all the bridges and low water on county roads. We put up roadblocks if necessary. There's a lot of high water tonight."

"Oh, yes. I have a draw on my property that's so dry it's cracked in summer but then it'll rise to four or five feet when it rains. I suppose it's the runoff from all these rocky hills that causes that."

"Yes, ma'am." he said.

"Are all the roads okay?" Marie worried about Alice and the kids, coming back after the movie.

"Yes, ma'am," he said again. "For now. After an hour or so I'll double back to check a couple of places that looked iffy earlier. I always hate to block a road unless it's absolutely necessary."

"I understand." Marie looked down at the food. An hour should give her plenty of time. "Listen, I was just about to fix myself a quick steak. Would you like to join me? That is, if you haven't already eaten."

One of his eyebrows shot up, but then he smoothed his expression into careful politeness. "Oh, that's all right, ma'am, I couldn't impose."

"You wouldn't be imposing. I have to cook anyway, and I hate eating alone."

"Where're the kids?" He turned and glanced down the flight of steps toward the den.

"Alice has them. B.J.'s at a friend's. What do you say?" She smiled. "I owe you a meal."

He smirked at the mention of his cooking. Rain drummed steadily on the roof and suddenly the air in the little mudroom seemed thick with humidity and with something else Marie couldn't name. She heard herself swallow, waiting for his answer. She wished he would stop looking at her as if he was sizing her up. She fixed her attention on the packages and said, "This sirloin is way too big for one person. I have all my beef cut big...with so many mouths to feed and all. I can't even remember the last time I fixed a meal just for myself—"

"I accept," he interrupted. "I'm cold and wet and very hungry."

She looked up into his face. His brown eyes crinkled with a slow smile. A sweet, sincere smile that melted Marie's heart and made her feel a bit guilty for what she was planning to do. But she told herself that she had every right to know what was going on in this county. Besides, maybe Alice was right, maybe he was a smooth charmer who had ladies fixing him steak dinners every night of the week. Maybe he always smiled like that.

She smiled back self-consciously then tried to adopt a casual air. "Good. Come on in."

She turned and walked the few steps to the kitchen, but he didn't follow.

When she noticed that he wasn't behind her, she poked her head around the door opening and raised her eyebrows in a question. "Something wrong, Sheriff?"

"Maybe I'd better do something about these." He

pointed at his boots. "I'd hate to mess up your nice clean floor."

Marie looked down at a pair of tan calfskin boots, which were at least a size twelve and solidly caked in Hill Country mud.

"You can take them off over there." She indicated the heavy antique brass bootjack affixed to the floor next to the back door. "That is, if you wouldn't feel uncomfortable in your socks," she added. She ducked around the doorjamb, giving him privacy.

"I sure hope I remembered to put on my perty silk stockings," he joked loudly as he tugged the boots off. "Oops. Looks like you'll have to put up with these holey old wool ones."

Marie smiled as she put the steak in the microwave to defrost. Carl had never been silly like that.

He came into the kitchen then, running his hand through his thick, damp hair. She watched the gesture with a flutter of fascination. He was the most handsome man she had ever seen. Perfectly proportioned. Relaxed and powerful. She looked down his long legs to a pair of olive-drab wool socks, which did, in fact, have a few small holes in them. She thought it charming that he was more concerned about her floor than he was about exposing those ratty socks.

He turned one foot and examined it. "I guess I ought to get rid of these old army socks, but they feel like a second skin."

"Sheriff, with four kids, I've seen my share of holey socks."

He smiled. "I expect you have. I like your kids, Mrs. Manning. Not a bad apple in the bunch."

"We're—I'm—pretty proud of them." She hated

it when she still talked in the "we" mode. She felt her cheeks flare.

She turned to the counter and busied herself preparing the steaks. "Make yourself comfortable. This'll only take a minute. I'd like one last look at Jillian's videotape before I turn it over to you. You can look at it with me, if you like, while the steaks cook."

"Fine with me," he said pleasantly. Then he sat down at the table and watched as she dotted asparagus with butter and grated some cheese over it. He sure liked the way her jeans fit. When his eyes came to her cordovan boots, he said, "I see your ankle's better—no more brace."

"Oh, yeah, my ankle." She shrugged. "The boot actually feels better than the brace if I don't have to get around much."

"By the way, were you okay when you drove home last night?"

"Oh, sure." She waved her hand dismissively, then continued grating the cheese. "I think I was just overly hungry, overly tired, and...I should have known those pain pills were too strong for me. The doctor gave me some tranquilizers after Carl died—I didn't wake up for twenty-four hours."

He frowned. He imagined she did need a few tranquilizers after a thing like that. She had probably loved her husband a lot. They were quite a couple in the community, always at the center of civic things.

He remembered the way she started crying after he caught her in that tree. At the time, he assumed it was mostly embarrassment, but maybe it went deeper. He wondered again what had caused her renewed interest in the circumstances of her husband's death. He had a feeling it had something to do with the McCombs case and he wanted to ask about that, but decided to forgo dredging up anything upsetting until after dinner. And he wouldn't tell her what the Dulane County sheriff had said this morning until after they ate.

Marie twisted dough into bread sticks and arranged them on a cookie sheet. ''Would you like a beer?'' she said over her shoulder.

''Can't. On duty.''

''Oh. Right. Speaking of duties, how's the murder investigation going?''

''It's going nowhere. I'm hoping the videotape will help.''

Marie popped the steaks in the broiler. ''The VCR's out in the den. Shall we?''

He followed her to the den and stood casting a long shadow down the little stairs while she switched on lamps.

She inserted the tape in the VCR. ''Oh. I need to rewind it,'' she said.

Jim padded down into the den and felt immediately comfortable in the cozy room. The wall around the fireplace was paneled in dark oak. The others were covered in muted wallpaper. The furniture was tasteful, homey. Several antique pieces caught his eye: a rolltop desk; a Waterbury mantel clock; a massive cherry-wood breakfront above which an entire wall was covered with family photos—pictures of cherubic babies interspersed with portraits of solemn-looking ancestors. His eyes were drawn to a large picture of Marie, radiant in white wedding gown and veil. The photographer had captured her soft, confident, Mona Lisa–like smile, the woman who had everything.

The wide windows across the back were curtain-less, but the rich oak woodwork prevented them from seeming bare. Lightning flashed over the valley below the hill and he was drawn to the atrium doors to ex-amine the night view.

Lightning flashed again and he got a bright, pho-toflash image of the barn, the outbuildings and the ponds. It invoked a sudden sorrow in his heart. The thunder echoed his sudden gloom. When he thought of Carl Manning growing up here and living here and night after night going to bed with *her,* he was seized with an irrational jealousy. *The guy is dead,* he told himself. *How can you be jealous of a dead man?* Besides, Jim had vowed to have a place like this someday. He'd have to get his the hard way, that's all. As for having a woman like Marie Manning, that was so far out of his reach that he refused to even imagine it. Even though he knew he was beginning to fall for her. Which was just plain crazy. He'd only known the woman a few days.

He turned from the windows and went to stand in front of the TV with her. She was fast-forwarding the tape. "Sorry, I rewound it too far," she explained.

Every few seconds she stopped to check the place on the tape, and images of the children, the horses, the dog, the woods, Marie in her garden, would flit briefly across the screen. He wanted to tell her to let it play forward slowly. He *wanted* to see these im-ages. Images of a family he had never had, thought he might never have.

"Jillian goes a little berserk with the video camera,'' Marie said. ''The part with Cudd should be coming up soon.'' She pressed the fast-forward button again. She turned her head to look at him. He was tapping his lips with his forefinger and he had the strangest look on his face. His eyes were narrow and she could see nothing of the happiness she had seen earlier. He looked almost bitter about something. Maybe she was detaining him too long.

She said, ''Sorry about all this family stuff.''

He winked at her then, changing his expression entirely. ''I happen to like it,'' he said.

At last a fuzzy image of Cudd appeared, bent over in his woods, shoveling furiously.

They both watched intently. Minutes went by as Cudd continued digging.

For lazy old Cudd, he sure was working hard.

''Do you know where this is on the McCombs property?'' Whittington's voice startled Marie.

''Uh…no, I don't. Toots and I looked at this and couldn't tell. Jillian couldn't tell us where it was either.''

''Mind if we back it up?'' he said, and as he reached for the rewind button, she reached up at the same time and their hands collided.

It seemed as if every time they touched, she felt it—the magnetism.

He must have felt something, too, because he quickly stuffed his hands into his jeans pockets. ''Just a little way, please.''

''Okay.'' She focused intently on the task of reversing the tape.

After some seconds he said, ''Stop.''

Then he watched as the picture pitched around dizzily, zooming in on a very fat cat and then pitching down a bank, through brush, up again, growing dim as it went into a woods. Then the tape interrupted and resumed, showing Cudd bent over his task.

"Cudd is digging just across your property line," he said, tapping the screen.

Marie was genuinely perplexed. She pulled her hair over one shoulder, wound it and asked, "How do you figure?"

"Jillian had her eye glued to the viewfinder with her finger on the button regardless of what she was filming, until she ran into Cudd. Something unexpected like that would cause a kid to lower the camera and look. Then she probably took a second to decide whether or not to film him."

"But Jillian tried to show us where it was and couldn't."

"Of course not. She had the camera to her face the whole time, until she saw Cudd."

"If that's true, then there should be a brief image of Cudd when Jillian first saw him through the lens." Excited by her own insight, Marie released her hair and pressed the reverse button.

They looked at the footage of the cat, the ravine and the endless dim woods again. Jim reached up suddenly and hit the pause.

"There he is," he said, pointing at the screen.

Marie stared. There, hidden in the tree trunks, was a shadowy image of a man, bent over.

Marie clamped her hand over her mouth. She looked at Jim and his brown eyes twinkled at her. She felt exhilarated at their mutual discovery. "Well, I'll be," she breathed.

He smiled at her and rewound the tape. "I hope you don't mind if I keep this a while," he said. "I'll want to check out that spot in the woods. One of the deputies, or myself, may need to cross your property."

Already Marie was thinking that she would have to get out there before they did. Maybe even tonight? There could be more money buried out there or...more bones.

JIM THOUGHT dinner seemed strained. The food was excellent and he caught himself having another twinge of jealousy as he compared the fresh, delicious fare to his own dinners of fast food or Chunky Soup. He had a bellyful of Chunky Soup.

He had been amazed at how deftly Marie got the meal on the table, and he'd enjoyed watching her do it. She was so skillful and lithe that he imagined she must be a very good nurse. She was definitely a good cook. The steak was perfect—and those bread sticks! He ate four, and would have eaten six if he hadn't felt sure she'd be stunned to see how much he could devour in one sitting, or how starved he was for home-cooked food.

But her small talk seemed forced, as if she was dancing around the real topic she wanted to broach. After a while he let his side of the chitchat dead-end. Why doesn't she get down to it?

"More tomatoes?"

"Yes, thank you."

"I raised these myself, you know. The last of the fall tomatoes. I always have a bunch on the vine when the frost hits and then I have to find time to can or freeze or rice them, which is a mess…the colander and all. Every year it's the same thing, too many tomatoes at the end of the season."

"I'm glad I can unburden you of them," he said as he dished several slices onto his plate.

Marie laughed lightly, throwing her head back. The flash of white teeth and the length of sleek neck distracted him and he let himself take in the sight of her. He couldn't believe he was sitting at a table eating steak with Marie Manning, and making her laugh.

She looked at him, sobered, sipped her wine.

He realized he was staring, and focused on his plate.

Marie chattered on. "Well, there's always something to do around here. I never have a spare minute in my day."

"I imagine," he said, and busied himself eating the last of his steak, letting another silence fall between them.

Marie bit her lip, as if casting about for something to say. Lightning flashed at the small-paned window above the kitchen sink. Thunder rumbled in the distance. Fresh sheets of rain pelted the window. Jim steadily chewed his steak, giving Marie an occasional glance.

Finally she said, "So, how's your campaign going?"

The question sounded a little *too* casual. This must be it. The loaded topic. His campaign?

"My campaign? As well as I can expect, considering I've got a murder to distract me."

"I guess that does complicate things. Is fund-raising a problem? They say fund-raising's always a big problem.''

Her voice was definitely too…bright. And, of course, she'd know about fund-raising. ''Not really.'' He kept eating.

''Well…um…who all's helping you?''

''The usual suspects.''

''Well, I mean, who are the *main* people involved in your campaign?''

What is she getting at? he wondered. Aloud he said, ''The main people? Well, my deputies and office workers, of course. They want to keep their jobs. And the good old boys who want to keep their party in power.''

She smiled and nodded. Then she concentrated on cutting a tomato slice into neat squares with her steak knife. Without looking up, she said, ''I guess every politician has those types behind them. Who are your good old boys?''

So that's what she was fishing for. Okay. He'd give her a big old bass.

''Bud Weimer's one.''

For a heartbeat she looked surprised, as if she indeed had been fishing for that name and hadn't expected it to surface quite so abruptly. But she kept her voice casual. ''Bud Weimer. I believe I met him once.'' She got up from the table and took the tea pitcher out of the refrigerator. ''Rumor has it that he intends to buy Cudd's land. Is that true, Sheriff?''

Now it was Jim's turn to look surprised. Weimer *had* seemed anxious to buy Cudd's land before it went to a sheriff's sale, seemed to know just how much Cudd owed in back taxes. He wanted Jim to handle it through "unofficial channels," but Jim refused. Weimer brought up the subject again last night in one of those weird, furtive meetings out on the courthouse-basement stairwell. But Jim sure hadn't mentioned this to anyone and he was positive the old man hadn't either.

Yet Marie Manning pops up with this "rumor" as though it was common knowledge. She was being a little too casual, getting up and pouring him more tea as she brought the topic up.

He held his glass up so she could fill it and studied her face. Two little cherries of pink formed on her cheeks as she poured the tea.

She smiled and glanced at him. "Have you heard that rumor, Sheriff? That Bud Weimer wants to buy Cudd's land?"

"Does that concern you?"

She set the tea pitcher on the table. "Are you asking me if I'm worried about it, or are you asking me if it's any of my business?"

"Both."

She sat down and wiped her hands on her napkin. "Well then, yes to both. It's my business because that property borders mine and naturally I want to know what's going to happen to it. And yes, I'm little worried about a man like Bud Weimer owning it. I don't want a toxic dump in my backyard."

"I see." Jim stalled a moment and drank some tea. He didn't want to get into the subject of Weimer tonight. For that matter, he decided, he didn't want to get into the unpleasant news from the Dulane County sheriff tonight, either. Perhaps it was time to leave. Outside, thunder boomed again and he regretted having to go back into the storm, but he couldn't risk revealing anything about Weimer's interest in Cudd's land. Weimer had asked him specifically not to discuss it.

Marie sensed a sudden shift in his mood. She watched him gulp his tea, and noticed a line of red climbing up his neck. His Adam's apple jerked up and down as if he was having difficulty swallowing. He was concealing something. Of course, that had only been a wild guess about Weimer wanting Cudd's land, but she must have hit pay dirt.

"Well, I hate to eat and run—" he set his tea glass down carefully "—but I'd better get back out there and check those low spots. Looks like this rain is never going to let up. This was a delicious meal. Thank you." He was already on his feet and pushing his chair up to the table.

He walked over to the counter and picked up the videotape.

Marie stood. "Sheriff, would you check into that rumor for me? I mean, ask Mr. Weimer about buying Cudd's land. Since you're friends with him?" She followed him to the mudroom.

He was already pulling on his boots. Looking at the back of his neck, she noticed that the line of red was all the way up to his hairline.

"I know him, he's active in my campaign, but I wouldn't say we're friends," he answered truthfully.

"But you could ask him and tell me what he says when I come in to get my copy of the reports on Carl's death—you will have the accident report and the autopsy results by Monday, won't you?" she pressed.

He let out an exasperated sigh as he straightened and took his slicker off the hook. First she has him bugging the Dulane County sheriff and now she wants him to pry into Bud Weimer's business. "Mrs. Manning, I'm working on that, but you'll have to be patient and trust me. Getting the reports is not as easy as you think. The Dulane County Sheriff's Office is being awfully touchy about it. When I asked about it this morning, the sheriff said that two of his deputies have already been deposed in that case and he wondered why I was sticking my nose into it." *Again,* he added under his breath, as he pulled on the yellow slicker, snapping it quickly.

"Deposed?" Marie said. "Why on earth are deputies being questioned about Carl's accident?"

Jim stopped the snapping. Now he would have to tell her the bad news. Either that or lie.

He studied her face. She looked bewildered...and worried. *God knows what she's imagining,* he thought. Well, she'd find out sooner or later. Maybe it would be better for her to hear it while the kids are away, so she could think about it in peace.

"Mrs. Manning," he said quietly, "the life insurance company is investigating your husband's death as a possible suicide."

Marie's green eyes grew huge. Her full lips made a soft oval of shock and a crease formed between her eyebrows. "My God," she whispered, looking away from him.

He felt like a dog.

"Mrs. Manning, I'm sorry." He tried to make eye contact with her. "I didn't want to tell you this tonight."

"A suicide," she said, placing her hand at her throat.

She looked up at him. Her eyes were shocked...hurt...beautiful. And filling with tears.

She swayed and repeated, "A suicide?"

He offered his hand, palm up, to steady her, and she reached out and touched his fingertips, only his fingertips. He cupped his fingers under hers lightly, just touching, but curved enough to hold them. She was trembling.

He thought that he should release her, but instead he tightened his hold and drew her hand closer. "It'll be all right," he said as he squeezed her fingers. "You'll be all right." His voice sounded suddenly hoarse.

She seemed to be trembling all over now, and closed her eyes. "Carl would never commit suicide," she said quietly. "He had too much to live for."

"Anybody could see that," he said gently. And he thought, *If only I could put my arms around her.*

And then he saw no reason not to do exactly that.

"Anybody could see that," he said again as he pulled her to him and enfolded her in his arms.

She didn't resist. Despite her height she felt small and fragile. She put her head on his shoulder—he was grateful for that—and her hair smelled faintly of the bread she'd taken out of the oven earlier. The yellow rain slicker crackled as he pulled her tighter to him, and then he felt her starting to sob.

He let her cry, grateful to be holding her, not knowing what else to do.

After a while she let out a shaky sigh and said, "You must think I'm a fool, always crying or faint-

ing, but—'' She wiped at her eyes, flapped at the air
around her forehead and tried to back away.

But he held her fast, now that he had her. "Listen.
You're under a lot of strain. And I don't think you're
a fool. I think you're very brave. In fact—''

And suddenly, his eyes held hers with that mag-
netic force, and the room seemed ten degrees hotter.
Even above the noise of the rain on the roof, he could
hear his own breathing, and hers, and his arms came
alive with gooseflesh. They seemed to tighten around
her of their own free will and, looking down at her
mouth, he knew he was going to kiss her, and vulnerable as she was, he knew he shouldn't.

But he did.

MARIE COULDN'T be sure, but he whispered something just before he brought his mouth down on
hers—what was it?—but she couldn't think clearly,
for never, *never* had she been kissed like this. In all
her years of marriage, she'd thought she'd done it all,
tasted every sensual pleasure. She tried to tell herself
that this was only a kiss, but it was fiercer, more passionate than any kiss she could have imagined back
on Stranger Hill. He seemed to suck the life out of
her one second and breathe it back into her the next.
Her whole body, every secret place, responded to his
mouth.

She heard him tearing the snaps of the slicker open
with one hand and then he wrapped his arms around
her and brought her full against his hard body inside
the slicker. She heard herself whimper, not in protest,
no, not that. In surrender. She had known, had *known*
they would end up like this. She had wanted it.

Then he stopped the kiss, but kept his face close over hers. His breath felt hot on her lips as he spoke.

"What are we doing?" he said, searching her eyes. But he didn't wait for her answer.

His next kiss stirred a greater firestorm than the first. He entwined his fingers in her hair and tilted her head back, giving himself maximum access, which he used to full advantage. In some ancient, instinctual reaction, she tilted her head sideways to accommodate him and he drove his tongue deeper. She moaned and he gripped her head between both palms and forced the kiss deeper still, took more, gave more. Marie was tall, nearly six feet, but he was taller, and somewhere in that massive rush of sensations she had a clear thought: we are a perfect fit.

What are we doing? The question echoed in her mind then. She hadn't meant to let it go so far; she hadn't meant to let it happen at all. But the wine, the shock, the grief…this man…she hardly knew this man. She tore her mouth away.

"Sheriff…" She found she could hardly breathe, much less talk.

She felt his arms release her immediately. "I know," he said, his breathing harsh. "What are we doing?"

They stood facing each other, hands hanging at their sides, only inches apart, not touching anywhere, and not looking at each other. She heard him release a ragged sigh, and the sound of it made her want to start all over again. To taste him. To breathe his breath. To test the depths of his passion, of her own.

"I think I'd better leave now," he said and she heard the rustle of the slicker as he turned away and

finished snapping it. He cleared his throat. "I promise
I'll get the report to you as soon as possible. In fact,
I'll help you read through it and try to answer any
questions you have."

"Thank you. That's kind of you." She folded her
arms across her middle to keep herself from flinging
herself at him again.

He tugged the collar of the slicker up.

They looked into each other's eyes once more. He
didn't want to leave and she didn't want him to.

He thought, *Why can't I treat her like any other
woman?* But he knew why. Carl Manning was why.
He might be dead, but her heart still belonged to the
man. She wasn't any other woman. She was still Mrs.
Carl Manning. He turned away and picked up the videotape off the freezer top.

She thought, *Why don't I trust him?* But she knew
why. Bud Weimer. Until she knew what kind of hold
Weimer had on him, she could never fully trust Jim
Whittington, and she wouldn't let herself get emotionally involved with him, no matter what his kisses
had just done to her body.

Aloud he simply said, "Well, good night."

And she simply said, "Good night, Sheriff."

He put on his Stetson, opened the door and ducked
out into the wind and rain.

She stood behind the screen and watched him
dodge puddles across the yard to the driveway. She
watched the shadowy yellow silhouette of him as he
climbed into the Bronco. She watched the headlights
cut on and fan over the sheets of rain and the dripping
trees as he backed the Bronco around. And then she

watched the two fuzzy red dots of the taillights disappear down the driveway.

And were it not for the ache in her breasts and belly, Marie would have thought the whole thing never happened. But she did feel that ache. And with it a yearning. And fear.

Because standing there, watching him go, she realized what he'd whispered just before he'd kissed her. He'd said, "My God. I'm falling in love with you."

CHAPTER TEN

JIM YANKED OFF the slicker and his muddy boots just inside his kitchen door. He tossed the dripping Stetson onto its customary perch—the finial of an old ladder-back chair—and carried the videotape straight to the living room. He hesitated after he slid it into the VCR—was there something unethical about watching a tape of her that he'd obtained in the line of duty?—then he pushed the rewind button.

From the moment he'd laid his hands on it, he'd known he would watch the entire tape, not just the part with McCombs. He'd thought about little else while he'd driven the dark country roads double-checking for high water. He'd thought about her eyes. And her mouth. And the feel of her slender body against his.

He pressed Play and watched the whole thing straight through, standing right in front of the TV, without even turning up the sound. Only watched them—their faces, their smiles, their movements. Their nights. Their days.

Her days. Her nights.

The second time through he settled himself in the old barber chair with the remote and turned up the volume. The kids were a riot. They all liked to look straight at the camera and say smart-alecky things in their Texas drawls. They staged an elaborate parody of "This Is Your Life" for their mother's birthday. Mandy in a nurse's cap with a Summa Cum Laude sign around her neck; Jillian in an old robe with pillows lashed to her abdomen, on her way to "have" the twins. The camera kept panning to Marie's face, catching her delighted laughter. He watched this scene three times. He laughed out loud, too, causing Amos to lumber over and study his master's face.

By 2:00 a.m. he knew every place where Marie appeared on the tape: looking down crossly from atop a horse telling Jillian to "get that camera out of this muddy barnyard"; opening her birthday presents, misty-eyed as she held up a pair of earrings; tending her garden, unaware of being filmed with that gorgeous fanny sticking up in the air.

He rewound to the place where she opened the earrings and froze the frame in which she looked up with love in her eyes. Who was doing the filming? Who was she looking at that way? He thought he knew, even though the only sound was Marie's "Oh, my," before she held up the earrings.

For a long, long time he sat in the dark, his face illuminated by the glare from the TV, studying the close-up of Marie.

So, he thought. *This is what it feels like to fall in love.* Really in love. How had it happened so quickly?

He thought of the other women he'd loved in his life. Or thought he'd loved. Hoped he'd loved.

This was so very different from those.

This wasn't like his relationship with spoiled Bethany Bishop. That was a lovesick young man's obsession. A hopeless dream. Torment.

Or like the one with Paulette. That was a compromise, not a marriage. A way to tick off the years after Bethany. A good time, a diversion, gone sour.

No, this wasn't like either of those. Because while Marie was rich, like Bethany, she was not spoiled. And while she was sexy, like Paulette, she was not provocative.

She was something else. Being with her made him feel…whole…happy… He couldn't find the word for what Marie Manning made him feel.

He stared at the face on the screen. A happily married woman, getting an expensive present from her beloved husband. A beautiful woman. What would a woman like that want of him? *Expect* of him? What would a relationship with her cost him, financially, emotionally, every other way? What was the expression? High maintenance?

Why was he even thinking like this? It was easier, saner, to seek the path of least resistance. On Monday, in Austin, he would see that foxy blond political consultant—what was her name?—who'd sent him all the right signals at the state convention last spring. He could hook up with her. Easier. Safer.

He got up and reached to turn off the VCR. Before he did, standing close to the screen, he studied Marie's face one last time. And then the word he'd been searching for came to him. The one that described his feeling around Marie. *Joy.*

FALLING IN LOVE WITH ME. Had he really said that? But he didn't have to *say* anything, what he'd *done* to her had conveyed it all. Even so, Marie didn't trust the message, didn't trust him, didn't trust *herself.* She turned and slowly walked into the kitchen.

Carl suspected of suicide. That explained why every time she called the life insurance company about the delay, they said they were still "investigating." With a ruling of suicide, they would not have to pay Carl's benefits: two million dollars. Without that money, she'd lose Manning Ranch, her children's future, their heritage.

She folded her arms under her breasts and paced, her mind whirling, fighting off panic. Maybe Carl's death was no accident, but it sure as hell wasn't a suicide. Carl had been distraught, not mentally ill.

She snatched up the phone and punched in a familiar number.

On the third ring she said, "Put down your dominoes, Toots, and answer the dadgum phone!"

As if on cue, Toots answered. "Toots here."

"Toots! It's me. Could you come over here?"

"In this rain? When I've got the best Moon hand I've had in months?"

"Whittington just left. I have terrible news about Carl. You've got to come!" Marie heard her voice, fueled as it was by fear, sounding almost hysterical.

"Okay, Missy, calm down. I'm on my way."

MARIE DRAGGED Toots straight to Carl's office. There she pointed to a pile of papers bigger than a bushel basket and told him to start looking for anything that had to do with bridges, Triple C Construction, or anything, *anything,* that looked suspicious.

Toots pushed his cap back and looked disgruntled. "Do we have to do this *tonight?*"

"Yes. You do the paper. I'll check the computer."

While they worked, Marie told Toots about seeing Weimer with Whittington at the courthouse, about finding the bone, about Carl being suspected of suicide. She told him about everything except Whittington's kiss. That didn't matter. It was not going to happen again.

When she was finished, Toots let out a slow whistle. "A finger bone? Are you sure, Missy?"

"Positively. I can show you the picture in *Gray's Anatomy.*"

"Maybe Cudd was burying something besides money on his land."

"Exactly. Speaking of the money. Did you go back and get it?"

"Yep. Had to be a little sly, though. Seems like there's been a deputy out there every minute. Told 'em I had to get my propane torch—I knew Cudd had one—out of the barn. Wore my big overalls and my high boots and made myself some money underwear." Toots smiled broadly.

Marie took her attention off the computer screen for a moment. "Good Lord, Toots. How much was there?"

"There was eighty-five thousand dollars in that old dresser, Missy. Cudd was getting mighty rich from someplace."

Marie was flabbergasted. "Eighty-five thousand dollars! What on earth did you do with it?"

"Well, I couldn't exactly mosey into town and make a little cash deposit, so it's at my place."

"Toots! Do you think that's safe?"

"I guess it's as safe as trusting the Law with it,

considering he's having cozy conversations with Weimer out behind the courthouse."

Marie thought of Whittington again, standing in her mudroom in his ratty old army socks with that charming smile on his face. She couldn't believe he was capable of evil. But her ambiguous feelings about Whittington were one thing she didn't want to share with Toots. "I suppose you're right," she said, and kept her gaze on the monitor.

Then she saw it: a file named 3C, right in the middle of a monstrous list of tax files.

"Toots, look!"

It was a subdirectory. Within it were files with names that made no sense to Toots, but that Marie was quick to decipher—LGT:bw, 3CTX, CC:BID and on and on. Marie scrolled the list. Carl had kept careful records.

She retrieved the file named LGT:bw because she suspected "bw" was Bud Weimer.

And she was right.

The screen lit up with a memo, dated a week before Carl's death. Above it a "note to file" indicated that Carl had received the memo from his "source" in the local D.A.'s office and scanned it into his hard drive.

Marie read aloud:

"Confidential memo to BW—San Saba Creek Project. HCC says Commissioner Manning requested documents on bridge steel delivery for San Saba project. HCC told Manning there was a problem on the bid quote of the steel supplier and he had referred it to me to check into possible price fixing. If Manning asks this office for documents, I am to indicate records have been sealed pending completion of investigation. Steel delivery quantities can be corrected when the records are returned to Austin. s/LGT.''

Toots scratched his forehead. ''Who the hell's LGT?''

''Leland Gillespie Tucker.''

''Oh. Our affable district attorney,'' Toots said sarcastically. ''Everybody's friend.''

''Yeah. Including the local criminal class.'' Leland Gillespie Tucker hadn't tried a major case in living memory. But it wasn't Leland she was worried about. He'd done dirtier things than hiding steel records, and everybody knew it. It was the people giving Leland his orders who worried her. BW was most likely Weimer, but who was HCC?

Toots looked at the screen. ''Something's damn screwy here, Marie. I can't figure why Leland was doctoring up delivery records.''

''There's a puzzle.'' Marie sank back in her chair.

''Yep,'' Toots agreed. ''But we know Weimer's probably padding Leland's bank account like a cheap bra.''

Marie sighed. ''So much for going to the local D.A.'' She chewed a nail. Then she sat up. ''Do you think we have enough here to make Mike Garrett do something?''

''You mean go to Austin and show these records to him?''

''Yeah. Wouldn't it be safer to go to someone outside the county?''

Toots heaved an exaggerated sigh of resignation.

"I expect this means you want to search all these files."

They looked until they were bleary-eyed and heartsick. At expenditures and materials lists that did not add up. At phony records of bridge and road repairs. Suddenly Marie understood all the Polaroid pictures of bridges she'd found. And she understood what Carl had meant by "something big." And she felt ashamed for her lack of understanding while he was alive.

When they finished it was close to 2:00 a.m. Marie hit the switch on the printer and printed out everything they'd found, being very careful to omit nothing. And while the printer hummed, she worried. Who was HCC?

CHAPTER ELEVEN

THE HEAVILY MADE-UP, middle-aged redhead behind the reception desk in Mike Garrett's office displayed a tasteless excess of billowing cleavage, which she fingered lightly while eyeing Toots. Toots took off his cap and frowned at the Massey-Ferguson patch as if he'd never seen it before.

Marie had to suppress a grin. Women were always coming on to Toots. "I need to see Mike Garrett, please," she said.

The woman reluctantly shifted her gaze to Marie. "Do you have an appointment?" she asked.

Marie bit her lip and shook her head. They'd driven straight to Austin after the kids had left for school. They'd checked into the La Quinta Inn and came directly to Garrett's office in the capitol building.

"Well, I'm sorry. You'll need an appointment to see Mr. Garrett," the woman said. She batted clumpy, jet-black lashes and pursed crimson lips as if to say the matter was closed. Then she proceeded to file her nails even though they were already honed to ridiculous little points.

Toots cleared his throat and leveled his bright blue eyes at the woman. "Could you do me a special favor, young lady?" he said, and stroked his steel-gray mustache.

"I could try," the woman said in a husky voice, and grazed the top of her cleavage with those pointy little nails.

"Could you just slip Mr. Garrett a message that Mrs. *Carl Manning* is out here?"

"I guess I could—for *you*." She woman reached for a notepad. "Now, this is Mrs. Carl Manning and you are...?"

"I'm Toots Daniels," Toots said softly. "And I sure appreciate your special attention."

"I'll be right back." She winked at Toots as she stood and straightened her skirt over fleshy hips.

"You're a mess," Marie whispered when she was gone.

"You gotta do what you gotta do," Toots mumbled. "If it takes the old Daniels charm to get us past that biddy—"

"Good news," the woman announced brightly as she bustled back into the room. "Mr. Garrett *will* see you immediately."

Toots and Marie stepped forward together but the woman placed a palm on Toots's chest. "I'm sorry, Mr. Daniels, but he wants to see Mrs. Manning *alone*. You'll have to wait out here with *me*."

Toots shot Marie a look that said he was pleased as punch about that and turned to take a seat. Marie followed the receptionist to Garrett's office.

MIKE GARRETT was standing with his face toward the ceiling-high windows in the old oak-paneled office. When Marie entered, he walked around the desk and took one of Marie's hands in both of his own. "Mrs.

Manning,'' he said. ''I hope things are going well with you and the children.''

Garrett hoped his face was properly solicitous and not betraying his anxiety at seeing her.

He studied her while he cradled her hand. She was even more beautiful than he remembered. The ivory skin. The huge green eyes. That hair. He recalled the first time he had seen her at the Bluebonnet Banquet. He even remembered what she was wearing, black velvet, contrasting with her milky skin, accentuating every mysterious curve of that tall frame.

She slowly withdrew her hand. Perhaps seeing him stirred up too many unpleasant memories. He wished for the hundredth time that he hadn't been the one to have to tell her about her husband. He feared she would always associate him with that moment and he hated that, knowing that he was infatuated with her.

He couldn't resist looking her up and down. Her hair gleamed against her expensive-looking emerald-green sweater. Her cream-and-black plaid skirt fanned over slim thighs, almost grazing her ankles—his eyes stopped. One foot was clad in a slim black leather pump, but the other was bound by some kind of in-flatable splint.

''Pardon me if this is too personal a question, but what is that on your ankle?''

''It's nothing. I had a little mishap on the ranch.''

''Oh dear. I hope it wasn't serious. Why don't we sit down?''

Marie nodded.

He touched her shoulder lightly and led her to a small leather couch, then sat down beside her. Not too near. He wanted to be careful.

"How may I help you?"

She blinked several times, then said, "Mr. Garrett, you knew my husband, Carl. I need to ask you some questions about the weeks preceding his death."

Garrett's heart hammered and his palms suddenly became damp. Why was she coming here with questions now? After all these months, he'd thought this nightmare was finally behind him. He crossed his long legs, trying to appear relaxed. "Of course, I'll tell you anything you want to know," he said, keeping his voice calm.

"Did Carl ever come to see you about problems in Carville County?" She sat up more erect, shifted her hips, folded her slender hands in her lap. How had Carl Manning ever convinced this totally classy woman to live out in a remote area, spending her days chasing around after a passel of brats and having mishaps on the ranch? He studied her eyes while he decided what to say. She was onto something, he felt sure. Why else would she be here, suddenly asking questions? How much did she already know?

He got up and walked over to face the windows, buying time and concealing his expression.

"Mrs. Manning," he said, turning to her, "as a Texas highway commissioner, your husband came to me several times to get answers to complex legal questions. But problems in Carville County?" He frowned at her, then turned back to the window. "Like what?"

"Problems at Triple C Construction."

Garrett watched a single raindrop break loose and careen down the windowpane. So she knew about the Carville County Construction boys. But what good would it do this beautiful woman to know the ugly truth about that mess? No one could touch Weimer, much less Dale Thornton, the new highway commissioner. Only a fool would delve into this. Carl Manning had been just such a fool. Garrett told himself he had to protect this delicate woman from making the same mistake.

"Triple C?" he said, tapping his lips with his index finger. "I believe he did ask us to look into some problems there, but I'm sure it was all cleared up." He turned from the window and gave her a reassuring smile.

"He didn't show you some files?" she asked.

"Some files?" He faced the window again. This was not going to be as simple as he had hoped. If she knew about those files—but how could she?

She opened her oversize clutch and pulled out a sheaf of papers. "These," she said.

He crossed the room to take the papers then sat down on the couch again.

"Well, let's see," he said, crossing his legs. "Let's see…I would remember something like this."

His hands shook slightly as he flipped through the documents. "This is very serious, very serious," he mumbled.

He grazed his teeth with his tongue as he examined the pages, then asked if there were other copies. He asked where he could contact her if he had any questions. She told him she could be reached at the La Quinta Inn.

Then the meeting was abruptly over.

After he closed the door behind her, he picked up

the phone and said, "Get me Dale Thornton on the line immediately."

THE REDHEAD behind the receptionist's desk was making Toots jumpy—repeatedly patting the haystack on her head and constantly fiddling with the nail file. Twice now she had doused herself with some concoction—rancid vanilla and dead roses?—and on top of that, she smoked.

He'd managed to keep his eyes fixed on an ancient issue of *Field and Stream*. What was taking Marie so damn long?

Just then Marie came flying out of the corridor to Garrett's office. She looked pale. She looked worried. "Let's go," she said as she sailed past.

The receptionist caught Toots's eye and slid the nail file down her cleavage. He tipped his hat cordially, wanting to say, "Careful, ma'am. Wouldn't want a blowout," when her phone intercom beeped. She picked it up and said, "Get Dale Thornton? Right away, sir."

Toots strolled casually out the door.

Out in the cavernous capitol corridor, even with her ankle slowing her down, Toots had to scamper to catch up with Marie. "Well," he said, "what'd you find out from Garrett?"

"I made him nervous," Marie said as she charged along. "He took my hand when I left and his palm was all sweaty."

"Could be you make him nervous the same way you make the honorable Sheriff Whittington nervous."

She slowed down to give Toots a withering look.

"I don't mean he's *attracted* to me. It was more than that. He was smooth as silk until I mentioned Carville County Construction—"

"What'd he say about Triple C?"

"That it was a tempest in a teapot. But when he saw the files, his body language told another story."

"What'd his body language say?"

"He tangled up like a bundle of barbed wire."

Toots frowned. "I overheard him ask the biddy to raise Dale Thornton, but that could be a coincidence."

Marie stopped. "Dale Thornton? Carl's replacement?" She pulled her hair over her shoulder and twisted it. "Well, between bodies and bones and files that give people the sweats, there's sure no shortage of coincidences lately."

"True. Now what?"

She checked her watch. "Now I need to call the kids."

ANN MILLHOUSE, Carl's former secretary, unlocked Carl's old office so Marie could use the capitol watts line in private.

Marie had not been in this office since Carl's death, and seeing the desktop and credenza, empty except for a fine layer of dust, disheartened her.

Ann patted Marie's shoulder. "It's stayed vacant because Thornton's using his own office, which is bigger. Tell you the truth, I don't think anybody's had the heart to move in here, after the tragedy."

Marie nodded, staring at the rocker in the corner. The one she'd refinished for Carl. She supposed she should have Toots and Henry haul it back to Deep

Springs before it disappeared. "Ann, thank you so much for taking care of everything here," Marie said.

"You thanked me at the time, dear," Ann said quietly. "Listen," she added briskly, "we're closing down for the day." She turned a lever on the doorknob. "You're locked in now, but just turn this lever back to get out, okay? Security will lock the outside door later."

"Thanks," Marie mouthed as she dialed the phone.

"Manning residence." Marie detected a note of long-suffering in Alice's voice.

"Alice, it's me. How're the kids?"

"Oh, they're darling, hon, just darling." A protracted sigh.

Darling, huh? Marie thought. *Translation: the little simian beings were driving Alice bonkers.*

"Well, put the darlings on. I'm using the watts line in Carl's old office. I can talk a while."

The twins came on the extensions, whining in tandem, Mandy claiming that Jillian was trying to "run her life," and Mark feeling persecuted because the heartless tooth fairy had forgotten him.

Marie felt genuinely sorry about the tooth-fairy omission. Once again, she doubted her sanity for chasing down some political intrigue when her family needed her at home.

The sun sank behind the rain clouds and the office grew darker as Marie talked to the twins longer than she'd planned.

Alice was back on the line, in the middle of one of her monologues, when Marie heard someone trying to unlock the office door. She started to jump up and open it, but a sudden realization halted her—there was no light shining through the transom from the outer office.

Wouldn't security or the janitor have turned on a light out there? She heard the intruder trying another key.

"Alice," she hissed. "Gotta go. Call you back!" She slipped the phone into its cradle and squeezed under the massive desk just as the door creaked open.

The person who had gained entry into Carl's office did not switch on a light. Marie listened intently. Maybe it was just security after all. But there was no flashlight. Then she heard rifling noises in the gloom. And muttering. It sounded as if someone was going through the drawers in the wall storage unit. She heard the hiss of a pressured sigh. The intruder snatched up the receiver of the phone directly over Marie's head. She heard the faint notes of the touch tone and then:

"I'm in. Everything looks the same. I don't think she got it here. I *told* you we searched his office when he died. It's empty."

At the reference to Carl, Marie's heart started to pound. She tried to remember where she'd heard this woman's voice before, breathy, cigarettey.

"Oh, hell! Would you like to come and do that yourself? It's a waste of time. The original's probably at Manning's house and how do you propose to get *that?*"

There was a long pause, then:

"All right. One quick look. I'll meet you in the parking lot in thirty minutes."

Marie heard the phone clatter into its cradle.

Marie's palms were sweaty as she clutched her

long legs and tried not to make a sound. She turned her wrist to check the time, but couldn't read her watch in the darkness under the desk.

She heard the woman moving a chair from the corner. The room suddenly flared with the glow of the computer monitor.

When Marie heard the clack of the keyboard, she let out her air soundlessly, a puff at a time and checked her watch by the greenish light: 5:28.

The hard drive whirred endlessly, with the intermittent clicks. The woman kept up her search for what seemed an interminable time.

What if she comes over and searches the desk next? Marie worried. Her mind flailed for a way out of this predicament and nothing came, except her own stern command, *Don't panic. Don't panic. Don't panic.*

More clicking. More whirring. *If she doesn't leave soon, my neck is going to break!* Marie thought.

Then she heard footsteps out in the corridor.

The woman said, "Damn!" causing Marie to jerk and bump her head. She froze, but the woman evidently didn't hear the thump because seconds later the monitor light was snuffed out, and then Marie heard the door lock click.

For a moment, boot heels and high heels blended in a cacophony in the marble corridor.

Marie stayed crouched below the desk, slowly exhaling.

Deciding to tail the woman to see who she was meeting in the parking lot, Marie reached for the doorknob, just as a sharp rap on the office door made her heart leap into her throat.

"Marie? You in there?" a male voice said. *Toots*. He'd been off in search of a sandwich.

Marie's shoulders sagged with relief then she threw the door open and yanked Toots inside.

"Marie! What the—"

"Did you see anybody when you were coming down the corridor just now?" Marie asked urgently.

Toots looked puzzled. "Yeah. That redheaded biddy from Garrett's office."

"I knew I'd heard that voice somewhere before. She must be that Billie Schmidt Ann told me about. Remember? Ann said there were only two people who ever had a key to Carl's office—herself and Billie Schmidt. Billie was in here, digging around for something, probably the originals of those files I gave to Garrett."

"She was in *here?*" Toots poked at the floor with the umbrella he was carrying.

"Yeah, but I was hiding under the desk."

"You were *what?*"

"Hiding." Marie checked her watch again. "No time to explain. Come on." She grabbed Toots and pulled him out the door. "We've got to go see who she's meeting in the parking lot in about five minutes."

When they got to the end of the corridor, Marie opened the door there a crack. They saw Billie Schmidt facing an elevator, impatiently punching the button.

Marie jerked her head back, and hit Toots in the nose.

He grabbed it. "Dammit, Marie!"

"Shh!" she commanded, pressing her ear to the door.

When they heard the ding of the elevator, Marie cracked the door open again just in time to see the elevator doors swish closed, and the indicator lights go to the basement. "We'll run down the stairs," Marie informed Toots.

He was still trying to rearrange his nose. Through his hand he said, "Why? So I can fall down the stairs and break my neck, too? What is the point of all this, Marie?"

"I'll explain later." She grabbed his arm and dragged him to the stairs.

Marie poked her head out of the exit of the stairwell and spotted Billie Schmidt's flaming red head ducking into the passenger seat of a black Scorpio Merkur sedan with gold-plate detailing. The driver sped off into the misty rain before Marie could get the license number. But it shouldn't be hard, she thought, to trace a car like that. Toots came up behind her.

"You didn't get a look at the driver, did you?" Marie asked.

"Nope." Toots popped up the umbrella and held it over Marie's head.

"Well, at least we saw the car," she said. "And whoever's driving is the person Billie Schmidt called from Carl's office."

"She called someone from Carl's office while you were hiding in there?"

"Yes. A very revealing conversation. I'll tell you about it later, after we talk to the security guard. That's probably him." Marie indicated a figure in a yellow rain slicker and uniform hat, standing by the guardhouse.

"Okay, let's go," Toots said. "Then what do you say we hunt up some grub? The cafeteria was closed." He took Marie's elbow.

"Oh. I bet you're starving," she said as they walked across the parking lot. "I promise I'll take you somewhere nice to eat. I know some great places."

"You got a deal," Toots said.

The guard was a young Latino, with macho looks and a build to match. Rain dripped steadily off his plastic-covered hat as he sipped steaming coffee from a disposable cup.

As Marie and Toots approached, he put the coffee on the ledge of the guardhouse window and touched the brim of his hat. "Evening. May I help you?" he said.

"Yes, please," Marie replied. "I was wondering if you're Mr. Hernandez, the guard who was on duty on the twenty-second of May—May of last year, not this year—on the day shift?"

"I'm Hernandez, but I can't answer your question without checking the duty log, and I'll need to see some identification."

Marie fumbled in her purse and produced her wallet. "I'm Marie Manning," she held up her driver's license, "and this is my uncle, Toots Daniels."

Toots touched the brim of his hat.

The young man glanced at Marie's I.D. and then his handsome eyes softened with recognition and pity.

"If you'll wait a moment, Mrs. Manning, I'll see if I can find that log." He picked up his coffee, stepped inside the guardhouse and flipped back through a stack of pages on a clipboard.

"Hey," he called out through the window. "I *was* on duty that day. I worked a double."

Marie stepped up into the guardhouse. Hernandez raised his eyebrows but said nothing.

The interior, barren except for two beat-up stools and a newish-looking coffeemaker, was thick with humidity and the smell of overheated coffee.

"I've got to ask you a couple of questions," she said as she smoothed the damp hair back off her face. "Do you remember Commissioner Manning leaving that morning?"

The young guard frowned. "Wasn't that the day Mr. Manning drowned? The twenty-second?"

"Yes, it was," Marie said simply. "And I…I need to know…" She looked down.

Toots stepped into the guardhouse and put an arm around Marie's shoulder. "It's important to Mrs. Manning to know as much as she can about the day her husband died," he explained.

"Of course," Hernandez said and settled himself on a stool, indicating that Marie should take the other one.

Toots leaned against the doorjamb.

"Do you remember anything about that day? What time Mr. Manning left? Did he say anything to you? Anything you can recall would help," Marie said. "Was he carrying any boxes?" she added.

"Well…" Hernandez looked thoughtfully out at the parking lot. "I've already been questioned by some life-insurance guys," he said after a minute. "I told them everything I know, but I do remember something else from that day, but it doesn't have anything to do with Mr. Manning. It's funny what sticks in your mind.''

''What is it?'' Marie prompted.

''Well, it's a little thing, really, but our coffeemaker was broken and coffee's pretty important out here, it's so boring most of the time—I always drink more when I'm working a double. I was dying for a cup and this guy I know walked by carrying a big thermos and I called out, 'Is that hot coffee?', and he nodded but kept on walking. So I took a few steps toward him and said, 'Could I bum a cup off you?' and he said, 'No,' kinda hostile like that. I couldn't believe it. I thought, what an ass, you know? Pardon me, ma'am. But it sort of embarrassed me, for asking. I've never said a word to the guy since, although I see him all the time. I remember it was the day I was working the double, so it must have been the twenty-second, but I guess that doesn't help you much.''

Marie was disappointed. ''You don't remember anything about Carl—Mr. Manning?'' she asked.

''No,'' Hernandez shook his head sadly. ''Commissioner Manning would usually just smile and wave—hey! I just remembered. He came out of the building right after the jerk with the thermos and he said something to *him.*''

''What did he say?'' Marie said, suddenly intent.

''He hollered, 'I'll meet you there,' or something like that.''

Toots stood erect. ''Who was the guy with the thermos?''

"As a matter of fact, he just drove off," Hernandez said. "In that black—"

"Scorpio Merkur," Marie finished for him.

Hernandez looked surprised. "Yeah," he said. "It was Dale Thornton. How'd you know?"

CHAPTER TWELVE

THE INSTANT she stepped inside the ornate carved antique doors and let the rush of nostalgia wash over her, Marie remembered why she loved the Old Lone Star Saloon. It was a hundred and one percent Texan.

The atmosphere was exactly the same as it had been in her college days: wagon-wheel chandeliers, hunter-green leatherette booths, Christmas lights year-round. All the same. And everywhere, replicas of the beloved Lone Star—flags, mugs, photos.

"This is exactly what I need," she shouted in Toots's good ear above the din of country-and-western music and rowdy young voices. "Someplace distracting and loud and awful."

"It's that, all right," Toots hollered back. A couple of urban cowboys in pointlessly long dusters elbowed past. "And crowded. Want to go someplace else?"

Marie poked him. "I suppose you'd prefer naked fluorescent lights and chipped Formica tables."

"Now you're talkin'." Toots winked. "Someplace where they dish out chicken-fried steak twenty-four hours a day."

They followed a sunburned girl with a bushy blond ponytail to a booth in a dark corner on the upper deck.

Marie smiled when she picked up the orange wall phone to place their order. The very same phones.

Where on earth did they ever find *orange* phones? "Two ranch burgers, the heap and two draft beers," she said succinctly and hung up. "This place gives me an appetite." She grinned at Toots.

"Yeah, it's pretty...stimulating," Toots said, eyeing the pretty coeds all around them. "Did you come here a lot in college?"

"Before I married Carl. But after we got married and he came back to Austin to study engineering, I was in the thick of nursing school and couldn't work much. We didn't have the money to go out."

"Not even for a burger?"

"Not according to Carl." Marie smiled. "It was okay, really. My grades improved dramatically after I got married." But it dawned on her that her world had become telescopically narrow the day she'd married Carl, and she'd missed coming to the Old Lone Star.

The light on the orange phone blinked.

"The food's ready," Marie said. "I'll get it."

"Nope. Better let me pay," Toots said, reaching back for his wallet.

"It's okay, Toots." Marie gave him a rueful little smile. "Carl isn't counting my pennies now." She hitched her purse over her shoulder and slid out of the booth.

Toots watched Marie make her way through the crowd to the pickup bar and tried to remember her as a nineteen-year-old coed, before she married Carl. How she made them all laugh, how she did everything with such gusto. He watched her bend over her purse, digging for the money to pay the tab. Though Carl had showered his family with luxuries, he had controlled every dime. Toots knew she was worried sick about losing that life-insurance money, but she needn't be. Old Uncle Toots would find a way to help her hang on to Manning Ranch even if it meant selling his own share of the Manning land.

He lost sight of her in the crowd, then spotted her again. She was walking back across the restaurant, but where was the food? Maybe she didn't have enough money to pay the— What the hell? Jim Whittington was walking behind her, carrying the tray! What in tarnation was Whittington doing here?

"Toots!" Marie called out as she approached the booth. "Look who I found!"

Marie's voice was a little high, and so was her color, Toots noticed. He slid out of the booth.

Whittington set the heavily laden tray down on the table and extended his hand. "Mr. Daniels."

"Sheriff." Toots gave him a firm, not entirely cordial handshake.

"I invited the sheriff to join us," Marie explained brightly, "since it's so crowded here, and all."

"Sure thing!" Toots said with forced enthusiasm.

Oh brother, what have I done, Marie thought. *Well, too late. Toots will just have to put his suspicions aside and be a gentleman.*

She slid into one side of the booth and started pulling napkins out of the dispenser.

The two men stood awkwardly as if they were choosing seats for the peace talks.

Then Toots zipped around behind Whittington and wedged himself in beside Marie. He gestured to the opposite side. "Have a seat," he said.

As Whittington lowered himself into the seat, Marie said, "The sheriff is in Austin for—what did you say?" She leaned across the table toward Whittington.

"A campaign seminar." He removed his hat and laid it on the seat.

"What kind of deal?" Toots said, screwing his hearing aid up.

"A class on campaign strategy." Whittington raised his voice for Toots's benefit. "More like a pep rally for county candidates in the last weeks of the elections. The state Democratic party sponsors it."

"Oh. The *party*," Toots said softly and popped a french fry into his mouth.

Marie rolled her eyes. Toots considered Democrats a bunch of cliquish little knee-jerk sheep, like Nazis, only not nearly as smart. "Just look at all this food," she said as she unloaded the tray.

"I wouldn't o' figured you for much of an organized-party man," Toots said, popping in another fry.

"I wouldn't say it's an *organized* party." Whittington winked at Marie. "We're just Democrats."

She chuckled. Toots did not.

"The old Will Rogers joke," Toots said flatly. "But you must be in pretty good if they're bringin' you all the way to Austin for a—what'd you call it? A seminar?" Toots wasn't letting up.

Marie started to squirm. Maybe it hadn't been so smart to invite Whittington to their table.

"It's really a mandatory indoctrination session. If I want their money, I have to attend."

Whittington's candor seemed to mollify Toots, at least temporarily. He nodded and attacked his hamburger.

Whittington did the same.

Marie took a nervous gulp of beer.

After a couple of massive bites, Whittington said, "I guess the kids all got home okay on Saturday night?"

"They're fine," Marie said, recalling how weird Sunday had been. Taking Mark out to the place where he found the cow bones, finding a gaping six-by-six-foot hole, which Mark insisted was not there before. Marie focused her attention on getting catsup from the bottle. She wondered if Whittington could sense that she was concealing something. "They're just fine," she said again.

"I'm glad to hear that," Whittington said. "And I'm glad you're feeling better, too."

Toots stopped chewing and eyed Marie.

"Well, it's like I told you Saturday night, Sheriff. That was a fluke." Marie could feel Toots's steady, scrutinizing gaze. "Oh, look!" She pointed at a large print of cactus and coyotes. "That silkscreen looks like it was done by a girl I went to school with. I'll have to go over and see if it's one of hers."

Toots was not deflected. "*What* was just a fluke?" he said.

"Oh, nothing," Marie said, and gave Whittington an embarrassed glance. She took another sip of beer.

"Mrs. Manning's ankle was bothering her when I saw her on Friday, but she looked *fine* on Saturday night." Whittington winked at Marie again.

A smooth dissembler, Marie thought. But she was grateful for his cover-up. Toots already fussed over her enough without knowing that she'd fainted. She took another hasty swallow of beer. It tasted cold and sweet. She couldn't remember the last time she'd sat in a bar and enjoyed a beer.

"This is a great place, isn't it?" Whittington said.

"Great?" Toots shouted. "If I wasn't deaf before, I will be now!" He cranked down his hearing aid.

Whittington smiled. "A lady at the seminar told me to meet her here," he explained to Marie. "But I haven't seen her." He craned his neck and looked out over the crowd.

"What does she look like?" Marie asked, immediately wishing she hadn't. It sounded nosy, which, of course, she *was* when it came to Whittington. She took a bite of her burger.

"Well, she's blond, tall. About twenty-five, I guess. It's funny. I can't tell you much else about her, and I looked at her all day."

"You looked at her all day?" Marie said, and wanted to chop her own tongue off.

Whittington stopped searching the bar and looked back at Marie, his eyes narrowed a fraction. "Yeah. All day. She was one of the instructors at the seminar." He glanced back out over the crowd. "I guess you could say she's average-looking, nice-looking."

He probably had scads of "nice-looking" females asking him to meet them all the time, Marie thought as she studied his handsome profile, his large powerful hands, his bulging forearms and shoulders, his square jaw, his thick brown hair. She swallowed, suddenly feeling old, widowed, out of it. She picked up her beer and took another swig.

"Well, right now I don't see hide nor hair of her," he said, flashing a smile as if that pleased him.

It was the same smile he'd given her Saturday

night, there and gone in an instant, but revealing something warm and unexpected. She recalled how his voice had sounded when he was talking to his dog in the kitchen. Warm. There was something very, very warm about this man. She finished the last of her beer with her eyes on him.

"Do you need another beer? Who's driving?" Whittington said, pointing back and forth between Marie and Toots.

"I'll be driving, Your Honorable," Toots said. "Go ahead, Missy, have another. It'll help you sleep."

"I guess one more won't hurt," Marie allowed.

Whittington picked up the orange phone and ordered two more drafts.

When he hung up, he smiled and said, "I haven't asked what you're doing in Austin."

"Just talking to insurance people," Toots said.

"I'm here to find out everything I can about the day my husband was killed," Marie said.

Toots poked her in the ankle with the toe of his boot.

Whittington's smile vanished. "I thought you were going to leave that up to the lawyers," he said.

"It's been over a year, and the Law isn't doing that much as far as I can tell," Marie said and Toots poked her again.

The crease between Whittington's eyebrows grew dangerously deep. "What makes you think we're not doing much?" he asked.

"I still haven't seen that accident report. And there are *other* things."

Whittington panned from Marie to Toots and back.

The crease between his eyebrows looked etched in stone now. "I explained the delay in getting the accident report to you, Mrs. Manning," he said.

"Marie, you've hardly touched your hamburger," Toots said. "Eat."

The red light below the phone blinked, and Toots fixed on it as if it were a signal from outer space.

"The beers," Whittington said. "I'll be right back." He eased himself out of the booth, then frowned down at Marie as if he might say something, then turned and walked away.

As soon as he disappeared into the crowd, Toots said, "Hoot damn, Missy! I thought you were going to blab everything for a second there."

"Is that why you booted me in my sore ankle?" Marie said, indignant.

"Well, *excuse* me. I was just making sure you weren't too charmed by our handsome, sincere sheriff," Toots said, acting equally indignant.

"Charmed? Now see here! I want him to feel some pressure not to sweep all of this under the rug. I want him to know *I'm* looking at it, too. *Nobody* is charming *me*."

"Oh, don't get your skirts all blowed up. I know how guys like that operate, asking about your kids and your health, and all. He's up to something if you ask me."

"Here he comes," Marie said.

Whittington walked up to the table carrying two mugs brimming with beer. "Here we go," he said and set them on the table, but he didn't sit down. He laid a palm on the table in front of Marie, leaned toward her. He looked directly into her eyes. "I hope you'll excuse me now. I really enjoyed eating with you—'' he was so close that she could smell the mixed aromas of aftershave and cigars ''—but I found that lady from the seminar. She's with those people down there.'' He inclined his head toward a group of smartly dressed urbanites on the lower floor. ''I really should join her.''

''Oh, by all means. Don't let us keep you,'' Marie said brightly. ''Do we need to reimburse you for the beers?'' *By all means? Reimburse?* Marie thought. *Why was she talking like a church lady?*

''My treat,'' he said, then reached into the seat for his hat, and looked down at her as he adjusted it on his head.

Marie felt thin and pale and small, sitting there below his gaze. She wanted to look anywhere but into his eyes, and ended up glancing at his big, western-style belt buckle. Mortified at this gaffe, she focused on her beer mug as he said goodbye and shook hands with Toots.

''Take care of yourself, Mrs. Manning. I promise I'll get that accident report to you as soon as I get my hands on it.''

''Thank you, Sheriff,'' she said without looking up.

As he worked his way through the crowd, Marie could not take her eyes off him. *Of course,* she thought. *He would rather be over there with a pretty blonde than with a suspicious little widow and her prickly old friend.*

When Whittington got to the table of laughing people, the blonde stood and hooked a hand on his shoulder, apparently introducing him.

That woman wasn't just pretty, Marie thought, she

was a replica of one of Mandy's fashion dolls. Her hair swung in a shiny white-hot sheet to her waist. She wore an expensive-looking cream-colored suit with a saffron silk blouse, unbuttoned an indecent distance. She stood with a tanned thigh peeking sexily out of a high side slit.

Marie looked doggedly at her beer mug again.

Suddenly she wished she were back on her ranch, in the kitchen, drinking hot chocolate with her kids, instead of here in this bar watching that woman plaster herself all over Jim Whittington. She took another swig of beer. Now it seemed flat, lukewarm, bitter.

Toots wanted to know if Marie wanted to go over and check out the print that she thought her friend might have done. She didn't.

Toots wanted to know if she wanted to get up and leave. She didn't.

She didn't know what she wanted. She burrowed into the booth corner, brooding, sipping beer and watching the dance floor.

The two-steppers were packed out there, all flowing in one direction, under a giant mirrored ball rotating over the center of the dance floor.

She spotted Whittington with the blonde. They seemed in perfect harmony. He moved her along easily, her ashen hair swaying behind her. A stud and his filly. The droplets of light sprayed hypnotically over her hair and his cowboy hat as he dipped his broad shoulders and tilted her back.

They danced through a couple of numbers and then an old Hoyt Axton number started.

At first, Whittington and the blonde didn't break stride, but then Axton was singing about lights at night, and memories, and dreams, and it seemed to Marie that Whittington suddenly lost his rhythm.

Then Whittington stopped dancing, with the blonde pressed awkwardly against him. The other dancers flowed around them like an oblivious river.

He looked in the direction of Marie's booth, and then Marie saw him bend down and say something to the blonde, take her elbow and walk her to her table of friends. She saw him turn and come toward her.

Marie sat up straight and pulled her hair over one shoulder. And suddenly, he was standing over her.

"Do you dance?" he said, his voice sounding deep and resonant coming from under the brim of the Stetson.

Marie looked into his shadowed eyes, her lips parted in surprise. Was he asking her to dance?

He put his hand out, palm up.

Marie looked at his hand and back into his eyes. They were utterly sincere, utterly serious. He meant it. He wanted to dance with her.

"Well?" he said.

"I'll be back in a minute, Toots," she said and put her hand in Whittington's. His palm felt firm and warm. His touch electric. He gently pulled her to her feet.

"You won't need this," he said and slid her tweed jacket off her shoulders. He folded it carefully, and laid it in the booth. Then he drew her hair back over her shoulder, lifted it off her neck, fanned it out.

Marie felt her cheeks grow hot as she wondered if it was wise to submit to having her hair handled this way.

Whittington smoothed his palm slowly down her

hair and rested it at the small of her back. "Ready?" he said.

"Wait." Marie was suddenly self-conscious. "I'm not much of a two-stepper."

"Don't worry," he said. "I'll lead." He slipped his hand around to her side and guided her onto the dance floor with his palm burning through her thin cashmere sweater.

He led all right.

The compelling two-step beat and the sea of dancers swept them along. It seemed at times that Marie's feet didn't even touch the floor. In fact, she felt a little light-headed as he swirled her around. Marie worried about the effects of the beer. She concentrated on her moves, hoping that she wouldn't do anything grossly clumsy.

"Oh!" he said, clutching her tighter. "Maybe we shouldn't be out here. Is your ankle okay?"

Truth be told, Marie hadn't even thought about it. "It's fine," she mumbled. "The air cast, and all."

He smiled. "Then relax. We're just dancing."

Marie, tall for a woman, was not used to being overpowered by men on the dance floor. But he did it easily. He was hot from his exertions with the blonde and his heat seemed to magnify his size.

This song was about dreams also and he leaned his head down beside her ear and said, "Do you ever have dreams, Mrs. Manning?"

Marie, still concentrating on her dancing, answered seriously, "Of course."

He smiled broadly and dipped her a little, giving her a dizzying half turn. "Well, that's a relief. People who don't dream go crazy, you know. Deprived of REM sleep, and all.''

He smiled knowingly and looked into her eyes. Then he pulled her into his chest and put his mouth next to her ear again. ''I was talking about a different kind of dream. *Dreams*. With a capital D.''

Marie kept her gaze focused over his shoulder. She couldn't think. His scent, his shoulder muscles, his strong legs pressing against her thighs, the clean line of his close-cropped hair on the back of his neck—it was all so very distracting. What did he want her to say?

He gave her a little squeeze and laid his cheek against her hair. ''Come on. Tell me. This is your chance to spill your guts.''

Marie laughed nervously and she felt his chest vibrate in an answering chuckle.

''Okay. I guess I dream about keeping Manning Ranch solvent, and raising my kids well.''

He leaned back and regarded her face skeptically. ''My, you dream some pretty serious stuff, Mrs. Manning.''

You don't know the half of it, Marie thought, recalling her nightmare Saturday evening. *I dream about Bud Weimer, and you, and death.*

''Well, if I had those kids and that ranch,'' his deep voice rumbled in her ear, ''I'd dream about them, too, night and day.''

''I dream other things,'' she said defensively.

''Like what?'' He tilted his head back and looked at her.

''Like, someday I want to finish my master's degree. I want to do something meaningful after I've raised my kids.''

''Well, I'll be,'' he breathed, and Marie decided *he* was a little mellow from the beer, too. ''Mrs. Marie Manning, the woman who has it all, actually wants more.''

Marie didn't know how to take that. Was he judging her for wanting more? And why was he insisting on calling her Mrs. Manning?

Just as she started to say, ''Call me Marie,'' the song ended.

They stopped, looking at each other with the droplets of light from the mirrored ball playing over their faces. Linda Ronstadt's version of ''Desperado'' started. Plaintive, slow.

He took her hand, and with his face only inches from hers, looked into her eyes and whispered, ''Can your ankle take one more?''

Marie allowed herself to be pulled close to his body and led to the slow, melancholy ballad.

He was so strong. She felt her breasts melting into his warm chest. She felt that chest heave with a sigh.

She tried to peek at his profile out of the corner of her eye. *Was* he tipsy? But he seemed very much in control. He held her securely. He covered her right hand with his left and pressed it against his chest. His right hand was flattened against the small of her back. Firm. Warm. Moving down by degrees.

His head bent toward her shoulder imperceptibly and she felt his breath, hot and moist, on her neck. His mood seemed suddenly as earnest as the song and Marie felt uncomfortable, compelled to say something.

"What about you?" she said. "What do you dream about?"

He looked into her eyes and held her gaze for an excruciatingly long moment.

"You," he mouthed.

Marie stared at him in genuine disbelief. Had he really said "you"?

They stopped and the sea of dancers moved around them, yet seemed far away. "Are we still dancing?" she whispered.

He shook his head no, then put a finger under her chin and angled her face up. Marie opened her lips to ask, "Then what are we doing?" but before her words formed, he covered her mouth with his own.

All breath left her. He raised her high into his chest, crushed her against him and forced his tongue deep into her mouth. She swallowed and a small moan escaped her throat. Oh, his mouth was wondrous!

She felt suspended, lost, free, wild, subdued all at once. The kiss continued for what seemed an eternity as the craziest sensations and thoughts flooded her: grinding desire, terrible wanting, blissful surrender.

He eased back and gently tugged first on her bottom lip, and then on the upper one as she breathed, "Oh, Jim."

"Yes," he said, and came down on her mouth for more. This time his kiss was so intense she thought she might cry out, right there on the dance floor.

The last languid chords of the song—about letting somebody love you—seemed to pull Marie's tears forth in a flood. She whimpered and he raised his mouth, studied her face. He was shielding her face with the brim of his hat as he held her protectively.

He said, "I'm so sorry. I...I had no right to do that. The last thing I want to do is cause you more pain."

Marie bit her lip, and shook her head, but she couldn't answer him. She couldn't even open her eyes. She could feel his hot breath on her cheek and he kept holding her tenderly, with her breasts just grazing his shirt, with her elbows cupped in his warm palms, as if he didn't know what to do with her.

"Why don't I take you back to your table?" he said.

She looked at the floor, and nodded. Another song had started, but Marie hardly heard it.

She tried to discreetly wipe away her tears as they worked their way through the crowd back to the booth where Toots sat waiting, chewing a toothpick and frowning at them. He'd probably seen the whole thing. Marie didn't care. She didn't care about anything but this amazing discovery: passion. Where had it come from? Where had it been all this time?

Passion.

When they reached the table, she managed to look into the face of the man who had inspired it. He said, "Thank you for the dance," as if nothing had happened. But his face looked concerned, sad, somewhat guilt-stricken.

"Yes. Thank you," she tried to say, but only a hoarse whisper came out. She nodded.

He tipped his hat at Toots, turned and was out the door of the Old Lone Star in less than thirty seconds.

"What's the matter, Marie?" Toots said when Marie finally lowered herself into the booth. He leaned forward and put a hand lightly on her wrist.

She withdrew her arm and fumbled in her purse for

a tissue. When she didn't answer, Toots pressed, "Did Whittington upset you somehow?"

Still looking into her purse, she shook her head and said, "No, Toots. He didn't upset me." And that was all she would say. And even that was a lie. Because Whittington *had* upset her. More than she could admit, even to herself.

CHAPTER THIRTEEN

JIM IMPATIENTLY tapped his cellular phone and counted five rings. Why in Sam Hill didn't she answer?

Six rings. The front desk at the La Quinta Inn picked up, informed him that the party in that room had already checked out. So, she hadn't waited for his call. The desk clerk said yes, he was certain Mrs. Manning got the message.

He tossed the phone into the passenger seat and cursed under his breath. Beautiful. Just beautiful. Marie Manning was the most confounding woman. Maybe after that kiss last night she didn't *want* to talk to him. Probably. He closed his eyes and her huge green ones came to memory, shimmering with tears. But then he remembered her stubborn insistence on sticking her nose into this investigation and his jaw clenched.

By God, she would *have* to talk to him. If she didn't want to have anything to do with him personally, fine, but the investigation was another matter. He merged into traffic. Maybe he could intercept her before she did anything too stupid.

When he turned into the parking lot of the La Quinta, he spotted Marie's Jeep immediately. Strange. A chubby redheaded woman stood beside it, tugging on the door. Who was this woman? Instinct told him her actions were sinister.

He parked on the opposite side of the lot, concealed between two RVs, and observed her in the rearview mirror. After trying all the doors, she dropped to her knees and groped around under the front fender. Then she got up and tottered as quickly as her high heels allowed to a waiting car, which sped off.

Jim got a quick ID on the vehicle: tag XTJ-101, late-model black Scorpio Merkur, gold-plate trim, no body damage. When they disappeared into traffic, he sprinted over to Marie's Jeep, put a knee to the pavement, felt under the front fender. His agile fingers soon retrieved a small electronic device attached to the frame by a powerful magnet.

He stood up and rolled the device around in his palm. Very interesting. He hadn't seen one this nice since his days at the Presidio, when he'd tracked drug runners from Mexico north to San Francisco, and those were the kind built only on a government contract. This little jewel had cost a bundle.

Congratulations, Mrs. Manning, now you've got them bird-dogging you. He slipped it into the inside pocket of his jean jacket.

He heard a female voice echoing off the hotel pool, coming from a passageway. Marie. A man's voice intermingled with hers, but it wasn't old man Daniels. This guy was younger. Jim bolted around the corner of a Dumpster. And watched.

He recognized the guy. Mike Garrett, a self-serving bastard if ever there was one. What was Marie doing with him? Making the same mistake her husband had? Jim couldn't hear what they were saying.

Garrett walked Marie to her Jeep and took her hand, enclosing it in both of his own. Oily skunk. Then Marie got into the driver's seat and Garrett folded her full skirt neatly inside the door and closed it.

When Garrett went around and got in the passenger seat of the Jeep, Jim couldn't believe it. That creep was actually riding off with her! Maybe somebody knew they were together and had been trying to track Garrett. He needed tracking, judging from the company he kept.

As Jim watched, Marie backed out and drove the Jeep around the side of the hotel, out of his view.

He stepped out of the shadows of the Dumpster into the bright morning sunshine and suddenly it was as if all the amorphous impressions that had been forming in the shadows of his mind came forward into the light also.

He had work to do in Deep Springs.

He thought of the blonde at the campaign seminar as he jogged back to the Bronco. He should go over there and explain his absence. He needed that five thousand dollars to win the election. He remembered the woman's words last night, "You have to have your priorities. Politics first. You have to *commit*," she'd said.

Commit? he thought. Oh, he was committed all right. But not to running for sheriff. Not even to *being* sheriff. He was committed to this and only this: nailing the bastards once and for all.

He reached in his pocket and pulled out the tracking device, took another look at it as he fired up the

Bronco. Might as well make this interesting. How about a little side trip to the Dulane county seat? He'd get that accident report *today*. He didn't care if it harelipped the governor.

CHAPTER FOURTEEN

WHEN BUD WEIMER'S call interrupted Jack Hess's snoring, Jack had little choice but to drag his portly frame out of bed and trudge down to the Swing Door to open up. Using the bar for these predawn meetings was all Weimer asked in return for keeping Jack afloat. That and Jack's silence.

He put on the coffee and set out an array of chipped mugs. Then he shuffled across the street to Dollie's Donuts.

Weimer and two men entered by the swing door, poured themselves coffee, then sat in a back booth. They slurped coffee and exchanged shifty glances over the rims of their cups before Weimer began. "Well, did you create a distraction?"

A wiry young man with a pocked ruddy face, scraggly blond hair and one earring said, "Don't worry. They'll be distracted."

"Enough to get 'em off the ranch?" Weimer insisted.

Garms squirmed. "If the deputy here does his part, they'll leave." He shot a sour look at the man on Weimer's left. Pruitt slouched in the corner of the booth. He even had his starched uniform on at this ungodly hour. Garms smirked into his coffee cup.

Pruitt cleared his throat and Garms jumped, slopping coffee down his front.

Weimer made a disgusted face at Garms's shirt. "Thornton's people couldn't find anything in Manning's computer at the capitol, so it's probably in the one at his home. That's how Mrs. Manning got ahold of it. I imagine there's some of those—what'd you call 'em—" He snapped his fingers at Garms.

"Floppy disks," Garms said.

"Yeah, floppy disks. That's where you come in. I don't like using you after the way you went berserk—" Weimer finished his sentence with beady eyes boring into Garms "—but you're the only one who can do the computer stuff. And you, Bobby, have to be sure they won't come back while he's doing his thing." He pointed a stubby finger at Pruitt.

Pruitt finally spoke, "I'll see that Garms has plenty of time to do a thorough check."

"*Dweeb.*" Garms didn't bother to conceal his scorn. "I don't need to do a *thorough check.* I delete all the floppies and disable the entire system."

"No!" Weimer jabbed the stubby finger at Garms now. "You find those records, and you make *me* some copies. I don't trust Garrett. This comes before a grand jury, Garrett'll cover his ass and sell me down the river. I don't like him being the only one with Manning's records. You take some of those floppy things and make me some copies before you destroy anything. And leave all of her stuff looking exactly as it was. Understand?"

Pruitt gave Garms a smirk.

"What about Whittington?" Garms said. "We have to make sure he's out of the way, too."

"That boy doesn't take a poot that I don't know about it." Weimer sipped his coffee.

"Want me to fix the election computers so he loses?" Garms said.

Weimer shook his head. "It's too late to run any opposition we could control. We'll find a way to disgrace him and boot him out after the election."

"That's doable. That's entirely doable," Garms said.

"Just don't underestimate him," Pruitt put in.

"Sh—!" Garms spun on him, "Don't tell me how to do my job!"

"Boys! Boys!" Weimer shouted, putting a palm up toward each of them. "I've got enough problems without this bickering. If you two can't get out there and destroy the evidence, I'll find me someone who will." Weimer reached into his shirt pocket and pulled out a roll of antacids.

"Whittington's in Austin and has to stay there until tomorrow if he wants the money I earmarked for him." Weimer sipped his coffee thoughtfully, then chewed the antacid. "And one of Dale's people is putting a homing device on Mrs. Manning's Jeep this morning. We'll know the minute she heads back to Deep Springs. In the meantime, only *one certain* deputy will be guarding the Manning Ranch." He reached up and clamped a hand on Pruitt's well-developed shoulder. "Ain't that right, Bobby?"

Pruitt fingered his walkie and nodded without taking his eyes off Garms.

"Fake an investigation," Weimer went on. "And then make that Croft woman take the kids somewhere 'safe'—not her place. She can see the Manning gates from there. Scare Honicker off, too. Then let Garms know the coast is clear." He turned his attention to Garms. "You do your thing and make sure nobody can tell you were in the house when you leave. Leave it all nice and neat."

Garms nodded, cocked an eyebrow and tugged on his earring.

Jack Hess slipped in through the swing door carrying a pink box of doughnuts.

"None for me," Pruitt said, brushing past Jack and leaving the swing door banging in his wake.

"I'm already having my breakfast, Jack," Weimer said, holding an antacid between his front teeth for Hess to see. "But I'm sure Garms here could eat a mess of doughnuts." He squeezed his potbelly out of the booth and slapped Garms on the back, baring all of his blunt coffee-stained teeth in a feral grin. "Couldn't you, boy?"

"Sure could." Garms grinned.

Weimer put on his cowboy hat and tossed a twenty on the table. "Thanks for the hospitality, Jack."

"No trouble, Bud. You all were never here." Hess did not look at the twenty.

"Enjoy your doughnuts, boy. One more little job, and we're home free." Weimer slapped Garms's back again and ambled out the swing door.

CHAPTER FIFTEEN

ON THE TRIP BACK to Deep Springs, Toots kept his hisses and his ''hoot damns'' to himself. Marie was in no mood for friendly advice. He studied her profile. Her knuckles were white on the steering wheel, her mouth a hard line, her eyes wide with fear. He pulled his cap down and slumped into the seat.

Alice Croft be stifled. Imagine that silly woman calling Marie in a hysteria about a prowler when Marie had more than enough to worry about in Austin.

''Let's stop in Wildhorse for a cup of coffee,'' he said, knowing it was a useless gesture.

''I had breakfast, courtesy of Mr. Garrett, remember?''

''Oh, right,'' Toots said, recalling the mood inside the Jeep when Marie and Garrett pulled around the corner of the hotel. Marie had acted as if that big breakfast threatened to come back up any second, and Garrett had acted like a fawning soap-opera actor. ''You have my *pledge* that I will take care of this,'' he had said, and ''I *assure* you there is no need to do anything further,'' and ''I *certainly* hope things are all right at your ranch,'' and on and on all the way to the capitol where she finally dumped him like a sack of feed.

Alice was waiting when they got to the ranch, pacing the porch, wringing her hands in her apron.

"Marie, honey!" she cried when Marie and Toots got out of the Jeep. "It's just plain awful. The children and I were asleep. Henry spotted him before dawn, when he went out to start the feeding. I feel so terrible, this happening when I was in charge of things—"

"Got any coffee, Alice?" Toots interrupted.

Alice regarded him icily over the rim of her glasses. "How can you be thinking of coffee at a time like this?"

Toots gave her a taut smile. "Now, Pie, even a war couldn't make me forget my coffee."

Alice looked as though she wanted to bean Toots for using the hated nickname from their high-school days—Pie. Short for Sweetie Pie, and the older Alice was anything but. She planted her fists on her wide hips. "You just shut your old biscuit hole, Toots Daniels. While you've been gallivanting around Austin we've had a prowler—"

"Stifle yourself, Alice—"

"Actually, I could use a cup of tea," Marie intervened wearily.

Toots and Alice looked at Marie, then aimed blaming glances at each other.

"Of course, honey," Alice said haughtily, and waddled up the porch steps.

"The kids went to school?" Marie asked as they entered the kitchen.

"Yes." Alice busied herself with the teakettle. "I tried not to make a big deal out of this in front of them. Mark and Mandy woke up Jillian and B.J., shouting, 'We had a burglar!', and by the time Deputy Pruitt arrived we were all pretty keyed up.''

"Deputy Pruitt was here?" Marie asked.

"Oh yes, honey. He hightailed it out here as soon as I called. Said I should take the kids somewhere safe, that the prowler might be back.''

"He said that?''

"Well, yeah, but I said, 'nonsense, in broad daylight?' I told him I was getting the children off to school, like always, and then I was waiting right here for you to arrive, that I'd already called you back from Austin. I told him the kids wouldn't want to go anywhere if it meant missing the Halloween parade. He got a little put out then, but I stood my ground.''

Marie dipped her tea bag, waiting for Alice to wind down.

"Then he went out and asked Henry some questions—it's funny, Henry said Bailey never barked—then Pruitt came back in here and wanted to know when you all would be back from Austin. He said to let him know immediately if we found anything else suspicious. Said he would check in with you later…''

As Alice went on, a chill crawled over Marie. Why hadn't Bailey barked?

She raised her teacup to her lips as she realized that Bailey hadn't barked his usual greeting when they drove up, either.

Suddenly, Marie set her teacup down and flew out the door into the brilliant October sunshine. "Bailey!" she yelled. She shielded her eyes and looked in all directions, then marched to the back of the house.

"Bailey!" she yelled again. "Baileeey!"

She whirled on Toots and Alice as they scurried

toward her. "Has anybody seen Bailey this morning?"

The older two stopped and looked at each other as if it had not even occurred to them to look for the dog.

"Now, Marie." Alice came at her with her arms outstretched. "We just missed him in all the excitement, that's all. He's probably got a squirrel treed out in the woods and won't give up."

"That's right," Toots said. "It's just a coincidence that he's missing. I'll go hunt him up right now." He trotted off toward the woods.

A foreboding gripped Marie. She wanted it to stop, all these terrible coincidences. She wanted everything to be safe and sane and *boring* again.

Alice patted Marie's arm while Marie tried to calm herself, to regain her bearings. The deputy had checked the ranch. Her children were safe at school. Toots would find Bailey. Garrett had said he would handle the documents.

This morning Toots's assessment of Garrett had been as skeptical as her own. "That fella's as jumpy as a preacher in a whorehouse." But Garrett had kept assuring Marie that she'd done the right thing.

She had done the right thing, hadn't she?

CHAPTER SIXTEEN

THE CHOPPER SWOOPED down over the crowd—*whap!
whap! whap!*—then flew in a low beeline over the
paraders as they snaked up Main Street.

Marie squinted up with irritation. "You would
think," she shouted at Alice above the noise, "with
a murderer at large, that the sheriff would have better
things to do than dive around showing off his helicopter!"

Alice pursed her lips, then leaned toward Marie and
added, "Especially when *prowlers* are running
around Manning Ranch."

Alice cocked an eyebrow at Marie. Maybe she
shouldn't have mentioned that prowler again. With no
sign of Bailey all afternoon, Marie had been edgy.

At least the costumes they'd rigged up for the kids
had cheered her somewhat. When Mandy came out
of her room as a sparkling pink princess, and Mark
stepped forward stiffly, dressed in a Styrofoam carton
as a space robot, she had clapped enthusiastically.

But when Mandy rapped Mark's helmet with her
wand, and Mark intoned mechanically, "I will va-
porize this pink alien," she'd managed only a faint
smile.

Maybe seeing her children in the Halloween parade
would get Marie's mind off her troubles. Of course,

the twins could be behaving better, Alice thought as she caught sight of them.

Mandy was whacking Mark on the helmet with her wand again, this time in rhythm with the band. He turned to give her a shove, but she dodged and Mark hit the pavement flat on his face.

Marie's hand flew to her mouth.

Mark struggled to get up, but couldn't because of the restrictive Styrofoam box and dryer hoses at his elbows.

The first-graders marched on, including Mandy, blissfully unaware of her brother's predicament. Coming up fast were the sixth-graders, swirling and hot-dogging on skateboards.

Marie started frantically pushing her way through the crowd when a man in a cowboy hat materialized from the other side of the street and scooped Mark up. Jim Whittington.

He stood Mark up at curbside just as the skateboarders careened by. Then he knelt on one knee, brushing off the little boy's face and straightening his pipe-cleaner antennae.

Whittington nodded his head and listened sympathetically as he wiped Mark's tear-streaked face and dabbed at his bleeding nose with a large hankie.

Marie darted across the street. "Mark! Are you all right?" she asked, breathless.

"Mom, make Mandy leave me alone!" He sniffed.

"I will, honey," Marie said, dropping to one knee in front of him. "I'll talk to her."

Whittington examined Mark's nose and said, "Listen, partner, looks like your nose has stopped bleeding. You go on, and tell Miss Fairy Princess that if she tries to cast any more spells, I'll arrest her.''

Marie was suddenly aware that Whittington's thigh was pressing against hers. After that kiss last night, she didn't trust herself to be anywhere near him. She stood up.

Mark dashed off to catch up with the first-graders.

Jim stood and faced Marie as little ghosts, witches and pumpkins poured past. She took a step backward. ''Thank you,'' she said, and her cheeks were suddenly hot in spite of the chill October air. ''Thank you for helping Mark.''

''He's a cute little boy. Here—'' Whittington took her elbow ''—let's get out of the street before we get trampled.'' He guided her onto the curb.

He continued to hold the back of her arm as the crowd at the curb pressed him near, too near. The heat in Marie's cheeks increased. She told herself she was just upset because Mark had nearly been hurt.

''I thought maybe you were in the helicopter. Did you come back from Austin to politick at the parade?'' Marie asked above the noise, not daring to look up into his face. She could feel him studying her profile.

''My deputy is flying the county toy. I came back from Austin to check on something…and to find you.''

''Me?'' Marie looked up at him. The crease between his eyebrows had deepened. She tried to ease her arm away, but his grip was sure.

''Yes, you,'' he said. ''We need to talk. Right away.''

Marie felt cornered. He'd left that message at the

La Quinta and she'd ignored it. She wanted to avoid this man until she could sort out her confusing feelings. For her, that kiss had been no small thing.

"If it's about what happened last night—"

"I only wish it were," he said. "When can we talk?"

Something in his tone alarmed her. She glanced at his face. "I promised to take my children to McDonald's after the parade."

"Fine. After the safety talk, I'll see you at McDonald's." He released her arm, looking self-conscious, as if he only now realized that he was holding it.

Marie opened her mouth to say, *Can't this wait?* but he touched the brim of his hat and disappeared into the crowd before she could speak.

She watched him as he worked his way down the street. People touching him, slapping his back, pumping his hand. He smiled and nodded at everyone who caught his eye and acted as if there was nothing more on his mind than making this little parade a big success.

She could never maintain such a cool facade when something was bothering her. How would she ever face him at McDonald's?

THE MCDONALD'S at Deep Springs had never been so crowded. Every kid in town was crammed inside, clamoring for their supper or at least a hot chocolate, creating a terrific din.

The franchise owner, Charlie Trochmier, hollered "Sheriff!" as Jim squeezed in the door and steered aside a wavering tuba and the skinny twelve-year-old attached to it.

"Come on over here, Sheriff," Charlie yelled. "I'll wait on you myself." He reached across the counter for Jim's hand. "If you ask me, we should have one of these Halloween parades every week!"

"I imagine this bunch would oblige you," Jim said.

"What'll you have?"

"Nothing now. I'm waiting on some people. If you see Marie Manning, would you tell her I'm back there?" He jerked a thumb toward the back booths.

Charlie's bushy eyebrows went up in mild curiosity. "You mean, Carl Manning's widow?"

"Yes."

"Uh…sure thing, Jim," Charlie said and was distracted by two hungry-looking vampires.

Jim took the booth he'd indicated, then immediately spotted Marie in the crowded parking lot.

The wind whipped her hair in all directions as she unloaded the twins from the back of the Cherokee. She bent from the waist and appeared to be having a discussion with Mark. Her soft apricot-colored sweater hugged her rear end and Jim followed the curve of her jeans down to her boots. She was a finely built woman, that was for sure.

He watched her cross the parking lot, holding a pink fairy princess by one hand and a spaceman by the other. Jillian followed in her band uniform, with Alice clucking along like a hen beside her. B.J. brought up the rear, looking disheveled and sweaty in a practice jersey.

Marie and her little entourage.

A smile dimpled one cheek as she turned her head and spoke to her little daughter. Her long, graceful neck flowed down to the vee of her sweater.

A satisfying feeling of warmth expanded and spread through him as he watched her. He hadn't felt this drawn to a woman since... *What the hell is the matter with you?* he thought sharply. Boy, he sure could pick the women to go gaga about. Here he was getting all wound up about a woman who probably wouldn't even speak to him under normal circumstances. He got up from the table slowly and went to intercept the Mannings at the door of the restaurant.

"This is my treat," he said as he came up behind Marie, who was digging in her purse while the kids plied her with requests.

"Oh!" She looked up, startled. "Oh, I couldn't. You bought the burgers and beer for Toots and me last night."

He smiled, glad that she had brought it up. "Was that just last night?"

Marie sighed. "Seems like a hundred years ago, doesn't it? Time drags when you're having misery."

He smiled, even though he wasn't exactly sure how to take her play on words. "You're having misery?"

She laughed. A low, musical sound that thrilled him to the core. *"No,"* she said. "The last few days have actually been a lot of *fun.*"

Her sarcasm surprised him. "Well, yeah, I expect so," he replied. "A dead body, a twisted ankle, my dancing—it doesn't get any funner than that."

She laughed that laugh again, and a wave of pure happiness washed over him. Damn. He was definitely fascinated by this woman. "Tell you what, you buy the boring stuff and I'll buy the sundaes," he said.

"Sundaes!" Mandy exclaimed, twirling in a whir of pink sparkles.

"Oh, all right," Marie said and laughed again.

If only he could keep her this way—happy.

Jim continued to study Marie as she stepped up to the counter and ordered for the twins, but then, out of the corner of his eye, he noticed Alice peering at him over her glasses.

"How are you, Mrs. Croft?" he addressed her politely.

"Fine, Sheriff. We were expecting to see you or your deputy back out at the ranch this afternoon, but I guess the parade overshadowed our troubles."

"I beg your pardon?"

"The prowler."

Jim was confused. "The prowler?"

"The prowler we had early this morning. Your deputy came out and investigated it. He said he would be back, but he never showed. Had to squire you around in that whirlybird, I suppose."

Jim's alarm level rose sharply. He hadn't told Pruitt about the homing device he'd removed from Marie's Jeep, but even so, Pruitt should have informed him of this new development. There had certainly been time for it before the parade. He studied Marie's profile as she bent to tend the twins. To Alice he said, "Mrs. Croft, would you mind if I take this up with Mrs. Manning?"

"Just so long as that's all you take up with her." Alice pursed her lips like a strict chaperon.

Why, you old biddy, Jim thought. But aloud he said,

"What are you having? I kind of favor the double cheeseburger myself."

Jillian and B.J. took their burgers to an area where the teenagers had gathered. The rest of the family returned to Jim's booth in the back. The twins flanked Marie on one side, forcing Alice and the sheriff to share the other seat.

The twins had almost wolfed down their food before the adults finished unwrapping theirs. "Can we go out to the playground now?" Mark pleaded.

"*May* we," Alice corrected.

Mark wrinkled his freckled nose impishly at Alice, "You want to go to the playground, too?" he said.

Jim suppressed a grin, but not before Marie caught it.

"Finish your milk and you can go," she said.

When the twins ran to the playground, the adults ate in an uncomfortable silence. Marie could see Alice sizing Whittington up, chewing her fish sandwich, and she suddenly wished Alice would vanish.

He must be getting tired of my friends giving him the eye, Marie thought. She knew, from the *way* he'd said it, that Whittington needed to talk to her privately, but it didn't seem possible with Alice sitting there, chewing and glaring.

Jim gave Marie a little covert glance. "Want to help me carry those sundaes?" he said.

Marie jumped up. "Sure. We'll be right back, Alice."

When they got to the counter, he said, "Your friends don't like me much."

She decided to be equally frank. "Alice thinks you're a womanizer."

"A womanizer, huh?" He was counting the cash for the sundaes. "I'm running a countywide sheriff's campaign almost single-handedly. I've got an unsolved murder on my hands—" his voice dropped lower, to a growl "—the local movers and shakers are down my neck, the state party's probably ticked off, to boot, and now I've got to figure out what to do about a widow and her retinue before one of them gets hurt. Lady, I wish to God I had time to womanize." He stepped up to the counter, and when he finished paying he looked at Marie with that crease between his eyebrows again.

The part about a widow and her retinue had stunned Marie. "You think we're in danger?" she said quietly.

"Don't you?" He handed her one tray of sundaes.

"I hate to tell you what I think." She avoided his eyes.

He let a heartbeat of silence fall between them, enough to signal to Marie that what he was about to say was crucial. "Mrs. Manning, I think you'd better tell me everything you know." He regarded her calmly, waiting for her response.

Marie frowned, deeply disconcerted. She thought again of the scene outside the courthouse, Whittington talking with Weimer. She thought of Garrett's warning not to discuss the documents with anyone else. She thought of the bone, the money, everything she had withheld from Whittington.

But then she thought of his honesty, how good he had been with the kids. She thought of him cooking those eggs. She thought, against her will, of his kisses. She closed her eyes and swallowed, wanting to trust him. She opened her eyes and said, "You're right. We need to talk. What'll we do about Alice?"

"Let me take care of Mrs. Croft," he said.

They carried the sundaes over to the booth where B.J. and Jillian sat with the other teens.

"I guess you guys could get rid of these for me," he said as he set a sundae before each of them. Then he said to B.J., "Would you do me a big favor?"

"Sure, Sheriff," B.J. said around a mouthful of ice cream and hot fudge.

"Would you and Jillian take this over to Mrs. Croft—" he took a sundae from Marie's tray and set if before B.J. "—and sit there so she won't be all alone while your mom and I go out to the playground and talk."

So direct! Marie thought.

But it worked.

"Sure thing," B.J. said and got up and did exactly as he was asked.

MARK AND MANDY were so involved in wild play that they barely noticed as Jim and Marie sat down at a small table with the sundaes.

"It's a little chilly out here." Marie shivered.

"I guess the kids generate plenty of heat ripping around like that." Jim smiled as he watched the youngsters. He looked back at Marie and frowned.

"Why don't you sit over here on this side and I'll block the wind." He scooted over on his bench to make room.

Marie hesitated. What if someone saw them sitting like that, nestled on the same bench?

"I'm fine." She folded her arms under her breasts.

"No you're not. You're chilled. What's more important, being warm and comfortable or looking proper?"

Marie's mouth popped open and snapped shut. He'd read her mind!

"That's right." He raised one eyebrow. "I can tell what's holding you over there in the wind. You don't want any of the upstanding folks of Deep Springs to see you sitting next to *the womanizer.*" He popped a huge spoonful of the sundae into his mouth.

"Oh?" she challenged. "Don't tell me that you, a politician, never worry about what other people think."

"I'm not a *politician,* and I learned a long time ago that what other people think is not nearly as important as what *I* think."

A gust of wind blasted Marie, plastering her sweater against her chest.

Jim let out a low groan and peeled off his jean jacket. "Here," he said. "At least wrap this around yourself."

Marie took the jacket and gratefully slipped into it. The sheepskin lining radiated his body heat. It smelled of him. She pulled the collar up around her chin and tried to breathe in his scent discreetly. He was watching her.

"Better?" he said, popping in another spoonful of ice cream.

"Yes. Thank you."

"Tackle that sundae," he suggested. "It'll be a while before the kids come in for a landing."

She nodded and started to pick at her dessert.

"Okay," he said, finishing his off. "First, tell me about the prowler."

"Not much to tell," she said and took a timid lick at her spoon.

"Strange that this happened during your trip to Austin. By the way, you told me you were there to get some answers about your husband's death. Find out anything?"

Marie made a business of removing the cherry from her sundae. "Nothing important."

"Look, you've got to stop holding out on me. Whoever was prowling around your place could be connected to the McCombs murder and they could also be connected to this." He reached across the table, pulled open the front of the jacket and dug deep into the inside pocket, the back of his hand brushing Marie's breast. Her cheeks flamed, but he seemed oblivious to the intimacy of his movements as he produced an object the size of a thick fifty-cent piece.

"Sorry," he said matter-of-factly. He held his palm toward her face. "Do you know what this is?"

Marie stared at the thing lying in his palm. "No."

"It's a homing device. A way to track *you*," he said, pointing at her. "I watched some gal plant it under your Jeep outside the La Quinta."

Marie struggled to understand. "My God," she said. "Why?" She looked up into his face and saw the deep crease between his eyebrows again.

"That's what I'm asking you," he said quietly. "Why?"

Marie felt pushed to a wall. The sight of the homing device panicked her, but what if that was the idea, to get her to tell him what she knew? Remembering his secret meeting with Weimer, she said, "How on earth should I know?" But she sounded unconvinced, even to herself. She looked back down at her sundae.

He made no reply, waiting. His hand lay open on the table, the device resting in his palm like an unspoken threat, fanning her fear.

She maintained her silence while her thoughts galloped around in circles as she tried to fit this new development in with all the other pieces. Who would have put that thing on her Jeep? And why?

He let out a long slow hiss, and settled back on the bench, pushing the device down into the pocket of his jeans. "Mrs. Manning, I thought we came out here to help each other. There are some things in the Dulane County coroner's report..." He hesitated, rubbed his forehead. "Let me tell you something about myself. I got my training at the Defense Intelligence Agency at the Presidio in San Francisco. I cracked drug cases for the army. Some real biggies. But I blew some biggies, too, and it was usually because a witness held out on me. When somebody holds out on me, usually because of *fear,* I can't help them." He waited.

Marie could not figure out where that first tear came from. She shook her head, determined not to cry in front of this man again.

"I don't want to scare you, Mrs. Manning," he said. "I want to *help* you. I'm not going to let anything happen to you or your family, but you've got to let me help you. You've got to tell me what you know."

"I don't know what's wrong with me," she said. "It...it seems like lately I'm always..."

"You're just scared," he said quietly.

It was true. She was afraid. Afraid of losing Manning Ranch. Afraid of what she'd found in those files. And afraid for her family's safety. But most of all, she was deeply afraid of knowing the truth about Carl's death. Was it really an accident? What had happened at the Lampassas River Bridge before he plunged to his death?

"I… B-Bailey's missing," she blurted, as if that explained all of her fears at once.

"Bailey?"

"Our dog. I know it sounds dumb," she said. "A missing ranch dog, but he's like a member of the family. No one's seen him since last night—he didn't bark at the prowler. He's a good, hardworking, happy dog. He's so sweet." She bit her lip, tears streaming. "He wouldn't hurt anybody…" Her voice trailed off.

He patted her shoulder. "Bailey will show up," he said, feeling helpless to make it so. Damn! Why did he have to browbeat her? Here she was, just trying to have a nice time at McDonald's with her little family and he throws a homing device in her face and demands answers. *What finesse you have, Whittington.*

"Bailey will show up," he said again.

Tears pooled in her eyes. Never had he seen such beautiful eyes.

He still needed to know what she was withholding, but he could wait until morning. "Mrs. Manning," he said, "I promise your family will be well protected tonight and we'll get to the bottom of everything." He stood and took her hand and raised her to her feet.

"The twins," she said.

"I'll get Mark and Mandy. You don't think I could

get out of here without buying them sundaes, do you?''

Marie excused herself and went inside to wash her face. Jim rounded up the twins, dealing with their delay tactics diplomatically. "Come inside *now*, or you don't get a sundae."

Once they were inside, he said, "What flavor?" and slapped the counter.

"Hot fudge!" the twins chimed in unison, wriggling between Jim and the counter and staring up at the menu, as if they could read it. At what age do children learn to read? he wondered. His own childhood memories were of struggling to make out the words in his primer under the glare of the streetlight outside the Swing Door bar while his daddy drank away their grocery money.

"Two broccoli sundaes." He winked at the teenage clerk.

"No!" the twins shrieked. "Hot fudge!"

"Oh." He smiled. "I guess they want that yucky old hot fudge."

Sometimes, when he hadn't been able to figure out the words, he'd pored over the pictures. Pictures of children sitting at kitchen tables covered with red-checkered tablecloths, while a mother in an apron baked cookies and a little spotted dog sat on the floor.

Always he'd flipped back to the pictures of the mother. Mother at the clothesline, or sitting in a cozy armchair, knitting. Mother walking down the sidewalk with her arm linked in Father's, Dick and Jane skipping happily ahead. Mother, her head bent low under the soft glow of a lamp, reading the sleepy children a bedtime story.

He had imagined that all the other children in the world lived in families like that, where the food was plentiful, the houses were neat and the mothers were attentive. When it got cold out on the steps of the bar, he would turn his collar against the wind and concentrate on the pictures harder than ever.

He especially remembered a book from fourth or fifth grade. The content was a little highbrow—Edna St. Vincent Millay and Tennyson—but it transported him far away from those gritty steps. He swore he would leave Deep Springs and never come back. But here he was in a McDonald's that hadn't even existed when he was a child, buying sundaes for a couple of kids whose mother, no doubt, actually did bake cookies.

Mark was poking something into his face. "See what I got in my Happy Meal?" he said.

Jim took it and the plastic thing broke in half. "Oh, gosh, Mark, did I break it?" He handed the pieces back to the child.

"No. It's okay. It's Lego. Lookit." Mark demonstrated how the Lego pieces snapped back together.

"Well, well," Jim said, snapping and unsnapping the little toys. "What'll they think of next?"

Mark wrinkled his nose and said, "You never seen a *Lego* before?"

"Can't say that I have."

The twins looked at each other in amazement. "Gosh, we got buckets, *gallons*," Mandy said.

"Yeah," Mark chimed in. "Me and my dad was gonna build a whole city out of 'em but...he never got the time."

"I'll help you build a city, Mark," Mandy said kindly.

"Nah. It's okay," Mark said, twirling the Lego listlessly.

"Maybe you can give me Lego lessons," Jim offered, "and then I'll help you build a city."

"Okay!" Mark brightened.

"It's a deal," Jim said. "Now finish those sundaes. I think your mom's had a long day."

When Jim escorted the whole family out to their Jeep, he came around to the driver's side and stopped Marie before she climbed in. "Is Henry out at your place?" he said.

"Yes," Marie answered. "When I left he was doing the evening chores."

"Good. Have Henry stay in the house with you tonight. Someone will be out to patrol the ranch."

Marie smiled and nodded. She climbed into the Cherokee, and he closed her door.

The wind had the bite of early frost. He pulled his collar up to block the chill and watched her back out of the parking space. He'd have to tell her the bad news from the Dulane County coroner's report tomorrow, but for tonight, he would assign someone to guard Manning Ranch. Himself.

CHAPTER SEVENTEEN

WHERE THE HELL was he?

Except for the greenish glow from the dash controls and radio equipment, the inside of the cruiser was dark now. The parade had been over for almost an hour, the sun had retreated behind the hills to the west and downtown workers had retreated to their homes. Through the dirty windshield, the limestone facade of the old courthouse glowed in the slanting sun, looking like an ancient castle on some forgotten moor.

The cruiser stank of stale cigarettes and stale fast food. Seized by a fit of asphyxiation, Bud Weimer shifted his considerable girth and rolled down the passenger's window. How could Pruitt stand to be confined in this plastic-and-metal coffin all day and all night?

The nippy evening air settled his stomach somewhat. The radio squawked back and forth—an exchange between the other deputy and that little dispatcher, Cissy. Garms leaned forward in the driver's seat and fiddled with the volume. Weimer grimaced. To think he'd been forced to trust this loser with the business of Manning's files.

He turned his attention back to the courthouse—now fading to rosy gray—searching for signs of Pruitt. Where the hell was he?

Weimer wanted to get home in the worst way. It was pork-chops night. Lord, he needed the old girl to putter around and pull off his boots and bring him a nice big piece of millionaire pie. If he could just relax, knowing that those files were destroyed.

"Where the hell is he?" he boomed, and Garms jumped.

"Geez! Don't shout, man. He'll be here."

This kind of talk normally would have gotten Garms a whack upside the head. But tonight Bud needed Garms. Without him, they were all headed to the hoosegow.

Bud fished a roll of antacids from his shirt pocket and popped a couple in his mouth—more for control than for indigestion relief.

Although Lord knows he had a roaring case of indigestion, honestly earned. The sheriff was enough to give any man an ulcer. Again he considered sabotaging Whittington's campaign, but it was too late. Whittington was about to win this thing on his own merits. Nothing to do but discredit and destroy him later. Pruitt would come in handy for that.

A door at the side of the courthouse opened and Pruitt emerged from the sunken stairway.

"Told you." Garms grinned, then, catching Bud's venomous look, added soberly, "I'll crawl in back."

Even before Pruitt had folded himself into the driver's seat, Bud started in, "So. The Manning woman made it back to the ranch before anybody realized she was coming."

"Yeah." Garms reached forward and jabbed Pruitt in the biceps. "What if I'd been in the house when the old lady drove up?"

Pruitt shot Garms a look that was as effective as a gag, and Garms sank back in the seat.

"Let's drive around," Bud said. "Sittin' in front of the courthouse with him—" he jerked his head toward the back seat "—gives me the willies."

Pruitt put the cruiser in gear and rolled away from the curb. After a couple of blocks, he said, "The homing device was with Whittington. They tracked him to Dulane County before the fools figured out they had the wrong vehicle."

"Whittington? What was he doing in Dulane County?"

"Digging around about Manning's death, probably."

Bud sighed, winced. "It's a damn shame," he said around the antacid, "that they had to get rid of Manning like that."

"Should've taken care of the source sooner. And I told you not to underestimate Whittington."

Bud felt a tide of color rising under his shirt collar. "It wasn't my idea to kill anybody. Is that the only way you geniuses can think of to handle these unfortunate people—murder 'em?"

In the back seat, the skinny youth was having spasms, stifling an attack of giggles.

"He's high," Pruitt said simply as he steered around a corner.

Bud felt his face getting purple, the way it did sometimes when his blood pressure threatened to erupt like a wildcat well. "He's *smokin'* somethin' and we're depending on him to destroy the evidence?" Tiny chunks of the antacid flew out when he spat the words.

Pruitt smiled, canine teeth flashing in the shadows. "He snorted it. And don't worry. I'll watch him. After tonight this'll all be over."

Bud sighed. Popped another antacid. *Calm yourself,* he admonished. *What good will all your millions do if you croak from a heart attack?*

The radio crackled to life, "Cruiser two, you there?"

Pruitt picked up the mike. "Cruiser two here."

"Sheriff's looking for you. Says catch him at his place."

"Ten-four," Pruitt said and replaced the mike. "That'll work out well," he said to Weimer. "What do you want me to tell him?"

"Tell him to meet me at the Swing Door. Then make it seem like his idea for you to cover Manning Ranch."

Pruitt looked in his rearview mirror at Garms, "Then, as long as our little computer geek doesn't screw up, we're all set."

"CISSY, bring me the report on the prowler at the Manning place," Jim instructed the dispatcher as he walked into his office. "And run me a check on this vehicle." He produced a scrap of paper from his jacket.

With its thick concrete walls and terrazzo tile floor, Jim's office was always cool, and in the hot, dry Hill Country summers, he liked it that way, but tonight it felt colder than a cave. The panes of the one high, narrow window were frosting over. A norther was blowing in. Good. That'd bring in the trick-or-treaters early.

He left the door ajar to admit some heat, poured himself a coffee, wrapped his hands around the mug and sat down at his desk, boots propped up on the trash can.

Cissy came in and laid some papers in front of him.

"Was Pruitt the one who investigated this?" he asked as he perused the brief report.

"I think so." Cissy leaned forward in a coquettish pose, craning her neck.

He swiveled his chair away and proceeded to check the document. When she didn't leave, he cast a glance back at her. "Isn't it your night off?"

"Yeah. But Amy's got PMS." She grinned.

"Do tell." He flipped a page.

"You want me to raise Pruitt?" she said, fidgeting. "You just missed him."

"Yeah." He did not look back at her.

Cissy left and closed the door behind her. He didn't get up to reopen it, cold or not. He needed to think, to piece this puzzle together, without silly distractions.

There wasn't much in the report. A routine description of the premises. Nothing disturbed. Statements from the family and Alice. Mr. Honicker's statement. Time call answered: 7:03 a.m. He turned the paper over to look at the signature. *Alice B. Croft.* Pruitt went out there, talked to kids and old folks and then put the whole thing on a back burner. No wonder Alice and Marie were miffed.

Marie. She was concealing something from him. But what? And now that she'd stuck her nose into this thing, how could he keep her protected without blowing his whole investigation?

He pulled a ring of keys out of his pocket, unlocked the top desk drawer and withdrew a document. He stared at it. This would be a shock, but she would have to be told.

He swiveled in his chair and picked up the phone. "Cissy, got that tag run yet?"

"Sure do, boss. Vehicle registered to a Dale Thornton."

No surprise. "Thanks. Tell Pruitt I'm headed to my place. Send him there."

He laid the document on his desk and ran his fingers over the embossed seal of the Dulane County Coroner's Office. He rubbed his temple with his other hand. Carl Manning using drugs. Never. But tracing the drugs had to be the key. Now, who the hell had the lock?

AT HIS HOUSE, Jim gathered supplies efficiently. In a duffel bag stenciled SHERIFF he put a blanket, binoculars, a heavy-duty flashlight with extra batteries, a camera, gloves and a camouflage rain slicker. He loaded a .22-caliber pistol with hollow-point bullets and slipped it in the top of his right boot. He put a nine-millimeter automatic under his belt at his back and stuffed two extra clips in the pocket of his jacket. When he got into the Bronco, he would move the M-1 carbine automatic from the concealed compartment in the back to the front seat and place the clips for it within easy reach between the driver's door and the seat.

He went to the kitchen, put on a pot of extra-strong coffee, threw together two white-bread-and-bologna sandwiches. Surveillance could get so damn boring.

He foraged around and found potato chips—he hated bologna without chips. He smiled when he discovered that he had one Snickers left. He filled a thermos with coffee and stuffed the provisions into a backpack.

Amos watched his master as he did these things, the soul of canine patience.

"Hungry?" Jim said, and filled the dog's food bowl and water dish. Amos didn't move toward the food and continued to stare resolutely up into Jim's face.

"No. You're not going. This isn't a hunting trip. Now go lie down." Jim pointed to Amos's bed near the stove.

The dog walked in the opposite direction and stood by the back door.

Jim picked up the duffel and the backpack and gave Amos a disgusted scowl. "You always get your way, don't you?"

The doorbell rang and Amos barked two sharp woofs.

Jim marched through the living room, dropping his bags on the couch as he went by.

Pruitt was at the front door, still in full uniform, even off duty. Jim wondered if Pruitt slept, showered and had sex in full uniform.

"You need to see me?" Pruitt said as he stepped inside and folded his arms across his chest.

"I just wondered what you found out at the Manning place this morning. Your report was less than complete."

Pruitt shrugged. "The only one who saw anything was old man Honicker, and he wasn't too clear. The old guy could have imagined the whole thing. They're a little spooked out there, after McCombs and all.''

"I see." Whittington put on his Stetson.

"That all you wanted, Jim? I was on my way home." He hitched his thumbs inside his gun belt. "Oh," he said, "I almost forgot. I ran into Bud Weimer and he needs to see you about something important to do with your campaign. Said to tell you he'd meet you at the Swing Door. That's politics, ain't it, Jim? You don't get a night off even on your night off."

Jim let out a sigh. "Okay. Raise Monty and send him out to the Manning place. You'll have to cover for him until I'm through with Bud, then you can go home."

Pruitt jerked his head toward the bags on the couch. "Were you getting ready to watch the Manning place yourself?"

"Yep." Jim started gathering his gear.

"Boss, if you don't mind my saying so, with the election only a week away—hey." He snapped his fingers as if an idea had just occurred to him. "Let me do the stakeout at the Mannings'. I know that property better than Monty. I've been out there several times. Really. I don't mind working on my night off. There's no reason to do all this shifting around."

Jim hesitated. "I appreciate that. Okay. Let me go see what Bud's stewing about. Come on, Amos." As he walked to the door, he added, "I'll be on my pager, at the Swing Door, if you need me," over his shoulder.

"Sure thing, Boss," Pruitt said. "Sure thing."

CHAPTER EIGHTEEN

TOOTS SLIPPED through the metal swing door, saluted Jack Hess as he cut through the greasy, smoky kitchen and slapped Danny Kane on the back as he settled at the bar.

He spotted Jack's daughter wiping a table near the front. "Jackie, honey!" he called. "Bring me a beer when you get a minute."

Jackie had long ago lost her little-girl charm under layers of flesh and bottles of hair bleach. But because she'd grown up around the bar and its men, few secrets were kept from her. Toots figured she could be a real gold mine if you talked to her just right, noticed her new hairdo, or the terrific amount of weight she'd shed since your last visit.

"Thanks for calling me about Clarence," Toots said when she brought the beer.

"He's over there." She glanced to a dark corner booth where a bald old man in wire-rimmed glasses sat slumped over a beer and a shot. "Gettin' three sheets to the wind." Then she raised one thinly penciled eyebrow and regarded Toots. "There's been a mess o' speculation about Cudd and his gambling debts. Clarence have anything to do with that?"

"You just leave it to me." Toots patted her plump hand.

"Take care of yourself." She squeezed his arm and waddled back to cleaning her tables.

Toots adjusted his cap and picked up his beer. He slapped Danny Kane on the back again and said loudly, "Yep. Looks like your little wife can cook pretty durn good after all," with his eyes on Clarence the whole time.

Everybody at the bar laughed and when Clarence turned his head, Toots took his opening.

"Well, if it ain't Clarence Goodnoe! Mind if I join you for a snort?"

"Toots Daniels! You old sidewinder." Clarence's eyes were swampy as he tried to focus on Toots. "Whell, Whell, one o' my ole army buddies is still around the ol' watering hole."

Toots pushed his hat back on his head as he approached the booth. Clarence was *really* plastered. Gray in the face and with the putrid stench of a drunk who was rotting from the inside out. He couldn't even hold the bottle steady as he sucked his beer.

Clarence lowered the bottle to the table with a shaky thud. "You know, the other day I was thinkin' about Metz."

Toots himself hadn't thought about that night outside of Metz in a long time. They'd walked into a German ambush like a bunch of Boy Scouts on a nature hike. To this day Toots could not understand why the company commander had sent him to pick off the nest of German machine gunners when Clarence and Cudd had been more skilled Texas sharpshooters. But wriggling up that gully on his belly, defilade raining down on him, twenty-year-old Toots had learned something. He'd learned that some things are more important than survival.

"What I was thinkin'—" Clarence raised the bottle to his lips, mumbled around it "—was, truth is, I lost my nerve in the war, Toots, and you got yours."

"That's crap," Toots protested and slid into the booth. "You always did wax melodramatic when you had a few under your belt."

"Naw." Clarence waved his knarled hand. "Here's to you, Toots, a real hero." Clarence raised his shot glass with a flourish. "The Silver Star."

Toots glanced around the bar. It was going to be tough to get anything pertinent out of Clarence in his state. Toots eyed the top of the ex-county commissioner's bald head as he stared dully into his shot glass. Toots had known Clarence Goodnoe many a year and Clarence definitely had something stuck in his craw. Something big and nasty.

Clarence tossed the shot down. "Damn," he said. "I done my beer before I done my shot." He cradled his head in his hands and his mouth went slack. The veins in his neck stood out like snakes and the top of his bald pate pulsed bloodred.

Toots was afraid the man might be having a stroke, but when Clarence moved his hands down, even in the dim light, Toots could make out tears in his eyes. "Nobody cares about an ol' drunk," he said. "Look at Cudd. Deader'n a tree stump. Nobody cares."

Toots glanced around the bar to see if anybody noticed Clarence's behavior. A couple of men squinted at him briefly, but the place was too crowded and noisy for one crying drunk to attract much attention. The strains of Willie Nelson and Merle Haggard singing "Pancho and Lefty" drifted out of the juke-box.

"I care," Toots said.

"It's all my fault…all my fault." Clarence covered his face with his hands again and a sob erupted from between his palms.

Toots looked around once more, grateful for the loud music. He studied Clarence for a moment then he leaned forward and spoke quietly. "Clarence, what do you mean, it's all your fault?"

"I mean, I killed Cudd, me and my big mouth," Clarence said through his hands. "Cudd shoulda never listened to me."

Toots felt his mouth go dry. "Shoulda never listened to you?" he said.

Clarence jerked his head up out of his palms. He blinked at Toots, then removed his glasses and started cleaning them on his shirttail.

Toots signaled Jackie to bring another shot and beer.

"Not too many more of these," she said when she brought the drinks.

"Just put it on my tab. I'll take care of him," Toots said.

When Jackie was gone, he leaned forward to Clarence, who was raising his shot glass, and said, "Shoulda never listened to you about what?"

"I told him about a business deal. It don't concern you, Toots. I done killed one friend with my big mouth." Clarence threw down the shot, then grimaced. "Yep. That's my song they're playin'. 'Breath as haaard as kero-seeen,'" he sang along.

Toots ignored the self-pity. "This business deal, you think it had something to do with Cudd's death?"

"I don't *think* it had somethin' to do with it." Clarence sniffed and rubbed his nose on his sleeve. "I *know* it did." He laughed a raspy *heh, heh*. "But there's folks wouldn't appreciate me talkin' about it. They'd probably just as soon see me dead, too. Only I expect it's easier to let ol' Clarence do *himself* in." He held up his beer glass. "You know, you didn't hafta put this on your tab, buddy. I got a benefactor buyin' my hootch."

Toots decided to take a stab in the dark. "Oh yeah? Who's that? Bud Weimer?"

"His humane way o' committin' murder." Clarence held the chaser toward Toots, then downed it in five straight gulps.

Then he stared as if he were in some kind of trance. He seemed like an exhausted child who had run out of alibis and excuses.

"You see," Clarence said so softly that Toots barely heard him above the music, "they wouldn't have killed Cudd if I hadn't told him about the deal."

"What deal?" Toots prompted.

"Weimer and Thornton's deal."

The reference to Thornton made Toots's chest go tight, but he had to keep Clarence talking. "Ain't those coyotes in on every deal there is? Which particular deal are you talking about?"

"The highway and bridge deal. Federal money," Clarence mumbled.

"Oh, that deal." Toots waved a palm. "Anybody who can stick it to the feds and get some of our tax money back is okay with me." Another wild shot, but looking at Clarence's changed expression, Toots could see he'd struck oil.

"Hey. We didn't get *some* of that federal money. We got *millions*. And all I had to do was say 'good 'nuff.'"

"Good enough on the work Triple C did?"

"Triple C and all the others. Proctor. Bueless. All the big construction firms were in on it." Clarence smirked, suddenly seeming delighted by the enormity of the fraud.

"And all you had to do was say that the work they did for the feds was okay?"

"An' say the materials was all top grade."

"When they weren't top grade?" Toots guessed.

"Hell, when they didn't even *exist!*" Clarence's face was purple and his eyes bulged.

Toots felt sick. This is what Carl's careful documentation had shown. How widespread was the corruption?

Clarence puffed up and leaned across the table, his breath practically burning Toots's eyes. "I made fitty-five thousan' dollars on *one* deal," he breathed. "Cudd got in on money like that and he...Cudd got greedy. He was..." His voice dropped to a hoarse whisper. "He was blackmailing Weimer." Clarence's eyes glassed over and he fell morosely silent.

Toots wanted to ask exactly what a no-account like Cudd could blackmail Weimer about. But not here. Clarence had said too much already. The real questions—who did the actual killing and how was Carl Manning's death connected—would have to wait. Although it didn't take a genius to guess the answers.

When Carl took over as highway commissioner, he must have been a real fly in their ointment.

Bud Weimer and some other fellow Toots didn't recognize came in the swing door and stopped in the kitchen, talking to Jack.

"Come on." Toots plunked Clarence's hat on his head.

"Whaa...why?" Clarence batted his hands around his head, suddenly transformed from the smooth operator defrauding the federal government into the confused old drunk he really was. "Where're we going?" he managed to say.

"My place." Toots stood and pulled Clarence's slack right arm over his shoulder. "Your song's over, buddy."

CHAPTER NINETEEN

ALL WAS QUIET.

The twins, coaxed down off their sugar high by warm milk, were asleep. Jillian was curled up in bed, reading, B.J. was zoned out before the bluish glare of the TV. Alice was decompressing in a well-deserved hot bath and Marie was folding laundry while she tried to stop the merry-go-round of fear and questions that wheeled through her mind.

One minute she wanted to rush back to town to tell Whittington everything she knew. And the next, she'd reverse her thinking one hundred and eighty degrees and commanding herself to sit tight. She'd given the files to Garrett; Henry was in the house with them; their protection would arrive soon; there was nothing to be afraid of.

She wished for Bailey again, and worried about his absence. She'd feel so much better if he were padding around the house, with his sharp hunter's instincts working to protect them. She stopped herself short as she started thinking "if only Carl were still alive" thoughts.

She gathered the folded towels and snapped off the kitchen lights just as headlights fanned across the walls. She peeked out the curtains and saw a deputy sheriff's cruiser rolling up the driveway.

Good. Their protection was here.

She flipped on the porch light. It was that nasty deputy—what was his name? Pruitt?

"Deputy Pruitt, isn't it?" Marie said as she opened the door.

"Yes, ma'am." He stood with his thumbs hooked into his gun belt. "Sheriff said I was to come and watch your place tonight in case your prowler comes back."

My prowler? Marie thought. He made it sound like a prowler custom-made for Manning Ranch. "Yes," she said. "I understood that we were to have protection tonight."

"Yes, ma'am. You'll be perfectly safe as long as I'm out here." He swiveled his head and looked over each shoulder. "Where's your man Honicker? I don't want to mistake him for the prowler."

"He's somewhere in the house." *Snoring in the big chair, no doubt,* Marie thought. "Do you wish to speak with him?"

He threw a palm up. "No, ma'am. Just make sure he stays *in this house,*" he said, pointing at the porch boards.

"How will we let you know if we need something?" Marie asked.

"I'll know." Pruitt turned abruptly and marched back to the cruiser. Marie closed the door and sagged against it.

"I don't care if he is the Law, that boy's weird," Alice said from behind her.

"I wish the sheriff had sent someone else. Where'd Toots put that gun? This might be a good night to have it handy."

"High in the mudroom, in a lockbox. The clips are next to it. Blast that man. He would pick tonight to go to the Swing Door for a soiree."

Marie didn't bother to defend Toots. She went off in search of the gun.

CLARENCE HAD PASSED OUT cold on the way to Toots's place and Toots figured getting him into the house was going to be like hauling in a dead horse.

Struggling mightily, Toots got the sagging, heavy man to a standing position beside the truck. Clarence pitched forward and banged his head on the open door.

"Clarence!" Toots shouted. "Hoot damn, you're no good to either of us."

"That's right!" Clarence's face popped up, wild-eyed. "I ain't no good." It seemed the cranial blow had roused him.

"Clarence! Don't go back out!" Toots yanked Clarence up straight. "We've got to get you inside and hide you."

Clarence fixed one bleary eye on Toots. "*Hide* me? Whaa for?"

"Clarence, I'm gonna pop you in the snout if you don't cooperate with me," Toots yelled.

"You always was a pushy li'l rooster," Clarence said with sudden indignation. "Jush take me home." He threw himself sloppily across the seat of the truck.

Toots jerked Clarence's arm up in a half nelson. "Now, get in the house like a good boy," he said through clenched teeth, "or I'll break your arm."

"Toozsh," Clarence said, his face smashed against the seat. "I'd hate to hafta hurt ya."

Toots gave the arm another vicious jerk.

Inside, he dropped Clarence in a heap on the couch, went to the phone in the kitchen and dialed Marie's number.

"Marie? It's me. I need to tell you something, but not over the phone... No, I can't come there. Can you come here?... What do you mean, the deputy won't let you leave?... No, it can't wait until morning. All right. Tell that deputy I'm coming so he don't blow my head off."

Toots satisfied himself that all the doors and windows were locked. Clarence looked like a puffy seventy-five-year-old baby as Toots tucked a blanket under his chin. He felt uneasy leaving his friend like this, but what else could he do? He had to make sure Marie understood the stakes, right away, tonight. If somebody had killed Cudd for knowing too much, why wouldn't they do the same to Marie? If they controlled the Law, what was to stop them?

He picked up his cap, stomped over to his gun case and took out his revolver, always maintained in top condition. A man could trust a revolver, he thought as he loaded it. Unlike an automatic, even if it failed once, a revolver would always fire the next time. He jammed it in the belt of his pants and left.

PRUITT HIT Toots's truck with the alley lights as soon as he pulled off the road, and kept them trained on him as he rolled back the large entrance gates and drove up to the back door. The beams bored into Toots's back as he pounded on the door and waited.

Marie opened the door and threw her hand up to shield her eyes against the white-hot glare.

"You did tell Barney Fife I was coming, didn't you?" Toots squinted over his shoulder.

"He's no Barney Fife," Marie said, tugging on Toots's jacket to get him inside. "Pruitt's more of a Robocop, only not nearly as sweet and cuddly. Enough about him. What's this all about?" Marie seated herself across from Toots at the kitchen table.

"I went to the Swing Door tonight. Talked to Clarence Goodnoe. You remember Clarence?"

"Vaguely. Used to be a county commissioner?"

"Yeah. Me and Clarence go way back—in the army together. Sometimes connections like that can blind you a little." Toots studied his hands for a moment and shifted in his chair. That's when Marie noticed the revolver sticking out of his belt.

She pointed at the gun. "What's that for?"

"Something real bad's going on here, Marie. Real bad."

"I know that, Toots," she said.

"I don't think you know how bad."

"Tell me."

"Bud Weimer, Dale Thornton and some other big boys have been gouging the federal government for millions of dollars. Clarence Goodnoe was in cahoots with them. When Clarence bragged to Cudd about their moneymaking deal, Cudd wanted a piece of the pie. And it looks like he got killed for his trouble." Toots gave Marie a sharp, appraising look.

Marie sucked in her breath. "That explains all of Carl's documents." Her thoughts fired wildly, clashing with each other. Could Carl have done something illegal, also? And could he have committed suicide because he couldn't face up to it? But even if Toots sat here and told her that right now, she would never believe it. "And Carl...did he...get killed for *his* trouble?" She braced herself against his answer.

"I imagine Carl becoming the highway commissioner was the very thing that messed up their little scam. They probably really scrambled to cover up, but not fast enough. Carl must have been onto them."

"Clarence told you that?"

"Not in so many words. He was pretty drunk, but he told me enough."

A horrifying thought hit Marie. "Do you think somebody besides Garrett knows about those records?"

"Seems likely. Could be they're trying to get them—you know—offa that machine somehow." Toots jerked his head in the direction of Carl's office and the computer.

Marie pulled her hair over her shoulder and twisted it. "Yes, the files. At least now we have Clarence as a witness."

Toots stood up. "That's right, and I hid him at my house. He's out cold, but I can't leave him alone too long. We need to decide what to do next."

"Why don't you bring Clarence over here? At least we have Robocop out there. Then I think one of us needs to go get Jim Whittington, have him bring Clarence into protective custody. I wonder, with Clarence's statement, does the sheriff have enough to arrest Weimer tonight?"

Toots pushed his cap back on his head. "What makes you so sure you should run to Whittington with this? It's Weimer's crews that put up all those Whittington-for-Sheriff signs all over the county."

"Well, what do you suggest?" Marie twisted her hair into a tighter knot. "That we just sit here and wait and see what they do next? Who knows—"

Three sharp knocks at the screen door startled Marie. The two stared at each other for a second before Toots nodded. Marie went to the door.

Pruitt stood there, hat in hand, with the porch light glistening off his wavy black hair. His forehead wrinkled in concern over the angry red line where his hatband had fit too tightly. "Ma'am," he said, "do you all have a dog?"

"Yes. He's been missing since yesterday."

"A black-and-white Border collie?"

"Yes." Marie's heart thumped an irregular beat.

"I'm afraid I found him, ma'am."

"Is he all right?" Marie said, already sensing that Bailey was not all right.

"No, ma'am. I'm sorry. He's dead."

Marie stared at the deputy. She wanted to slap him out of the way, run out into the misty night and scream "Bailey!" at the top of her lungs. Instead she put one hand over her mouth and one hand on her stomach.

Toots came up behind her, put a hand to her back and looked over her shoulder at Pruitt. "Where did you find him, Deputy?"

"Out in the draw. His throat was slit."

"Oh my God!" Marie said, feeling her own throat constrict as tears welled up.

B.J. appeared from the den. "I thought I heard— Mom! What's wrong?"

"Oh, B.J.!" Marie cried and grabbed her son in a tense hug.

"It's Bailey," Toots said, looking into B.J.'s bewildered face. "Pruitt here found him—"

"With his throat slit," Pruitt repeated.

"Deputy," Toots said loudly, "I think you'd better go back outside now." Toots grabbed Pruitt's upper arm and compressed it as he shoved the man toward the door.

Pruitt jerked his arm free and said, "Ma'am, in my professional judgment it is not safe for you to stay here. I have no choice but to evacuate you."

Marie was crying quietly on B.J.'s shoulder.

"Deputy," Toots said, interposing himself in front of Pruitt, "we'll discuss this *outside*."

Pruitt frowned at Toots. "Exactly who the hell are you, old man?" he said.

B.J. released Marie and stepped up beside Toots with fists clenched. "Now just a goll durn minute," he said. "Nobody talks to my uncle Toots that way."

"Oh, you're Manning's uncle," Pruitt said without even looking at B.J.

"I am," Toots said. "And I'm asking you to step outside. Now."

Pruitt looked from Toots to the glowering B.J., then at Marie. "I guess we can go outside and let Mrs. Manning collect herself," he said.

Pruitt opened the door and started down the steps. When B.J. followed, Toots grabbed him and said, "You stay inside and get your mother a glass of water."

"Yes, sir," B.J. said, but he shot Pruitt a final threatening look.

"Now see here, Deputy." Toots began when they got out on the driveway. "I'm not sure it'd be such a great idea to move this family tonight. The little kids are already asleep and Mrs. Manning has had enough upsets."

"I will make the safety and security decisions, and I say they go into town. And you go back to your own house." Pruitt turned to go back inside.

"Hold on there just a minute." Toots hopped up the steps and held the screen door shut with his palm. "Are you still gonna stay out here and guard the place?"

"That would be my duty, sir," Pruitt said. Toots eyed the perfectly creased uniform and decided there was no point in arguing with Bobby Pruitt. Maybe it would be better for them to get out of here, after all.

CHAPTER TWENTY

BERNICE MANNING took four mincing barefoot steps across her living room to the couch where her niece, Marie, sat digging nightwear out of a gym bag. "What is this emergency Toots mentioned on the phone?" she said. Then she yawned delicately. "Oh my. I'm afraid my medication has started to take effect."

Bernice's slack expression had already informed Marie that "Auntie Bernice" had indulged in her usual nighttime concoction. Marie sighed. But even if Carl's aunt didn't have the sense God gave a flea, where else could they go in the middle of the night on such short notice? The old Manning "Sunday house" in town was the only logical place.

"Medication, schmedication," Alice muttered as she stepped up to help Marie and shot Bernice a look that could singe hair. "I don't suppose you've got beds ready?"

Bernice yawned again, looked confused. "Beds?"

Marie intervened before Alice slapped Bernice silly. "The kids brought their sleeping bags and Alice can have the spare room."

"Oh my." Bernice turned to Alice. "If you sleep in the spare room, where will Marie sleep?"

"I'll just slip in later and take the couch," Marie

said, then bit her tongue. Feeling her cheeks go pink,
she turned to pull out Mark's pajamas.

"Where're you going?" Bernice suddenly sounded
alert.

"Marie has to—" Alice was heroically succinct
"—do something."

Marie knew Alice would choke before she'd toss
one shred of fodder onto Bernice's gossip heap, but
wouldn't Bernice just love to know where Marie was
going right now? Wouldn't the whole town?

THERE WAS CERTAINLY no lack of parking when Marie pulled up in front of the bar. She parked the Jeep
and killed the engine. She took a deep breath, then
shuddered and buttoned her corduroy barn jacket up
to her neck as she surveyed the place.

Except for the streetlight, the only illumination on
the edifice was a small sign, blinking BAR in a sickly
shade of blue. She could hear the pulsing strains of
country-and-western music vibrating through the
Jeep's windows. She got out and punched the remote
clicker to lock the vehicle.

Biting gusts of wind pushed the drizzle into swirls
as she hurried to the door, but she hesitated an instant
before going inside. Maybe she shouldn't go in to
hunt the sheriff down—like Dickey Wayne Bauer's
goofy girlfriend? No! She'd been incensed when she
asked Pruitt if he was reporting this latest disaster to
the sheriff and he'd said the sheriff was in an important political meeting at the Swing Door and
"couldn't be disturbed." She was going to *disturb*
the sheriff, by God. She jerked the door open.

The place was even darker than she'd imagined,

the air was foul with smoke and the music was deafening. She felt naked, silhouetted in the glare of the streetlight. She inched inside and closed the door. A couple of cowboys sitting at the bar turned their heads. One said something to the other and they turned back to their beers.

A large woman in a hideous blond wig made a beeline toward Marie. "Marie Manning, is that you?" she shouted above the music. "It's me. Jackie Hess. Remember?"

Marie blinked. There had been a Jackie Hess a couple of years ahead of her in high school. She was a voluptuous, pretty girl. Could this woman be the same Jackie Hess? "Yes, I remember you," Marie said and shook the woman's hand, feeling enormously relieved to find another female on the premises. "I wonder if you could help me," Marie spoke to the side of the blond wig. "I'm looking for Sheriff Whittington. It's...it's...kind of an emergency."

Jackie turned to her with a look of alarm. "Emergency? What kind of emergency, sugar?" she questioned loudly.

"Private," Marie muttered and looked around, wondering if anyone heard.

"You just have a seat right there," Jackie pointed to a bentwood chair at the front. "I'll get him right now."

Marie sat with her spine rigid and her boots planted firmly together and watched as Jackie squeezed through the crowded bar. She craned her neck, looking for Whittington.

She spotted his dark head and one shoulder just as Jackie came up beside a booth in the very back.

Jackie spoke to him and pointed at Marie. He turned, took a cigar out of his mouth and stared at her. Marie's heart did a little skip. The two other men in the booth leaned out and looked at her also.

Bud Weimer!

He was drinking with Weimer! She saw him lean across the table and listen while Weimer said something. Toots was right. Better to sit tight at Bernice's and go back to Garrett with their witness in the morning. She decided to leave, immediately.

Whittington stood and Marie lurched out the door.

He followed her into the parking lot and grabbed her before her nervous fingers could dig the clicker out of her purse.

"Mrs. Manning. What is it? What's wrong?" He gripped her shoulders.

"Oh, Sheriff. I...I suddenly realized how foolish it was of me to come here and bother you, when you have an election to worry about and all." She pushed a frizzy curl out of her mouth and finally managed to locate and press the clicker. "I...you see, the deputy, he...he found my dog. Bailey. Remember? Bailey? Well, he—the deputy—he found him...dead—"

"Dead?"

"Yes. Someone slit his throat...and I..." Marie faltered and looked down at the keys in her hand.

"Someone killed your dog?" He moved in closer, only inches from her, blocking the wind.

Marie nodded, not looking up.

"That's terrible!"

"Yes. He—the deputy—he didn't think we were safe out there and he made us come into town. We're staying at Bern—" She bit her lip.

"I agree with his decision. Did you want me to go out there myself? I was planning on that. Or is there something else you needed to see me about?" His voice was low, gentle.

"I...no, it was a mistake for me to come here." She pressed the clicker again, frowned. "This clicker's not working."

"Let me," he said, covering her shaking hand with his warm one and taking the keys with the other.

He unlocked the door manually. "Thank you," she said.

"It wasn't locked." He frowned at her clicker as he handed it back to her.

But before she climbed into the seat, he blocked the door. "You changed your mind about why you came here, didn't you? Just like you changed your mind about telling me everything at McDonald's."

"Sheriff, I really should go. You must be getting damp and cold. So...so, goodbye now." She moved to get into the Jeep but again he stopped her with his body.

Between them, the gusts of damp air were thick with his scent. His breath rolled out steamily as he let out an impatient sigh and spoke quietly. "In there—" he jerked his head toward the bar "—Weimer said to make sure you went back to *Bernice's.*" Marie glanced sideways, surprised. "That's right. He said *Bernice's.*"

She looked up, startled.

Whittington held her gaze, his expression cool and unreadable. He waited for her to say something. It was as if he were seeing through her, seeing her fear and confusion. She started to tremble.

"Let's warm you up," he said.

He walked around the Jeep and she climbed in and started the engine. He got in, slammed the door and stared out the windshield, concentrating. The blinking blue light reflected off his clean square features and when he turned his head and looked at her, his eyes were alert.

"You're right," she said. "I did have something to tell you in there, but when I saw you with—"

Without warning, he grabbed her arm with one hand and pressed the fingers of the other to her lips. Very slowly he slid the ashtray open and pointed at a barely visible object the size of a button. A thin wire, no longer than an index finger nestled in the crack in the dash. She wondered how he'd seen it in the dark, but, of course, he'd been looking for it.

"With Bud?" he said, and his demeanor suddenly changed as if he were acting.

He looked out the windshield and laughed a short, bitter laugh. "You know, I used to sit right there and make out with Jackie Hess." His voice was casual, but he squeezed her arm and gave her a wild-eyed look, gauging her reaction as he continued. "As far back as I can remember, I waited on my father to stumble out of that bar. He disappeared into the good old Swing Door several nights a week to drink up his puny paychecks."

He was checking the interior of the Jeep with eyes and fingers as he talked, looking for something else. Another tracking device, Marie supposed.

"It was my job to make sure Daddy found his way home. It wouldn't do for my mother to come down to the men's hangout and get him, he would have beaten the daylights out of her. So, as soon as I was old enough to zip my own pants, she sent me. If he hit me, at least I could squirm away and leave him staggering around on a sidewalk somewhere. Night after night, I sat right there on that stoop.'' He jabbed a finger at the windshield. ''Reading my little books.''

He kept searching as he spoke. ''Every man in this town saw me sitting there. They all knew my father and what he was, and to them, I was just pathetic little Jimmy Whittington, Floyd Whittington's neglected pup. But eventually I made it off that stoop, and I thought I was through with Deep Springs.''

He stopped and rubbed his forehead; Marie sensed that the acting and the harsh reality of what he was saying were getting mixed. ''Then, I had to come back and take care of my mother when she got sick. She was always sick, but this time it was terminal.''

Marie's forehead creased in pity, but he wasn't looking at her. He was still searching. ''It took her a long, long time to die. I was lucky to get a job in the sheriff's department, and I wouldn't have gotten that without Bud. I guess he liked something about me. Anyway, when the old sheriff retired, Bud made sure I replaced him. Bud's a good guy.''

He fell silent then, eyeing her, pointing at the bug.

JIM HELD HIS BREATH waiting for Marie's response. Would she understand what he was doing? He thought of how this whole operation would break open if she made a mistake. He thought of the long road to getting Weimer, and the others put away. And he thought of all his work going to waste. Of his having to leave Deep Springs, having to start all over again in a new place. He thought of someone finding them together—conveniently dead.

Rain pattered softly on the roof of the Jeep as he waited for her reply. He could read the fear in her eyes. He studied her face in the mosaic of bluish light and shadowy tracks of raindrops, and he waited.

Finally she spoke. "When I saw you with Mr. Weimer," she said as she goosed the engine and turned up the heater blower full blast, "I didn't want to interrupt anything important. I'm just jumpy, especially after the deputy found Bailey, and all. Brrr! I'm freezing!" She switched on the radio and hit the scan button. "I wonder how bad this norther's going to be?"

"I'm not sure," he mumbled, cooperating with her strategy.

She stopped the scanner on the loudest station. "Would you hold me again?" she crooned. "I've been so scared. Warm me up." She snuggled up to him, positioned her mouth by his ear and whispered, "They're watching us, right?"

He nodded against her cheek, and drew a huge breath of gratitude.

"What about your house?" she whispered.

"Bugged, too, probably," he whispered back.

"And your Bronco?"

He nodded, tilted her jaw so he could whisper directly in her ear. "Even if there's a homing device on it, I can go anywhere in the county without arousing suspicion, as long as it's not Manning Ranch. Of course, we can't put our two vehicles together."

She backed her face up from his, her eyes bright. Then she mouthed, "A horse," and pointed at herself.

He could have quirked his mouth at that, but he

merely nodded his understanding solemnly, then whispered, "Be careful." He squeezed her fiercely, no longer faking the embrace.

"Where?" he whispered.

She put her mouth back by his ear. "You know Stranger Hill?"

He nodded, then pointed at his watch. Below the level of the dash he flashed ten fingers twice. She shook her head no, flashed ten three times. He nodded again, then whispered, "Let's make this convincing."

Marie didn't know about any onlookers, but the kiss he gave her convinced *her*.

"Feeling warmer now?" he said with gusto. His eyes conveyed his real meaning.

"Much better," she managed to say in a normal voice.

"I want you to go straight back to Bernice's."

He got out of the Jeep and said, "Go straight there," very plainly before he slammed the door.

"I will," she said aloud to the rain-streaked windshield, to the microphone under the dash, as she watched him duck into the bar.

CHAPTER TWENTY-ONE

JIM ORDERED a beer on his way to the booth where Weimer and Thornton were waiting. The crowd had thinned to the after-ten bunch. He walked slowly to the back, as if in no particular hurry.

"Mrs. Manning's all upset about this prowler they had out at her place," he said as he slid into the booth.

"But you, uh, calmed her down, didn't you, Jimmy?" Weimer popped an antacid into his mouth.

That told him what he wanted to know. Where were they listening from? Jack's back room?

"Poor little thing," Weimer continued. "I expect she feels insecure since her husband's death, and I reckon it didn't help, finding that old bum…" He was tsking around that antacid in a way that made Jim want to knock his head off.

"There's a rumor in Austin that they're investigating Manning's death as a suicide," Thornton said.

"I wouldn't know about that one." Jim squinted at Thornton.

"Well, I guess Pruitt's watching her place tonight, ain't he?" Weimer said.

"That's right, and Mrs. Croft and the children are moved to safety," Jim said.

"And you made sure Mrs. Manning went over there too?"

"Yes, over to—what'd you say that woman's name was?"

"Bernice. Bernice Manning. The aunt."

Exactly, Jim thought. *And there is only one way you would know that.* "Oh yeah. Bernice. Well, I made sure she was going straight there."

"Then they'll be all right. Well. I reckon it's time for me to go. You okay on this sign vandalism, Jimmy?"

"Sure."

"I'll tell the boys not to clean up a thing tonight. You can make a statement for tomorrow's paper. A photographer's lined up to get pictures at first light. Hell, this won't hurt your campaign a bit. It makes you look better than ever, as long as we can get enough press off it."

"Sounds like you *planned* it," Jim controlled the sarcasm in his voice. He was convinced that Weimer had indeed planned tonight's destruction of all his rural campaign signs.

"The Lord works in mysterious ways, Jimmy." Weimer winked. "And we got to take advantage of his handiwork. You keep your mind on the election. Let Pruitt sweat this Manning business." Weimer rolled out of the booth. "Go home and get some rest. You look beat." Weimer slapped Jim's back and walked off toward the metal swing door.

"Guess I'll be leaving too," Thornton said. "Long drive to Austin." He stood up.

"I'm much obliged to you for smoothing things out with the state party, Dale," Jim said as he got out of the booth. "I just couldn't make that campaign seminar. And thanks for driving this check down. When Bud said he had something important for me at the Swing Door, I never figured it was the five thousand dollars."

Thornton slapped Jim's back also. "You just keep on doing a good job for us, Jim."

"Sure thing, Dale."

They shook hands. Then Thornton pointed as if suddenly remembering something. "Did you ever figure out who killed that old bum? What was his name? McCudd?" he said.

Jim rubbed his fingers across the label on his beer. "State lab's doing a DNA workup, but so far, nothing," he said.

"Well, it was probably one of McCombs's gambling buddies. Saw Clarence Goodnoe in here tonight, rantin' and ravin' as always." Thornton glanced around the bar. "Old boy drives drunk, I expect. Better watch him, Jim."

Jim nodded and took a swig of beer. He'd intentionally not corrected Thornton when he called Cudd McCombs *McCudd,* and he wasn't surprised when Thornton used the correct name on the second reference. What puzzled him was Thornton's interest in the old man. What did reprobates like Cudd McCombs and Clarence Goodnoe mean to these high rollers?

"Well, good night." Thornton put his hat on.

"Good night, Dale. Take care on your drive back to Austin. It's pretty foggy out tonight."

Jim watched Thornton leave and then he sat in the booth for what he thought would pass for a leisurely amount of time, tipping his beer up occasionally. He checked his watch frequently.

Out of the corner of his eye, he saw Russell Garms slip in the back entrance and slide into a booth where Jackie Hess sat rolling silverware into napkins. Garms was trouble. Jim didn't want to be bothered with any of his shenanigans tonight.

Jackie and Russell's conversation quickly flashed into an argument. Jim thought it unusual to see the ever-smiling Jackie arguing with a customer. He walked down to the far end of the bar, pretending to need a better view of the TV and listened in.

"...and I told *you* I don't never say I seen somebody in here that wasn't really in here. I'll say they ain't here if they are, but not the other. Got it? Making up alibis ain't part of my job," Jackie said.

She started to squeeze out of the booth, but Garms grabbed her fleshy forearm. "One little problem here—" Garms jerked his head toward the kitchen, and out of the corner of his eye, Jim saw the single earring flash. He remembered the earring he'd found beside McCombs's body and tried to get a closer look at this one.

"Your daddy owes Mr. Weimer," Garms continued.

"I think you'd best leave, Russell."

Russell's face twitched, shot fire red. "Suit yourself, sister. But don't blame me if somebody gets hurt." He sprang out of the booth and stomped out toward the kitchen. A few customers followed his exit with wary eyes.

Jim walked over to the booth where Jackie sat with

her hands clamped together on top of the pile of napkins. "What'd Garms want?" he said.

"Do you always take so long to get to the point?"

"Come on. I heard most of it."

"Our noble sheriff eavesdrops?"

"Our noble sheriff is up to his hind end in alligators. Now, what'd Garms want?"

Jackie sighed. "He wanted me to claim that he'd been in here tonight until past midnight."

CHAPTER TWENTY-TWO

MARIE PARKED Alice's station wagon behind the tall crepe myrtle bushes. Her Jeep, with its bug and tracking device, sat where it was supposed to be: mute in Bernice's driveway. She ran into the mudroom, grabbed her heavy down jacket and a stocking cap, then hurried down the hill to the barn.

She chose Cinnamon, her strongest mare, because with a sore ankle and the rough nighttime terrain ahead, she trusted Cinnamon to be surefooted. She led the horse out of the barn and spotted Pruitt's alley lights fanning in the misty distance. *A hell of a guard Pruitt is,* she thought as she hushed the mare. She quietly urged her into the dense woods.

Cinnamon did not disappoint her. They splashed along shallow Canyon Creek part of the way, then crossed the highway on a shadowy stretch.

When she got to the turnoff to Stranger Hill, she stayed to the crumbling edges of the winding road up. If anyone came along, she would see the headlights in plenty of time to steer Cinnamon into the low clusters of live oaks.

At the top, he was waiting.

His old dog was with him, and Cinnamon balked and whinnied at the barking Amos. Jim made a low command and pointed, and Amos quieted, then stayed a nonthreatening distance from the horse.

Jim took the reins and held the stirrup steady while Marie dismounted. "Your ankle okay?" he said as he held her waist.

"My ankle's the least of my problems," she said.

"True." He tied the horse to a bush.

He had a blanket and a flashlight. He aimed the beam toward a boulder at the edge of the clearing and led her by the hand.

"Stranger Hill was a good choice," he said as he wrapped the blanket around her. "If they're tracking me, it looks like I drove up to this vantage point to check on your ranch." He pointed toward Manning Ranch below. The house was black, and the outside lights looked cold and eerie in the mist.

"And we can see anyone coming." Marie pointed at the turnoff from the highway below. "You know," she said as she scanned the nightscape, "I can always think better up here." She sighed and sat down on the boulder.

"You come up here often?" He sat down beside her.

"Not as often as I'd like, but often enough to see the seasons change."

"Me too." They looked at each other in surprise, the clouds of their breath mingling.

Marie could not read his eyes in the shadow of his Stetson, but she knew a bond was forming, and she wasn't sure she was ready. She turned her head back toward the view. She pulled the blanket tightly around her shoulders. "This weather is so rare for the Hill Country, the mist, and that moon—" She stopped abruptly and shuddered. "My God. Murder and electronic surveillance. What's going on?"

"I don't know, but they must be damn serious to tap your Jeep at every opportunity."

"When I was inside the bar?"

He nodded. "I figured it out when your clicker didn't work."

"And Bailey? Why Bailey?"

He wrapped his arms around her. "I don't know. But hang in there," he said. "We've almost got them."

"We?" She looked back at the deep-set eyes under the Stetson, and again she couldn't read them, but his mouth seemed sad, soft with sympathy.

"Shortly before your husband's death, he came to me—"

Marie gasped.

He nodded slowly, gave her a second to absorb the shock. "He knew of my investigative background—your husband was very smart, Marie. A good man, a really good man—"

He gently pulled the blanket up to her ears as he continued. "I told him I would help him any way I could, but we were just getting started—"

"You were working with Carl?" Marie finally said, hardly able to believe what she was hearing.

"In a manner of speaking. He came to me two days before he plunged off that bridge. He said he had a source in the local D.A.'s office, and that he had some information that he wanted investigated, but not publicly, not yet. Then he never came back." She shuddered in his arms and he tightened them. "I thought I found out who that source was, but then he left town—they had a lot of turnover in the D.A.'s office all of a sudden. The source was suddenly nowhere to be found. That's when I realized your husband was onto something big.''

''Oh God!'' Marie said, and covered her mouth.

''I'm sorry you have to hear this.''

He doesn't understand, Marie thought, *that I already know it.*

''I've had this feeling ever since he died that someone has been two jumps up on me—''

''You don't understand,'' Marie interrupted. ''The source—what if he didn't leave?''

''You mean he's still around here?''

Marie shook her head. ''No! What if someone killed him?'' She tried again to look into his eyes. ''Mark found a human finger bone buried on Cudd's land.''

She thought his eyes narrowed. ''A human finger bone?''

''Yes. I found it under Mark's bed right after Cudd was murdered.''

''Why didn't you tell me this?''

Marie was silent.

''Never mind,'' he said. ''I know why. What can I say to make you trust me now?''

In the next few seconds, Marie fought a mighty inner battle. What if this was all an act to get her to tell the rest of what she knew so he could cover it up? ''I must know the whole truth about your relationship with Bud Weimer before I can reveal what I know,'' she said.

YOU DON'T KNOW what you're asking me to reveal...to relive, he thought, an icy tightness gathering in the pit of his stomach. But when he looked into her eyes, he saw her sense and intelligence, her sincere desire to do the right thing—and her fear.

She would probably be through with him when she heard why Weimer thought he could use him. Through with him? Hell, she had never even started with him. The truth was that he had this crazy thing for a beautiful widow who probably thought he was dirt, or at least she would think so in a minute.

''What I told you outside the bar is only part of it. Weimer made sure I won my first election as easy as a cakewalk. But you're not really vindicated in politics until you win your second election. Bud keeps telling me he'll make sure of that, too. But old Bud doesn't make heroes for sport. He always cashes in his chips. Bud owns me because he pulled me up from my sorry past. Don't make me go into that. It was some trouble I got into when I was a kid living out on Bishop Ranch.''

He sighed, scanned the night sky. ''Weimer got me out of it. That's when I joined the army. Now Weimer's been throwing money at me with both fists. Every mishap imaginable has taken place in my campaign; mishaps that a good old boy like Weimer could have controlled. I don't know what he's up to. There's a missing piece of information that I can't seem to get at.

''For some reason,'' Whittington continued, ''Weimer wants me to be too busy with the campaign to delve into Cudd's murder—I can't figure out the connection to Cudd—but they're buying time to cover something up. And after the election, Weimer expects to have even more control over me.''

''Why does he think that?''

''Politics is complicated. I just want you to understand that, to crack this case, I'm going to have to destroy my career along with the very man that made me.''

After a moment Marie said quietly, ''Bud Weimer didn't make you, Jim. You made yourself.''

He turned his head slowly and looked at her. Had she really called him Jim? In the shadow of the blanket he saw her sad, wise little smile, and he thought her eyes were shimmering with tears. Had she really called him Jim? He narrowed his eyes, studying her face, trying to understand who this woman really was, and why he was so obsessed with her.

''You must have been just kicking the slats out of your cradle when I went off to the army,'' he said softly. ''I think I remember you playing in the band when I was a senior quarterback and you were a—what—eighth-grader? How old are you? Thirty-two? Thirty-three?''

''Thirty-four. Actually, I think I was a ninth-grader when you were a senior, but I was immature. You don't have to say you remember me, but I remember you from back then.'' She looked down, felt herself blush. ''You were a big football hero. No one would have ever guessed you had such a...a...sad home life. I'm so sorry.'' Her voice resonated softly in the misty air.

He stared straight ahead, fearing that if he looked into her eyes, he'd see pity there.

She looked at his profile and continued in that

soothing voice. "Childhood should be an innocent and happy time. I believe every child deserves all the love and care imaginable, with nothing held back. After all, children are at our mercy, don't you think?"

He nodded, still afraid to look at her. She was amazing. After all the garbage he'd unloaded on her tonight, this woman was able to ignore the things he thought would shock her and to focus on what had hurt him the most: his childhood. With a sudden tightening in his chest, he realized that before tonight, he'd never told another person, not even his ex-wife, Paulette, what his childhood had been like, although he assumed everybody in town knew. But how could people really know what it meant to not have a toothbrush in the house, or even enough food?

"I'm really in awe of you," she went on, and his chest tightened even more. *Awe?*

"When I think of what you were like in high school and then consider what you must have been living through at home. Didn't you make really good grades as well?" She didn't wait for him to answer.

"I think you're brave. It doesn't matter if it was a long time ago. The fact that you were only a child makes you even more so." Her voice became almost a whisper. "How did you ever endure?"

He was still looking out at the dark valley, toward the lights of Deep Springs, remembering. "I just did," he said flatly. It was true. He had survived; he'd never really examined how.

His left hand was splayed across his thigh and she reached out from under the blanket and laid her own gently over it. He felt the warmth and thrill of it all the way to his shoulder. He looked down at her slender fingers, glowing white in the darkness, and slowly turned his hand up. When their palms connected and their fingers entwined, they seemed fused with heat. At last he looked into her eyes, then down to her lips.

"You really are incredibly beautiful," he whispered. She looked down, but didn't pull her hand away. He guided it around to his back as he turned to her. She leaned toward him and before they even closed their eyes fully, their lips joined.

And this time when they kissed, there were no questions in his mind. Only her mouth, her taste. Only fire. This time when her head went back, and she made that small sound, like the mew of a kitten, he let it fill him with a desire so strong that he wanted to crush her, and his muscles quivered with the exertion of restraint.

He felt her whole body respond to his kiss, and he wanted to devour her, all of her. To get control of himself, he broke off the kiss, breathed in her scent and opened his eyes a fraction to savor her beauty.

Her eyelids fluttered open. "What are we doing?" she whispered.

"I asked you first," he murmured against her lips.

"I think...I think we're falling in love," she said.

That tore away any restraint he'd managed so far. He groaned and fastened his mouth on hers again. He pushed the blanket back and wound his hands into her hair. That glorious hair. From the first, he'd longed to touch it, craved the feel of it. Was all of her this wonderful? He had to know.

Her hands found their way under his jacket, and he trembled as he brought his arms down and held her tighter, tighter. He wrapped one huge hand around her slender thigh and pulled it up high on his powerful one, then pinned it there with one arm while he found the fullness of her breast under her layers of clothing.

And then it was as if the limestone boulder became their pedestal while they held that timeless lovers' pose and kissed, tasted, explored, melted into each other's hearts, into each other's souls.

After a while he whispered, "I'm not *falling* in love, Marie, I'm already there."

Marie felt herself open to him in a way that filled her with simultaneous fear and joy.

And then, in a slow dance that seemed to echo the surrender that was happening to them emotionally, he pulled her off the boulder onto the thick grass at its base. He placed her gently on the blanket and knelt above her as he unsnapped her layers of jackets, and threw his Stetson aside. At last she could see his eyes, flashing with passion in the moonlight. He looked her up and down, then kissed her forehead, her cheek, her chin, and slowly lowered himself on top of her, conqueror and protector all in one.

He was mighty and sure in his movements, and Marie was swept away by his boldness. His hands, his mouth seemed to bring each place they touched to a sharp point of feeling so intense that she wondered if anyone, ever, had felt this way. Even through their clothing, it was as if their bodies were already one, and when Marie opened her eyes, the stars shifted and shone, shifted and shone, under the moving clouds.

One of his large hands cupped her bottom and the other arm encircled her back with his fingers coming around to splay tenderly under her breast.

"I want you to hold me like this forever," she said as he pressed his lips to the pulse in her throat.

He raised on one elbow and studied her face. In the moonlight he could see that her breathing was rapid and shallow and a tiny vein pulsed at her temple, and he was thrilled that he'd aroused her as much as she had him. But the shadows under her eyes reminded him of her situation, her fatigue, her fear. Suddenly she seemed delicate, fragile in his arms. He thought of all she'd been through.

Another time. Another time when she was not vulnerable. Another time when she would have the strength to meet him each step of the way, passion for passion.

"Marie," he whispered, stroking her hair back.

"Yes?" she said and her eyelids slid closed as she turned her soft mouth up to his.

"Open your eyes and listen to me," he said, waiting for her to look at him.

She opened her eyes and he studied their depths, realizing that he had never wanted a woman so fiercely in all his life, and he vowed that he would find a way to make that happen. But not now.

He smoothed her hair back again. "You've got to trust me. You've got to tell me."

She sighed, turned her head to the side. "All right," she said quietly. "What I came to the Swing Door to tell you was..." She stopped and closed her eyes. He reached up and tucked the blanket around her head, waited patiently. "What I wanted to tell you was I found out what Bud Weimer is covering up."

He smoothed her hair back under the hooded folds of the blanket, brought his hand down and framed her jaw. "I figured it was something like that." His expression was calm, accepting.

She swallowed. "I found out that for years they have been conducting kickback deals, bid-rigging and the like, and getting filthy rich on federal money. They've been doing shoddy construction, or worse—faking it all together...at least they were until Carl came along."

Jim said nothing. He turned his head and looked down the hill again. She studied his profile and could discern nothing from his controlled expression.

"They must have paid off everybody who would take a buck," she continued. "Cudd apparently blackmailed them for tens of thousands of dollars. Toots thinks that's why he was murdered."

He turned his face to her, frowning. "What makes him think that?" he said.

Marie felt her throat constrict. She prayed one final prayer that this was not a horrible mistake. She tried to think, but it seemed impossible with his heart beating, steady and strong, against her breast and the hot evidence of his desire against her thigh. Could this man's feelings for her be anything but real? She pushed herself away from him and sat up, with her back facing him.

"For one thing, I found a large sum of money that day you caught me poking around in Cudd's barn." She looked over her shoulder to see how he would take this.

He seemed unperturbed at her deception, only continued to watch her as he leaned on his elbow and listened attentively.

"And a man told Toots the rest—"

"Someone told Mr. Daniels that Cudd took black-mail payments?"

"Yes. Someone who knows the whole deal, all the players, all the names." She turned to face him fully, leaning against one palm.

"Who?"

Their eyes locked. Marie held her breath. This was the moment, she thought, when there was no turning back. If she gave him Clarence's name and Whittington was on the wrong side, Clarence was doomed. A wave of fear rocked her again. She shuddered.

"Marie," he said calmly. "Tell me. I have to protect this witness...and you."

Marie looked into his eyes, then nodded. "It was Clarence Goodnoe."

"That kind of figures," he said quietly. "Thornton made a point of mentioning that Goodnoe's a no-account."

"Dale Thornton?"

"Yeah. Tonight at the Swing Door. He's mixed up in this somehow. The woman who bugged your Jeep at the La Quinta made her getaway in Thornton's car. Did Mr. Daniels tell this to anyone besides you?"

"I don't think so."

He sat up on his haunches and rubbed his forehead, then exhaled a frustrated burst of air.

"Do you have any idea how Bud Weimer would know that you and the kids were supposed to be at Bernice's?"

She frowned, sighed, turned her head to the side, looking down at her dark ranch. "I can't figure that. Pruitt was awfully insistent that we get off the place after he found Bailey."

"I see," he said. He, too, studied the darkened ranch below them.

"Jim?"

He looked down at her. "Yes?" He'd almost said "sweetheart," or "baby," but later, later, when she wasn't afraid, when she wasn't vulnerable, he would use those words.

"What are you going to do?" she said, searching his face.

"I'm going to find Goodnoe and take him into protective custody," he said.

"Toots took him to his house."

He raised his eyebrows in surprise. "Okay. That makes it easy," he said. "I'll have to get over there right now. I want you to go back to Bernice's and stay there tonight." He reached out and stroked her cheek with the backs of his fingers, studying her face again. "I wouldn't want anything to happen to you, Marie." His breathing halted in his throat, his chest constricting at such a thought. But she reached inside his jacket and laid a warm hand on his chest and it soothed him. He put his hand over hers, then raised it to his lips and kissed her palm.

There seemed nothing more to say, unless it was the "I love you" that she was still afraid of and that he was saving for a better time. She handed him his Stetson. He put it on. Then he took both her hands and pulled her to her feet.

He walked her to her horse, kissed her and held her one last time, then helped her mount. He grabbed the bit as she started to turn and said, "Marie, do you have any idea why there was a prowler on your ranch this morning?"

He sensed a shift in her mood, a subtle withdrawal, as if a barrier had gone up between them. He thought her color changed, brightened, but he couldn't be sure in the moonlight. He watched the billowing vapor of her breathing as it became irregular. The horse seemed suddenly skittish.

"No. I don't have any idea," she said, but her voice sounded shaky, unsure.

If she had any idea what the prowler had been looking for, she wasn't going to trust him with it. His heart sank. Had he really expected to break through her fear and mistrust in just one night? If only he could communicate the force of his love in the most direct way he knew. Perhaps when this was all over, he could begin again with her. In the right way, with flowers and dates and little jokes. For now, the best he could do was to keep her safe.

"Well, if I can get a clear statement from Goodnoe at least *some* of the people behind this will be locked up. I'd like to follow you when you take the horse back, but that'd put both vehicles together."

"I took Alice's station wagon to the ranch—"

He smiled up at her. "Good. Okay. Come on." He turned in the direction of the Bronco. "I'll follow you to the barn."

"No!" The horse startled and nickered when she shouted.

"No," she repeated more calmly. "You go get Clarence." She reached down and patted the horse's neck. "He's our only witness. I'll be fine. There's no one to see me but your deputy, and he's an idiot. I slipped away on Cinnamon, didn't I?"

He hesitated, then nodded. "I guess the sooner I

get Goodnoe the better. You'll go straight to Bernice's?''

"I will," she said. But she already knew she wouldn't.

CHAPTER TWENTY-THREE

As soon as she turned the horse and rode away from Jim, all of Marie's old doubts closed in like the dark thickets around her. But now those doubts mixed crazily with a strange adrenaline high that made her want to gallop down the hill, shouting for joy.

He loved her. She had known. The memory of his kisses suffused her and she could almost feel the imprint of his chest against her breasts. Even at the thought of him, sudden yearning swept through her. She bit her lip as she reined the horse in. There was no room for denial now. She wanted him. And she loved him. Loved him in a way she had never loved before. Her hands went slack on the reins, waiting to feel disloyal to Carl, waiting for guilt, but she felt none. Part of her would always love Carl. Perhaps she would never have gotten over his death, had she not met Jim.

Why, then, hadn't she trusted him with the files? But Jim wasn't the only one she didn't trust now. She wasn't sure of herself. She'd made enough mistakes already. Besides, Mike Garrett had said—

Marie jerked on the reins so sharply she almost flipped herself out of the saddle.

Oh my God! *HCC stood for Highway Commission*

Council. Garrett was cooperating with them! Carl had documented it.

She kicked Cinnamon, and the misty woods blurred past her as she galloped down the shortcut to the ranch.

She struggled against panic, exhaustion and the throbbing in her ankle as she hurried Cinnamon into the barn. She threw a blanket on the horse and apologized for not rubbing her down, then ran up the hill to the house, keeping an eye open for Pruitt. She did not want to bump into him.

Fortunately the deputy was nowhere in sight. Inside, Marie stumbled through the house by reflected yard light, went straight to the office. She slapped the switch on the computer, peeled off her jackets, inserted a floppy disk and muttered, "Come on, come on" aloud to the screen as she waited for the list of files. The glare burned her eyes, and she rubbed them, fighting tears and fatigue as she scrolled down, marking the coded files for copying.

Her hand froze on the mouse as she marked LGT: bw, the file where HCC was mentioned. Why hadn't she made the connection before? She started to shake as she thought about Garrett betraying Carl. Had he also killed him? Tears threatened, but she used her rage to stem them. Garrett, Weimer and the rest of them would not get away with this! Until the grand jury convened, she, and she alone, would know where these copies were.

She changed the names on the subdirectory to "recipes," finished the copies and pushed the disks down into her boot. These would not leave her person until the bastards had been brought to justice.

She picked up the phone—to tell Toots what she had realized—then, aware that her phone might be tapped, she chose her words carefully:

"Toots. It's me. Listen. I'm...I got a copy of that secret hot chicken chili recipe. You know, the one they call HCC?"

There was a second of silence and then Toots, bless him, caught on. "You talkin' about the chili we ate in *Austin?*"

"Yeah."

"Hoot damn! Guard that—recipe—with your life. You at Bernice's?"

"About to be."

Toots's voice became as bland as if he were talking about the weather. "That's good. Listen, I'm expecting company right now." She assumed Jim must have called Toots's house as soon as he got in the Bronco.

"You're a wonder, Uncle Toots."

"Yeah. One in a million."

They hung up, and Marie relaxed a little, knowing that the copies were safe with her and that Jim was on his way to pick up Goodnoe.

She noticed her ankle throbbing then and decided she'd better put on the inflatable cast. She went to the bedroom. The yard light on this side of the house was moonlight bright.

She sat on the bed and eased off her boot. Her ankle felt swollen. She needed to rest it, just for a second. She pulled the drapes closed to shut out the yard lights, threw her ankle up on a pillow, flopped back on the bed and closed her eyes. Just for a second, before the long drive back to town. Just for a second...

MARIE'S EYES popped open. She wasn't sure what she'd heard. Maybe nothing. Had she been dreaming? Had she actually slept? How long?

There it was again. A noise outside the window by her bed. Like something hitting—scratching?—the screen. As soft as an insect, or a raindrop. Except it wasn't.

There it was again. Sneaky-sounding. She bit off the urge to call out.

Could it be Pruitt checking around in the dark? But wouldn't he be using a flashlight?

She sat up in bed, listening intently, her ears humming in the dark silence, and heard it again.

Noiselessly, she lowered herself off the bed and onto the floor on the side away from the windows.

She froze and listened again: more noises.

With the heavy chintz drapes drawn, the room was pitch-black, but she knew its proportions well. She crept on hands and knees around the foot of the bed. Years of stealing away from the beds of sleeping babies and patients had taught her to move absolutely soundlessly. She stopped below the windowsill, drew two halting breaths and listened hard.

Tap. Ping. A long rasp.

She huddled under the window, struck numb with terror. Someone was definitely breaking in.

Where the hell was Pruitt?

More sounds. Whoever was there was having trouble getting through the storm window. She forced herself to breathe. To think.

She'd parked the station wagon behind the giant crepe myrtles and she hadn't turned on any lights; whoever was out there wouldn't know *she* was in here. Thank God the children are safe with Alice. *Where was Pruitt?*

She forced herself to take another breath. Okay. Her keys were in her pocket. The gun was in her purse. She crawled over to get it, then crawled across the room to the door, intending to make a run for it, but she stopped before she opened it, wondering whether she had turned on a light somewhere. A change in lighting might alert the intruder to her presence.

She heard the storm window being lifted off, and then the squeak of the lock on the inside window being jimmied.

Her dressing room! She darted to the dressing room, latched the door. Then she stood on the needlepoint stool and peered over the transom. Even if he looked up, the beveled stained glass and the darkness would cloak her.

The old window screeched on its way up and the chintz drapes billowed out with a gust of night air. A pool of yard light spilled onto the rug.

With a shaking hand, Marie slipped the gun out of her purse. She unzipped the compartment where she kept the clip as she watched a thin, darkly clad figure ease himself inside. He closed the window, flicked on a blinding-bright flashlight and panned the beam around the room. Just before it hit the stained glass, Marie jerked her head back.

The light moved on, and she edged her head around the transom, tried to make out his face, but couldn't. She saw something near his head—an earring?—flash.

He left the room and she heard him move down

the hall. The door to the girls' room squeaked open, then closed. She thought she heard him in the vicinity of the office, but lost the sound. She dug the clip out of the zipper pocket, then lowered the purse to the floor.

The ring of the phone split the dark, almost knocking her off the stool. It rang again. Then again. With each ring, every muscle in her body twisted into tighter knots. She wanted to scream as she counted them. Four. Five.

Whoever it was, they were not giving up. Alice? Toots? Jim? Only Toots knew she was here. Maybe he would come. But with each additional ring, her hopes sank. He'd assume she'd gone on. Then she had a thought. If she answered the phone, she might have a chance to get help. She wondered where the intruder had gone, weighed whether to risk coming out of hiding to grab the phone.

The door crashed open, bounced off the wall.

"All right, lady," a young male voice called out. "I'm afraid you'll have to come on out now." He said it with dispassionate regret, the way a doctor says, "I'm afraid we have to do surgery."

Marie didn't move, didn't draw or release breath.

The phone rang a final time and fell silent.

"I said come *out!*" He kicked over the small round table by the bed and sent the family pictures crashing.

Marie started to tremble violently. She clutched the gun to her middle, bit her lip, tasted blood. He charged across the room and kicked at the locked door of the dressing room. It splintered and flew open. He shone the high beam directly into her face and Marie's hand flew to her eyes. He grabbed her wrist and jerked her down off the stool. Her bad ankle crumpled under her on impact. He wrenched her arm high and back, twisting her wrist viciously, and the clip in that fist clattered away on the floor behind her.

She tried to look up, to see his face, but he forced her head down, then extinguished the flashlight.

He pinned her wrist to her back, then wrenched the gun from her middle with his free hand. "Pretty high-tech," he mumbled. "Whittington's? Now—" his breath was hot, foul, on the side of her face "—get in here and show me which of these floppy disks contain those files."

Marie stumbled forward in the dark. Her mind clawed in terror. The files he wanted were in her boot, but if she gave them to him, he might kill her. Her only hope was to lead him on until she could get away from him.

Dear God, help me! she prayed.

When they got to Carl's office, the greenish glare from the computer was irradiating everything with eerie light. Over her shoulder she said, "I don't understand. Tell me what you want." She tried again to get a look at him. He had greasy blond hair, bad skin.

"The files you took to Garrett. We figure they're in your computer."

"I don't—ah!—"

He twisted her wrist again, higher against her back.

Marie gritted her teeth, struggled to remain calm. "I took all of my husband's papers to the capitol. I never use the computer—"

"Lying bitch!" She saw the flash of a knife on its way up to her throat. "Oh, don't worry," he said raspily in her ear. "Yours has to look accidental, like your old man. No cuts this time."

"You'd kill the mother of four children?" Marie was amazed at the strength in her voice.

He grabbed her hair and jerked her head back. "Lady, I'd kill my *own* mother for those files. Now where are they?"

Paralyzing terror shot through Marie, but she knew that as long as she withheld the files, she'd stay alive.

"Where?" He yanked her hair again.

"I don't know." It came out in a frightened whine as her terrified mind lurched around for a better stall.

The knife disappeared, but before she could move, the blow of his flashlight hit her square on top of the head. She was aware of a sensation like hitting the water headfirst off the high dive and then she was on her knees, her ears ringing, but she could still hear him.

"I swear, lady, I will *kill* you with the next one."

His voice echoed like thunder through Marie's waves of nausea. She managed to say between gasps, "The disks are in…the storage shed…beside the garage."

Blessedly, he didn't question this and hauled her up by the hair and shoved her forward, knifepoint in her back.

Her head was screaming with pain but the cold night air cleared it as she stumbled over the gravel driveway. The shed. She'd lead him to the shed where somehow she'd escape and run into the woods.

He kept his grip on her hair. She realized as the rocks poked through her sock, how difficult it was going to be to outrun him with only one boot on. She tested the ankle, found it weak.

"Let go of my hair so I can work the lock," she said when they reached the shed.

He released her and flicked on the flashlight, aiming it at the lock. Her hands shook badly, but she succeeded in working the combination. She pushed on the door and over her shoulder said, "Careful. We're always finding copperheads out here."

"Perfect," he said, and shoved her into the darkness ahead of him. "Get the disks," he ordered.

Marie knew the configuration of junk in the shed by heart, and her timing was precise. As he moved in behind her, she toppled an unstable pile of boxes and toys. He came lunging, grabbing at her, but she'd already slipped around another way and was out the door before he got his bearings.

Heedless of her ankle, she bolted across the driveway, the empty field and into the woods, flying like a wild animal, leaping, knocking limbs and brush out of her way like so many cobwebs. Finally, she stopped, gasping, crouched behind a large log.

Her lungs burned. Her head pounded. Her wrist throbbed. Her ankle hurt like the devil. She ignored it all and peered into the mist.

Nothing. No beam of flashlight. No sound. Only the chill, the damp, the silent darkness of the woods.

CHAPTER TWENTY-FOUR

TOOTS PRESSED the phone to his good ear, wriggled into his down vest, and out of the corner of his eye, watched Clarence starting to rouse on the couch.

"Henry!" Toots hollered toward the bathroom where Henry was answering the call of nature. "Get out here. Clarence is waking up!" Then he muttered, "Dammit. Pick up the phone, Marie."

Henry barreled out and strong-armed Clarence back to a supine position. "You ain't going nowhere," he said quietly.

Clarence cast a wary look at Henry, rubbed his face and said, "Where the hell am I?"

Toots banged the phone down. "You're at my place, you old drunk, and you are staying put 'til the sheriff gets here. Henry, this—" he shoved a shotgun into Henry's hands "—is locked, loaded and ready to blast. If Clarence tries to leave, shoot him...in the foot o' course."

"Now just a damn minute!" Clarence bellowed, straining against Henry's paw.

"Please don't give me no trouble," Henry said, pressing Clarence down with one hand, dangling the shotgun in the other.

Toots pulled on his cap. "I'm going to go see what's become of Marie. If she's not at Bernice's and the sheriff's telling me to load up, there's trouble afoot.''

Henry nodded, ''I'll tell the sheriff you're there.''

''No! Don't do that,'' Toots said. ''You just keep your trap shut and stay with Clarence.''

''Even after the sheriff takes him into custody?'' Henry seemed unsure.

''The sheriff can only keep him as a material witness—so stay with Clarence and see that nothin' happens to him, and don't take no guff from Whittington.''

''Gotcha,'' Henry said, fixing a glare on Clarence like a bead-eyed watchdog.

THE FOGGY, WINDING ROAD down from Stranger Hill seemed ten times longer than it had on the trip up.

When Jim pulled onto the highway, he had a sudden urge to turn off in the direction of Marie's, but he suppressed it and drove toward Toots Daniels's place instead.

He had used his binoculars to watch her as long as he could. He'd caught a last glimpse of her on the horse, crossing under a barnyard light, and then she'd disappeared into the barn.

Right now he had to get to Goodnoe before Weimer's bunch did. The highway seemed endless, ominous. He increased his speed and flipped on the rotating beacons. Objects leaped out of the ghostly mist as he vaulted along.

He snatched up the radio mike, maneuvering the hairpin curves with one strong arm, ''Cissy, cruiser one here,''

''I read you, cruiser one. Over.''

''Get on the horn to cruiser two at Manning Ranch for a status report.''

''Copy… Cruiser two left to check out an abandoned vehicle. Reported everything secure at Manning Ranch.''

''Copy. Out.'' Jim hung up the mike and muttered ''Beautiful,'' then slowed his speed, concentrating on finding the narrow driveway to the Daniels house.

A red pickup careened in front of him from out of the mist. Tires squealed and skidded, both horns blared, and the two vehicles barely missed each other. Whittington saw the taillights of the pickup in his rearview mirror as it righted onto the road, then peeled off in the direction of Stranger Hill and the turnoff to Marie's.

Jim gunned the engine. If that was old man Daniels—and he was certain it was—then Goodnoe was alone, or worse, in the hands of that ranch hand of Marie's. Where was Daniels going in such a hurry? Marie's? A wave of alarm coursed through him. It was about a five-minute drive to Manning Ranch. He could be over there and back in less than fifteen. But Goodnoe might be their only witness. As long as he was right here at Daniels's driveway—he rubbed his eyes. Exhaustion from the harried trip to Austin and the campaign in general weighed on him. He wondered if fatigue was impairing his judgment.

He picked up the cell phone and dialed Marie's number. After ten rings he hung up, satisfied. As long as Marie and the kids were safe in town, what could be happening at Manning Ranch that was more important than this witness? He pulled the Bronco onto the road and turned into Toots's driveway.

THE RUSHING AND POUNDING in Marie's head threatened to drown out all other sensation. Pain zinged across her forehead like lightning.

She was squatting, and her legs cramped, but she feared if she relaxed, she wouldn't be able to spring away fast enough if the need came. *When* the need came. She forced down her anxiety and concentrated.

This guy, she guessed, had killed Cudd and Bailey. And maybe Carl. Would he kill her too? Again, she pushed down the fear. *Don't think about it,* she commanded herself, shaking her head. Pain lanced through her skull. *And don't shake your head.*

Had the intruder accessed the computer and not found what he wanted? If Garrett was HCC, then Weimer and crew knew exactly what was in those files, but Carl had buried them in subdirectories under obscure names, and she'd disguised them even further.

Her eyes grew accustomed to the darkness, and the moonlit outlines of a thicket of spiky sycamore and cottonwood trees told her that she was close to the draw, not far from the McCombs property line.

She thought about making her way into the draw. It was about six feet deep in most places, dry most of the time—how much water would it have in it from the recent downpour? And it would surely hide her better than this log.

But how long could she stay out in the cold like this? Her sock was soaked, and her sweater was thin. The shivering made her head throb violently; each wave of chills seemed to explode through the top of her skull. She ran her fingers lightly over her head. It felt sticky. She felt her pulse. Rapid, of course, but weak also. She felt her face. Clammy. She might be headed for shock. *Don't panic,* she warned herself. *Don't panic.*

She thought of her children. What if she never saw them again? She fought back tears and prayed for their protection.

Then she thought of Jim.

She hadn't had any time with him and now that she'd found him, she wanted that time so badly. But she thanked God anyway, for that one moment of beauty on Stranger Hill. Then she prayed for Jim's protection. And for her own.

TOOTS PULLED OFF the highway, doused his headlights and sat in the idling truck, studying the Manning house at the crest of the hill. Something was wrong. There were no lights on, and he couldn't see Marie's Jeep. Could be she'd left already. He spotted the shed! Its door stood wide-open and debris spread out in front of it.

He killed the engine, tucked the revolver in his belt and pulled the shotgun off its rack behind the seat. He checked the bolt, dropped it and crammed some extra rounds into his jacket. He slid the halogen flashlight from under the seat.

His plan was to approach the place from the draw, unseen, and figure out what the hell was going on before anybody spotted him.

He climbed out of his truck, and as the chill of the night air settled on him, he felt every one of his seventy-plus years. It had been a long time since he'd been in a situation like this. At least when he was sneaking up on Nazis, he'd known what he was facing. This time he was groping in the dark, and this time he was an old man. *But you're still one tough son of a bitch,* he thought and set his mouth in a hard line, pulled down his cap and stayed low in the mist as he crept down into the draw.

MARIE FEARED that the longer she delayed, the worse her condition would become. Blood seeped out of her hair and dripped down her face onto her shoulder. Superficial head wounds bled freely, she knew, but even so, this was an alarming amount of blood. She decided to make her move while she had the strength.

The leaves seemed to make a hideous racket as she inched unsteadily through the brush toward the draw.

A ribbon of moonlight lit the ravine. Was this good or bad? She could see better, but might not be able to hide as well. She lowered herself as quietly as possible, holding on to saplings. At the bottom, her feet sank into the soggy bottom. Mist swirled around her knees as she picked her way along, testing each step in the inky loam before applying her weight, concentrating on moving silently and staying out of the narrow trough of moonlight.

She had progressed fifty yards or so when she heard a sound—farther down the draw. Like a twig snapping. She froze, instantly regretting the noise she'd made.

WHITTINGTON LEFT the Bronco running in Toots's driveway, with the high beams and alley lights trained on the house. No other vehicles were in sight, but all the lights were blazing in the house. He took the nine-millimeter automatic from his back and circled to the rear.

He edged up to a picture window, which was uncovered except for a half-drawn venetian blind. An overhead fluorescent bulb illuminated the interior like a stage.

Honicker was standing over the couch with a death grip on the stock and trigger of an antiquated shotgun, his eyes zigging around wildly in their sockets. The riot lights on the Bronco had spooked him, no doubt. *Beautiful,* Whittington thought.

On the couch, a rumpled-looking old man slept with glasses askew. Jim assumed this was old man Goodnoe.

He stole noiselessly around to the other end of the house, and, satisfied that everything was secure, tapped softly on the back door, so as not to set off Honicker, with his finger on the trigger of that shotgun. "Henry, it's me. Whittington," he said in a low voice.

Henry's head popped over the edge of the small window in the back door like a scared rabbit's. Relief washed over his face as he opened the door wide enough for Jim to squeeze in.

"Is he asleep or unconscious?" Jim said, pointing at Clarence.

"Sleepin' off a drunk," Henry answered. "Didn't give me no trouble. What's Clarence done, Sheriff?"

"Nothing for you to worry about, Henry. I'm just taking him into protective custody. Can you help me get him into my Bronco?"

"Yessir, I'm supposed to go with you." Henry

walked over and picked up Clarence's boots and jacket.

Whittington stuck his gun back in his belt. *Fine, if it makes them all feel better, Henry could go along as security.* "Was that Daniels I saw tearing out of here a minute ago?" he asked as they wrestled Clarence's boots on.

"Yessir."

"Where's he headed?"

Henry looked perplexed and scratched his bald pate, then fingered the bib of his overalls. "Cain't say," he said, looking sideways.

"Can't or won't?" Whittington said, pushing his Stetson back on his head.

Something akin to stubbornness transformed Henry's features. "Won't," he said and his chin went up.

Whittington struggled not to lose patience. "Henry, if there's a problem, shouldn't I know about it?"

Henry's face crinkled in consternation. "I reckon. But Toots said not to tell you. Besides, your deputy's already over there."

"Marie's? Toots went to Marie's? Why? Is there some trouble?"

Henry looked pained.

"Answer me!"

Under Whittington's intimidating stare, the dam of Henry's resistance broke. "Marie called Toots and she was there...doin' something. But when Toots tried to call her back—he figured somethin' was a...afoot and all—and he couldn't raise her at Bernice's neither, he went over to make sure she was okay.'' Henry's face was tortured, agitated. ''I wasn't supposed to tell you.''

''Beautiful,'' Whittington muttered under his breath. So she'd gone to the house instead of straight to Bernice's. Why in the hell would she do that?

''Henry, you lock up behind me,'' Whittington said as he headed for the door. ''I'll send a deputy over to get Clarence. Keep that shotgun handy, and don't let anybody else in.''

''Cain't me and Clarence go on with you, Sheriff?'' Henry took two steps toward him. ''I'm about to go crazy out here, with Toots tellin' me to shoot Clarence and you talkin' about protective custody and all.''

Whittington looked at the two old guys, thinking how they would slow him down, but Henry's anguished expression undid him. It might be best to keep Goodnoe with him, anyway.

''All right. Let's get Sleeping Beauty out to the Bronco.''

''Yessir.'' Henry yanked Clarence to his feet and hauled him out to the Bronco like a sack of potatoes. And Whittington fervently hoped he wouldn't regret having these two old fossils in tow.

MARIE REMAINED absolutely motionless, listening. She held her breath until she thought her lungs would burst. Far off, she heard the solitary woofing of a large dog.

She started to shiver.

Then she heard the sound of brush moving again. Closer than before. He wasn't using the flashlight, perhaps realizing that she could elude him forever if she always saw light coming. Then a soft crunch. Very near. Up on the bank, not down in the draw. He seemed to be moving haltingly, listening after each step perhaps. Waiting for her to move and reveal her location.

Soundlessly, she eased herself up against the steep bank and inched along, hoping for an indentation, finding none.

She heard more rustling sounds, directly above her. If he came sliding down the bank, he'd land right on top of her! She hugged the bank, fingers clutching cold mud.

A flare of white-hot light engulfed her.

She leaped out of the circle of light and clawed along the bank, but he snared her in the glare again. She heard him crashing through the underbrush as he kept her in the scope of the flashlight even as she frantically clawed her way up the opposite bank.

She tore blindly off into the woods, but almost immediately, she ran into a meander in the creek and went rolling down another steep bank. She landed at the bottom in a heap. She heard him coming down the bank right behind her, the torch of light getting dangerously close, but she couldn't seem to move, couldn't even scream. A new pain burned in her side, and before she could catch her breath, he was on top of her.

He pulled her up with an excruciating jerk and crushed her back against him, animalistic in his power. He stank of sweaty denim, his arm clamped around her so tight she could hardly breathe. And she felt the knife, cold and thin at her throat, tipping her jaw up. She dared not even swallow against it. One slice and she would be left out here to die. Like Cudd. Like Bailey.

He was panting, grunting horribly. "All right," he gasped. "Enough…games in the woods, Mrs. Manning. We're going to…get those disks now. Let's make a deal…you pull anything else, and I'll find your kiddies…and fix *them* like I did the dog."

Marie's heart contracted, came up in her throat. Every beat was for her children now. Keep them safe. Keep them safe. Keep them safe.

TOOTS HAD SEEN the faint pinpoint of light just in time to come up short. He heard someone thrashing, farther down the draw. Then he heard a male voice, but couldn't make out the words. The deputy? He waited. Patience had never been a problem for Toots. He lowered himself behind a pile of muddy brush and driftwood. He cocked the shotgun, and waited with his finger on the trigger.

The light swung unsteadily around a curve in the draw. He thought he heard more than one person clumping through the brush, then he heard a woman cry out. Marie? Damn his old ears, he couldn't make out any of it clearly.

Suddenly the cone of light whirled around, flashing right past Toots's hiding place. When the light passed, he eased his head up to see the unmistakable silhouette of a woman, struggling with a male figure. It *was* Marie! The flashlight beam blazed around wildly, up on the bank, into the inky sky, over the twisted black tree limbs and back down. Toots did nothing to betray his position.

The struggling stopped abruptly, and all Toots

heard then was Marie's fast-paced, frantic breathing in concert with her assailant's deeper, hoarser gasping.

Then Toots heard Marie's sharp cry.

They were close enough now that Toots could finally make out the man's words. "That's to remind you that I *like* cutting people."

He has a knife on her, Toots thought.

The light moved on as they stumbled through the brush.

Toots followed, staying low, matching his sounds and movements to theirs, keeping his finger on the trigger, waiting for his chance. The beam of the flashlight veered off to the left, deep into the trees. He heard the male voice mumble. He heard Marie's reply clearly, "No...I'll find them, I swear. Just take me to the shed. Down this path."

Toots kept sight of the flashlight. When they got to the shed, he'd figure out something.

JIM TORE DOWN the short stretch of highway to Marie's with Clarence propped between himself and Henry on the bench seat and Amos panting over his shoulder from the back. Clarence roused a few times, making impotent gestures, and Whittington rolled the man's lolling head away with irritation. Henry clutched the dash with one hand and the shotgun with the other and said nothing.

Fifty yards before the turnoff to Marie's driveway, Jim spotted Toots's truck in the headlights. He slowed just enough to make sure the truck was empty and roared off, anxious to find Marie and make sure everything was all right.

But when he turned into the driveway, he knew everything was definitely not all right. The house was in darkness, and the door to the shed was open with rubble scattered everywhere. Amos barked once and Jim silenced him.

He trained the high beams on the house.

Just as he flipped the switch of the Bronco's alley lights, he saw a figure—*two figures?*—jerk back into the shadows beside the shed. He drew his firearm, jumped out and crouched behind the Bronco door. "You out there!" he shouted. "Come out into the light with your hands on your heads!"

"Jim!" It was a female scream.

"Marie!" he called back.

Marie didn't answer. Russell Garms did.

"Got your little lady friend, here, Sheriff. Got my knife at her throat. You know how I can be with my knife... You 'member that, don't you, Sheriff?"

Jim remembered. A bad knife fight at Wildhorse a few years ago. And now Garms sounded shrill, unstable. Now his knife was on Marie.

"Let her go, Russell."

"Can't do that, Sheriff. The lady's got something we need. Something Bud needs. We're on the same team. You know that."

So Garms was one of Weimer's boys. Figures. Where was Pruitt? Where was old man Daniels? Jim hoped if he stalled long enough, one of them might show up behind Garms. Whatever Marie had, Weimer had already demonstrated his willingness to kill for it. Weimer must have been pouring on the pressure these last few days, aware that this whole mess was unraveling. "What's she got that you and I need?" he said.

"Some stupid little diskettes," Garms hollered back. "Bud wants 'em real bad. And you need Bud real bad. I mean, you ain't gettin' elected without Bud, ain't that right?"

"She'll give them to me, Russell. Let her go."

"She won't give *you* a damn thing. She ran to Garrett and didn't tell you. You're taking the side of some little broad who likes to play games and you're making Weimer real mad. You better decide whose side you're on, Whittington—Bud's or this little *broad's.*"

Jim heard Marie give a muffled squeal, and a stab of fear lanced through him. Garms had flipped.

"Russell, Weimer's finished. I have a witness here who will put him away. He's finished, even without the diskettes. You don't owe him anything. Don't do something that'll cost you the rest of your life."

"You're lying!" Russell screamed.

"No, I'm not. Whatever you came out here to get, it can't save Bud now—"

"The hell it can't. You're being real stupid, Whittington. When Weimer finds out you messed with me, *you'll* be finished."

"Maybe so," Whittington replied calmly, "but I can't let you hurt her. Let her go—*now.*"

"Who—" Russell's voice cracked, "Who do you think rigged the election-board computers for you? You owe me!" Russell's shrill voice bounced off the woods and outbuildings.

Jim felt something inside himself shrivel and seal off. Weimer had rodents like Garms rigging his election and Jim hadn't even known it? And now Garms's knife was on Marie. Marie, the only true and beautiful thing in his whole life. When he spoke, his voice was cold, controlled.

"You're right, Russell. I owe you. That's why I won't let you hurt this lady. Let her go."

There was a long silence, then Russell's high-pitched voice echoed again. "You've been in the dark, Whittington. Weimer kept you in the dark."

Abruptly, Garms shoved Marie around the corner of the shed into the blinding light. He forced her toward the shed door, with his back to the shed wall, a fierce grip pinning her against him.

Jim made a quick assessment of Marie: hair matted with blood, legs caked in mud, one boot missing. She looked pale and frightened, and a small cut on her jaw oozed blood. The knife blade sent a sickening beam from her throat.

"Garms!" A voice rang out from beside the house and Toots stepped into the light. He had a shotgun trained on Garms with his right hand and he held out something small and square with his left. "These are your files," he said in a clear voice.

Garms blinked at the apparition of Toots for a split second, then stared at the object in his hand. He made a jerk against Marie's jaw with the knife and a fresh bead of blood appeared. Marie squelched a terrified cry.

"These are the files," Toots said calmly. "Everything is here. Everything Weimer wants. My nephew gave it all to me before he died."

Garms jerked his head, spraying an arch of glittering sweat droplets. "Put it on the ground," he said.

Toots did so.

"The shotgun, too."

Toots carefully placed the shotgun a little distance from the disk.

"Now go stand in front of the headlights." Garms jerked his head, indicating the Bronco.

Toots walked with a measured gait and stood in front of the truck, keeping his palms facing out.

"Now you, *Sheriff,* come out into the light beside the old man—without your gun."

There was a long silence from the blackness behind the white-hot lights. Then Jim came around the truck and stood directly in the path of the alley lights with his legs spread wide and his hands raised, palms out.

The sight of Jim's powerful silhouette gave Marie sudden strength. She tried to read his face against the glare of the lights, tried to send him wild signals with her eyes, wasn't sure he read her. *Dear God,* she prayed. *Help me now.*

"Okay, lady, pick up that disk." Garms inched Marie forward to where the disk lay on the gravel.

When they reached it, he bent her forward, one hand tightly entwined in her hair, the other forcing the blade against her throat. "Pick it up," he said.

Marie reached forward shakily. Swiftly, she clutched all the gravel, chat and sand her fist could grab and flung it into Garms's eyes.

Garms cursed and his knife hand flew up. Marie lunged, but was snapped back by the hair. Almost the same instant, Jim dived forward into Garms's side, taking him down, Marie with him.

Marie felt her body thud on the driveway, felt gravel grind into her face and felt something jolt into her injured side. Jim was pressed against her, mashing her to the ground with his back, fighting off Garms from the front. She labored for breath as she frantically struggled to get out from under Jim. Then she was thrown, somehow, off the driveway into the mat of leaves beneath the hedge.

She rose onto her knees, gasping, and saw Garms doubled up, but floundering to his feet. He still had the knife.

Now, like bulls pawing the dust in an eerie, obliquely lit arena, Jim and Garms slowly circled on the driveway.

Toots was standing in the shadows with his revolver trained on Garms. The shotgun lay where he had placed it seconds before, a couple of yards to the right of Jim's foot. The knife blade gleamed in Garms's right hand, sure and steady, aimed at Jim's middle. They circled. Jim a little closer to the shotgun. Garms a little closer to his prey.

From the shadows, Toots said, "Drop the knife, boy," and cocked the revolver's trigger.

Marie saw Garms's eyes flash wildly at Toots just before he dived into Jim, jabbing the knife into his left biceps.

Jim crashed his right fist into Garms's jaw, knocking him back, then plowed into him with his shoulder.

But Garms did not fall. He seemed possessed.

He wheeled the knife around and drove it into the left side of Whittington's lower back. Somehow Whittington straightened, hurling him off balance and grabbing Garms's knife arm with both hands, twisting it. Smeared with blood, the knife flashed silver, high above the struggling duo. Garms aimed the blade steadily down and clawed at Jim's eyes as they grunted and shuffled in a deadly dance.

Toots circled and pointed the gun as Garms kept the knife trained on Jim's neck and Jim resisted the downward force with waning strength, blood pouring from his slashed side.

Then Jim managed to bring his boot down on Garms's instep, stopping the dance. Toots snatched his chance, charged forward and planted the gun at the base of Russell's skull. "Drop it!" he screamed.

Garms roared, and flung his left arm back, releasing Whittington and knocking Toots to the ground. The knife remained so firmly in his hand that it seemed part of his anatomy. Toots rolled away, scrambling to locate the dropped gun. Garms lunged at the old man just as Whittington grabbed the shotgun.

The boom of the shotgun echoed in the dark woods and hills. Garms jerked, then sank forward.

Then the echoes fell to the mist and there was only silence.

Whittington lay on the ground with his shotgun poised in the air, unfired, his face glistening sickly white, uncomprehending.

At the edge of the shadows, Russell Garms lay bleeding on top of Toots Daniels, and behind them, deeper in the shadows, Henry Honicker stood with a smoking shotgun leveled at his shoulder, and a look of pure horror on his face.

CHAPTER TWENTY-FIVE

"I DON'T KNOW," Alice clucked, and pulled her big sweater tight. "This morning air is a little chilly for a horseback ride. That wind is sure up."

"Now, Pie, that's a *breeze*. A little spring breeze isn't gonna hurt her."

Marie didn't mind that Alice had smothered her in a ton of clothes—thick cable sweater, down vest, leather gloves and this suffocating skull cap—but she hated it when they talked about her in the second person, as if she were still debilitated, which she absolutely was *not*, as she was about to prove if they would just get out of her way. She jerked the leather gloves on and hollered toward the barn—to remind them that she was standing behind them. "Got her saddled up, Henry?"

Henry emerged from the barn leading Harmony, Jillian's tame little mare.

Marie frowned. "I thought you were saddling up Cinnamon."

Henry's features set stubbornly. "I reckon Harmony is horse enough for your first ride." He turned to check the flank cinch.

She didn't argue. Henry had earned the right to be overprotective. She shook her head in amazement as she studied his bulky back. That their own quiet

Henry could have performed so heroically. What would have happened if—she pushed these thoughts from her mind.

She started out in a steady canter, going east.

The sun was radiant, the sky unblemished. The junipers already looked greener, and within a week the sand plums along the creeks would bloom. Wildflowers were popping up everywhere.

More than any other sign, the first bluebonnets nodding their lupine heads told Marie that her long-awaited spring had finally come.

In the hushed and ominous cave of the Intensive Care Unit, she'd lain and wondered if she would live to see another spring. Even if she hadn't been a nurse, she would have known she was in grave danger by the determined faces of the doctors and nurses. But here she was, riding a horse, surveying her property as it came back to life.

She came to a fence and reined the horse in, wondering if Harmony could take it as easily as Cinnamon. She rode up and down the sagging barbed-wire line, letting the horse assess it.

It had been a seemingly endless four-and-a-half months. The surgeries. The grand jury. The agonizing investigation of Carl's death—murder, not suicide. And finally, grief counseling. Because she couldn't stop imagining Carl's final moments: Thornton meeting him at the end of the bridge construction, handing him a cup of drugged coffee, rolling his idling car into the shadowed river. She kept seeing Carl's face, sleeping peacefully in the driver's seat while the murky water covered his rugged handsome features.

Hadn't she promised herself she wouldn't think along those lines this morning?

She reached down and patted the horse's neck. "Well, girl, are we gonna do this fence, or are we gonna go all the way around like a couple of old ladies?"

She delivered a brisk kick to Harmony's sides and off they flew. Marie felt no hesitation in the animal as they approached the low fence and sailed over as one unit.

She kept going at a hard gallop until they neared the road on the far side of the field.

A black Ford Bronco was parked on the shoulder. Her heart jumped into her throat and she pulled Harmony up short, hardly able to believe her eyes. At last he'd come.

Jim Whittington leaned against the fender, his long legs crossed casually at the ankles, regarding her from under the brim of his Stetson.

He took off the hat and waved it high over his head, and as she watched him slowly waving, all her feelings came flooding back. The thrilling, obsessive, passionate feelings, and the pain and sorrow...the memories. The therapist had said, "Don't be afraid of your feelings."

He strode across the pasture toward her now, looking magnificent in the morning sun. He was so tall, he moved so easily. Marie had forgotten. As she watched him coming toward her, her heart would not be still.

"Hi!" he called out cheerily as he got nearer. "I was coming to your house when I spotted you from the road." He smiled and came alongside the horse.

He took the reins and patted the horse's neck. Then he brought his hand down over the crest of her mane and patted her withers. "This is not the same mare you rode to Stranger Hill that night, is it?"

Marie closed her eyes, then opened them quickly.

She turned her head in the direction of the sun and squinted. "No, it's not. This is Harmony, Jillian's mare. Henry thinks Cinnamon's...she's too spirited for me...right now." *Stranger Hill,* he would bring it up immediately, just like that. He stays away for four months and now, the very first time they'd seen each other since that night, the first thing out of his mouth is *Stranger Hill.*

"I'm glad to see you out on a horse—" he continued to pat the animal "—enjoying yourself," he stopped and looked into Marie's eyes, "looking so well."

"I'm feeling much better," she said.

"So I see." He gave her a teasing little grin. "Are you supposed to be jumping fences like that?"

Marie felt her cheeks grow warm. "Well I...I guess I can do anything I feel strong enough to do," she answered.

His smile was replaced by a concerned frown, which Marie found wonderfully attractive. "I guess you can," he said. "But be careful. You were a pretty sick girl."

"I'm fine now," she answered seriously. "I heard you had a rough time too...with your kidney and all..."

They looked into each other's eyes for a second, but he broke the contact and resumed patting the horse. "Marie...I wanted to come and see you in the hospital but…I…I didn't want to take any time away from the kids—and I…I, well, the truth is, I wanted to give you time to sort out your feelings, to—''

''To grieve over what happened to Carl?'' Marie said quietly. She'd yearned for Jim during her recovery, but she understood why he hadn't come. For a while, in another hospital in Austin, he'd been too sick to come, fighting his own battle to survive, and then she'd assumed that for him, too, everything that had happened to them must have seemed surreal. ''I understand. For a while, I didn't know who visited and who didn't. But once I started to rally I thought about you—''

He glanced up at her from under the Stetson, as if checking her meaning. ''I thought about you—''

''Thanks for the flowers,'' they both said at once, and smiled, then checked each other's eyes again for a flicker of a second.

''Marie,'' he said, turning his gaze to the horse's neck so that all she could see was his mouth and the side of his jaw under the hat, ''I didn't just think about you, I…I prayed for you.'' His lips were tight, turned down at the corners, as if he were confessing some weakness. ''Prayed that you'd live. That's all I wanted. When I was lying in the hospital, you were all I could think about. I didn't care about anything else. Not the election, the grand jury, the murder trial…not even my own life. I just wanted you to be okay.''

He tilted his face up to her, his eyes narrowed with emotion, the line of his mouth still tight as he continued. ''When I got out of the hospital, my friend Roy brought me over to see you once—''

Marie was surprised at that and the horse skittered when she fidgeted in the saddle. Jim pulled the reins to bring the horse under control. "You came to see me?" she said sadly, wondering what else she'd missed during that dark period.

"You never knew I was there. I sat in my wheel-chair, looking at you—you looked so frail—and I thought, I have no right to be here. This woman hardly knows me, this is her family's place, beside her bed. Toots kept me informed about your progress. He said you were having a hard time coping, emotionally, with everything and I…I didn't want to make things more difficult for you. I wanted us…"

Marie stared down at him, wide-eyed. *Was he saying what she hoped he was saying?*

His speech became rushed, pressured, "I hope this all makes sense, because it's the absolute truth. I wanted to wait until you were really strong again and then I planned to do it right—flowers and candy and—you know, court you. I hope I'm not rushing things now, but I just couldn't stay away anymore."

He was looking back toward his Bronco, so that he didn't see her coming when she threw her leg over the saddle. She flung herself down on him, clasped her arms around his neck and plastered her mouth on his.

He staggered backward with his big hands clutching her sides, trying to say "whoa!" around her lips without much success. His Stetson had fallen off and he stepped on it as he tried to regain his balance.

Marie kept up her wild kissing, nearly bruising his lips. She wet his nose, cheeks and forehead with kisses, more kisses. When she made it to his mouth again, he was ready, and pulled her to the ground with him while their lips were still sealed.

He pinned her shoulders back, flattened her chest under his, and when she'd been thoroughly kissed, he raised his head and said, "Does that mean you understand?"

Marie tilted her chin up and closed her eyes in ecstasy. "I thought it was just *me,* just a crazy woman." She looked in his eyes. "That night up on Stranger Hill, I thought that we were caught up in the crisis, or that you felt sorry for me, or that I'd imagined it. Time went by and the whole thing started to seem unreal—"

He kissed her again. This time slowly, tenderly, with the most exquisite pressure, the most gentle probing tongue. "Oh, Marie," he whispered as he feathered his lips over hers. "Tell me, does this seem real?"

They lay for a long time in that field of wildflowers, and savored the feel and the taste of each other, and the same thing, the very same transformation, happened to them in the same way as it had on Stranger Hill. And Marie thought, *What will it be like when we finally do make love? Will I die from it? Can a body die from joy?*

"Would you think I was strange," she whispered, "if I told you that I felt like we've already made love even though we've never had sex?"

He smiled. "No. If you promise not to think I'm strange for falling in love with you before I ever even touched you."

"Now, Sheriff, I believe we'd have to say you

touched me when you carried me out of that draw the morning we found Cudd's body.''

''That's true.'' He grinned. ''But that was *after* I fell in love with you.''·

''Oh, sure. You were in love with me that first morning? I got the impression you didn't even *like* me. The way you kept tipping your hat and calling me ma'am.''

''I admit I had some stupid ideas about you. I thought you were a spoiled rich woman, a hothouse flower. But I was wrong. You're more like these wild-flowers.'' He stretched out his arm and swept his palm over the tops of the bluebonnets. ''Resilient, too beautiful to be tamed.'' He picked one and caressed her lips with it.

For a while they were quiet, then his expression grew solemn. ''Marie, while we're alone I need to tell you something.''

Marie's heart skipped a beat, but he touched his fingers to her lips and said, ''It's okay. It doesn't af-fect us. The state lab has finally identified that finger bone you found.''

''Yes, the one from Cudd's property,'' Marie said sadly.

''I thought I should tell you while the children aren't around to hear. I thought you'd want to know.''

''Of course I do.''

''Well.'' He lay on his back and pulled her head to his shoulder, as if it might be easier to tell her this if they were looking at the clear blue sky. ''Pruitt confessed that Weimer had forced him to remove the skeleton from Cudd's land and destroy it—he burned it—but he claimed he never knew the identity of the victim. State lab was able to determine it was our whistle-blower.''

"Carl's source in the D.A.'s office?''

"Yeah. A paralegal. A single lady who moved around and changed jobs a lot. Her parents were dead. She was new in town, had some friends, but they were all over the country. Before anyone got too concerned, Weimer had covered the trail pretty well, except for Cudd—''

"Who demanded more hush money in exchange for burying her on his property,'' Marie finished for him. Tears came to her eyes. "That poor woman. She tried to help Carl.''

"Or he tried to help her. Either way, she was a good person.''

"Oh, God,'' Marie said and covered her eyes, "What was her name?''

"Sandy. Sandy Hall.''

"Sandy Hall,'' Marie repeated, wiping at her tears with a leather-gloved hand. "I'll remember her name.'' She drew a fortifying breath. "So. They had already committed one murder before they—''

They were both silent then. It was a moment of silence for Carl, for Sandy, for themselves, for all the terrible things that had happened.

Marie looked up at the perfect blue sky, so pure, as if no evil had ever happened on the earth below it. "Kiss me,'' she whispered.

He rolled over and kissed her with everything he had, with everything he could give to make up for the pain.

After a while he helped her to her feet, scooped up his hat and poked it back into shape. They walked, with their arms around each other's waists, to where the horse was grazing.

"Guess what?" he said after he helped her mount. "I brought you a present."

"A present?"

"Yeah. For all of you. Are the kids home?"

She nodded. "Saturday-morning chaos is in full swing. Alice is making pancakes. Want to join us? That is, if you think you can handle Saturday-morning chaos." She said it teasingly, like a dare.

He grinned. "Well, I'm a pretty delicate type, but I *think* I can handle it."

"I'll make 'em go easy on you," she called over her shoulder and took off at a hard gallop, hoping that the spring breeze would cool the fire in her cheeks before she got to the house.

HE FIGURED she'd have to spend a little time in the barn with Henry and the horse, and decided to go in and say hello to Alice and the kids. He walked around to the back of the Bronco and peeked in the rear window. The present was sleeping soundly.

As he tapped on the screen door and stepped into the familiar mudroom, he felt as if he was coming home.

When he came out here to meet with Henry, Alice and Toots before the grand jury convened, Marie had still been in the hospital and the children were staying with their grandmother in Austin. The house had been immaculate then. And empty.

But this morning the smell of bacon, pancakes and coffee drifted out of the kitchen. Piano music vibrated from the direction of the living room, and the sounds of cartoons drifted up the short stairs from the den. All that was lacking was the barking dog. Jim smiled.

Alice offered him a chair, poured him a steaming mug of coffee and launched into a review of the trials, the worries, the miracles of the last four months. He removed his hat, sipped the coffee and smiled again. It wasn't hard to have a conversation with Alice Croft.

"People," Alice was saying as she bustled about the kitchen, "were so shocked when you withdrew your name from the sheriff's race and disclosed the vote rigging. I tell you, they just couldn't stop talking about it."

He fingered his bent Stetson, remembering. He'd called the press to the side of his hospital bed, and in a prepared statement that had lasted less than sixty seconds, he'd cleared the slate and ended his career. Or so he'd thought.

"But I guess nobody was more surprised than you when folks voted you in anyway."

"Yeah," was all he could say. He frowned into his coffee cup.

Mandy popped her head into the kitchen and looked shy when she saw him sitting there. She went to the stove and huddled next to Alice, fiddling with her braids.

"Hi, Mandy," he said, smiling and feeling a little awkward himself. "Remember me?" he asked.

Mandy nodded. "Why'd you come to see us?" she asked quietly, not budging from Alice's side.

"Well, now." Jim set his coffee down and raised his eyebrows. "I came because I brought you all a surprise."

"A surprise?" Mandy said.

"Yep."

"Jillian!" the little girl yelled and darted off to the living room. "Sheriff Whittington brought us a surprise!"

Alice turned from her pancake-flipping and peered over her glasses. "This surprise wouldn't require feeding and training and cleaning up after, would it?" she asked.

"Why, Mrs. Croft, wherever do you get these evil ideas?"

"Sheriff—" Alice waggled the pancake turner at him "—I have it on good authority from Bernice Manning that Janie Dorn's black Lab had a litter of ten, and that mutt you're always hauling around is the daddy. I figure it's just about time to unload those pups."

"Goodness!" Jim feigned shock. "That *Bernice Manning* sure keeps abreast of the reproductive doings in this town."

Alice rolled her eyes. "Don't evade the issue. Have you or have you not brought a puppy for me to worry over?"

"A *puppy!*" It was Mark, standing on the den steps, his eyes wide behind his thick lenses. "Did you bring us a *dog,* Sheriff?"

"Nobody said anything about a dog," Jim said, winking at Alice. "All I said was, I brought a surprise."

"Oh boy, can we see it? The surprise, I mean."

"Well...what say we wait 'til everybody is here," Jim said.

"I'll go get B.J. and Henry and Toots," Mark hollered, and dashed out the door without a jacket before Alice could grab him.

The screen door had hardly banged shut before Marie reopened it and stepped into the mudroom. "What's with Mark?" she asked Alice through the pass-through window as she removed her bundlings.

"The sheriff brought the kids a *surprise*," Alice said sarcastically. "But he isn't telling what it is until everybody is properly assembled. Mark is running to fetch the men."

"Oh, yes, the surprise." She smiled knowingly at Jim, then turned her back to him, surveying the food. "Breakfast almost ready? I hope you don't mind, I asked Jim to stay." As she spoke, she reached up and slowly drew off her stocking cap and shook out her hair. What there was of it.

Her hair—her beautiful hair—was no more than a couple of inches long all over her head! Jim's next thought was to hope that he hadn't made any shocked sound. What had he thought was under that turban of bandages when he saw her in the hospital? They must have shaved her head right down to the scalp.

Marie nibbled at a piece of bacon. "Yum. Alice, this is perfect."

Alice looked from Jim's face to Marie's hair and back to Jim's face. Then she snapped her fingers. "I think the thing we need is some of my crabapple jelly. It didn't jell right—" she addressed Jim brightly as if this was terribly interesting information "—and it's so runny, the kids think it's syrup. But it's pretty good on pancakes, even if I do say so myself." She glanced over at Marie again, who was staring out the window above the sink. "I'll just run out to the shed and get some." She cast another meaningful glance at Jim and ducked out.

Marie turned and leaned back against the counter, facing Jim. "So," she said, looking around with exaggerated interest, "where're the girls?"

A bad rendition of "Cavern by the Sea" answered.

Marie turned and started to pull things out of the cabinets: juice glasses, a sugar bowl, salt and pepper shakers. He came up beside her, standing very near. He could smell her fragrance and, as always, it made his heart beat faster.

In the living room the piano playing stopped. He wondered if the girls would burst in on them now, wondered if he should wait. But he felt he had to say something to her right now, something reassuring. He lashed at his mind for words. Marie wheeled away and jerked the refrigerator door open.

"Here," she blurted. "Would you mind pouring the orange juice?" She thrust the cold pitcher into his hands.

He stood there holding it, dumbly. *Say something funny,* he prodded himself. *Say, "Did Toots take one of his combines to your head?" Say, "Your hair looks kind of nice that way." Say, "Your hair..."* Oh, Marie. Your hair.

What finally came out of his mouth was a croaked, "Your hair."

She looked at him matter-of-factly, smiled and said, "Yes. My hair. It'll grow back."

At that moment Mark and B.J., Henry and Toots came clumping into the mudroom. "Mom!" Mark said breathlessly. "The sheriff brought us a surprise!"

"Oh, did he?" Marie raised her eyebrows and made big eyes at Mark. "Where is it?"

"In my Bronco," Jim said, stepping toward Mark. "Why don't we all go out and get it now?"

"Come on, girls!" Mark bellowed in the direction of the living room.

Marie took the pitcher from Jim. "I'll stay in here and help Alice set the table." She turned away and started pouring juice.

Jim's heart sank. Had he hurt her feelings? Maybe this wasn't going to be as smooth as he'd hoped.

THE PUPPY WAS a chubby little clone of Amos: solid black, wiggly and very enthusiastic about the children. They carried him into the mudroom, petting and fussing over him until, with considerable coaxing, Jim managed to get him bedded down in the wicker dog bed he'd brought along.

Breakfast was noisy and tasty and cozy, and it would have been a delight for Jim except that, as much as he tried not to, he caught himself stealing glances at Marie's hair. He wanted nothing so much as to hold her, to tell her how beautiful she was, how much he adored her.

When the meal was finished, Marie pushed her chair back and said, "Well, I guess I'll go out and get acquainted with my new baby now."

The children all jumped up to go with her.

"Whoa there!" Alice said. "That puppy's been wooled around enough. You urchins are going to stay right here and help me clean up this mess. And I imagine you menfolk have got chores to finish." She poked B.J. in the shoulder.

"Do I qualify as a menfolk, or do I have to clean up with the urchins?" Jim asked.

The kids giggled.

"If you make a habit of eating here, you'll have to do K.P. duty, or head to the barnyard." Alice winked at the twins. "Just like everybody else. House rules."

Jim surveyed the messy table, made a disgusted face and said, "I'll take the barnyard."

They all laughed again. Then the younger children started to stack dishes noisily and Toots, Henry and B.J. donned hats and jackets.

"Come and introduce me to this puppy," Marie said to Jim.

They went out to the mudroom.

"He's beautiful!" Marie cried as she got down on her knees and stroked the puppy while the little dog licked her hand with his tiny pink tongue and wagged his tail happily. She scooped him up in her arms.

For a moment, Jim stood above her, enjoying her response to the puppy, then he got down on one knee beside her and said, "I started to get you another Border collie, but then I decided no one could ever replace Bailey in your heart—" he looked into her eyes "—and no one ever should. I thought I'd get you a brand-new love, from me and Amos."

That brought a sudden prickle of tears to her eyes. Weren't they really talking about more than Bailey? "So, you think I'm ready for that?" she said, and looked down. "A brand-new love?" Her hand trembled as she continued to pet the puppy.

"Do you?" His voice was very gentle.

She met his eyes full on. "I don't know," she said. But it was a lie. She did know. She wanted him.

He gently brushed her cheek with the backs of his fingers, then folded her in his arms and rested his chin lightly on top of her head. "I think you do know, deep down, but maybe you're still afraid. We have all the time in the world. The worst is over, Marie. You've been very strong, and you're going to be fine now. The kids will be fine. Everything will be fine."

She felt his deep voice reverberating against her shoulder and back, and his body seemed to enclose her in a cocoon of strength. He was right, of course. The worst was over. The painful truth about Carl's death had been faced. And the insurance company had paid up, so their future on the ranch was secure. What was there to be afraid of now? A brand-new love? "Yes," she whispered. "Everything will be just fine." She relaxed into his chest and he tightened his arms around her.

"Hey! The sheriff's hugging Mom!" It was Mark's voice, booming above them. He was hanging over the sill of the pass-through window from the kitchen, looking down at them with an onery gap-toothed grin.

"Mind your own beeswax, young man," Alice said from the kitchen side and pulled the child down.

Marie smiled. "I have no privacy, Jim. I hope you're prepared for that."

"I've had about all the privacy a man can stomach," he answered.

She laid her head back against his chest. "Jim, you are so special," she said. Then she turned and slowly stood up, still cradling the puppy. "Want to help us name your surprise?" She smiled.

He stood, reached over and stroked the puppy in

tandem with her. "Oh, this little fella already *has* a name," he said.

"He does?" she said.

He nodded, his brown eyes solemn and sincere.

"Well, my goodness, are you going to tell me what it is?"

Jim Whittington broke into a grin that was both boyishly teasing and eminently wise. "This is Cupid," he said.

"Oh, Jim." She laughed and cried all at once.

He reached up and caressed her cropped head tenderly. Then he brought the backs of his fingers down her cheek and down the length of her slender neck.

Fire went through her. Just from that simple touch. She closed her eyes as Jim slowly wrapped her and the puppy in his arms again.

"Hey, everybody!" Mark yelled from the passthrough window. "He's doing it again! And hey! This time he's *kissing* her!"

HARLEQUIN SUPERROMANCE®

MEN OF GLORY

They're ranchers, cowboys, men of the West!

O LITTLE TOWN OF GLORY

by Judith Bowen

**Visit the town of Glory in December 1998!
A good place to go for Christmas...**

Calgary lawyer Honor Templeman makes a shocking discovery after her husband's death. Parker Templeman had another wife—and two children—in the small town of Glory. Two children left to the care of their uncle, Joe Gallant, who has no intention of giving them up—to Honor *or* her powerful father-in-law.

Available wherever Harlequin books are sold.

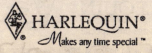

HARLEQUIN®
Makes any time special ™

What do you want for Christmas?

A DADDY FOR CHRISTMAS

'Tis the season for wishes and dreams that come true. This November, follow three handsome but lonely Scrooges as they learn to believe in the magic of the season when they meet the *right* family, in *A Daddy for Christmas*.

MERRY CHRISTMAS, BABY
by Pamela Browning

THE NUTCRACKER PRINCE
by Rebecca Winters

THE BABY AND THE BODYGUARD
by Jule McBride

Available November 1998
wherever Harlequin and Silhouette books are sold.

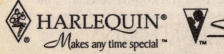

HARLEQUIN®
Makes any time special ™

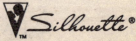

Silhouette®

Look us up on-line at: http://www.romance.net

PHBR1198

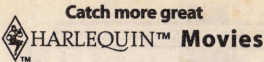
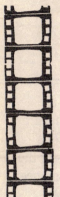

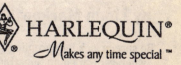

HARLEQUIN SUPERROMANCE®

Love **THAT MAN**

He's the guy every woman dreams of.
A hero in every sense of the word—strong, brave,
kind and of course, drop-dead gorgeous.
You'll never forget the men you meet—or the
women they love—in Harlequin Superromance®'s
newest series, **LOVE THAT MAN!**

BECAUSE IT'S CHRISTMAS
by Kathryn Shay, December 1998

LOVE, LIES & ALIBIS
by Linda Markowiak, January 1999

Be sure to look for upcoming **LOVE THAT MAN!** titles
wherever Harlequin Superromance® books are sold.

HARLEQUIN®
Makes any time special ™

COMING NEXT MONTH

#814 O LITTLE TOWN OF GLORY • Judith Bowen
Men of Glory
Honor Templeman is a Calgary lawyer, who makes the
shocking discovery that her husband, Parker, had another
wife, another family…in a small ranching town called Glory.
Now that he's dead, she wants to meet Parker's children—but
their uncle and guardian, Joe Gallant, is fiercely protective of
them. Inevitably, when Honor fills in because Joe's desperate
for a nanny, she grows to love these kids. *And* their uncle….
He's a man for all seasons, from the heat of a prairie summer
to the joys of a Glory Christmas.

#815 BECAUSE IT'S CHRISTMAS • Kathryn Shay
Love That Man
To most people in the small town of Bayview Heights,
Seth Taylor's a hero. But Seth can't forgive himself for a
mistake in his past. And neither can Lacey Cartwright—the
woman he loves. If Lacey takes his side, she'll lose what's
left of her family. It's a risk she can't take—and a choice Seth
can't allow her to make.

#816 LET IT SNOW • Sherry Lewis
Marti Johansson has brought her troubled teenage son to
spend a quiet Christmas on his grandfather's Colorado ranch.
Unfortunately, the holiday is anything but peaceful. Her father
is feuding with his neighbor, Rick Dennehy. Her son wants
her to forgive his father, who has his own reasons for wanting
Marti back. And then there's Rick….

#817 THE HEART OF CHRISTMAS • Tara Taylor Quinn
Abby Hayden is at loose ends until Nick McIntyre persuades
her to spend the Christmas season helping out in a home for
pregnant teenagers. This place is where Abby learns about
trust and happiness and letting go…. And this Christmas is
when she falls in love with her very own Saint Nick! By the
author of *Father: Unknown*.